CRIKEY!
HOW DID THAT HAPPEN?

CRIKEY!
HOW DID THAT HAPPEN?

The [refreshingly unauthorised]
Biography of Sir Bertram Wooster, KG

Ian S.

IAN STRATHCARRON

Published by Affable Media Ltd
Hampshire

ISBN 978-1-78926-295-7

Design by Vivian@Bookscribe

Printed and bound in India

Contents

Dedication

To the memory of P.G. Wodehouse, with untold thanks for the many happy hours of chuckling and wonder; and in the hope you might enjoy our old friend Bertram's further adventures, too.

CHAPTER 1

Change of Circumstance

December 1907
Easeby Park
Easeby-on-Severn
Shropshire

The Rev. Aubrey Upjohn
Malvern House Preparatory School
Bramley-on-Sea
Kent

6th December 1907

Dear Reverend Upjohn,
Ref: Bertram Wooster

I am writing in connection with your pupil and my nephew Bertram Wooster. As I'm sure you have read in *The Times*, my brother-in-law Sir Bertram Wooster GCSI KCB, until his demise H.E. The Governor of Bombay, has recently succumbed to consumption in India. My sister and I had an agreement that in the event of her and her husband's death, I would be their children's ward and guardian. This arrangement I believe will be enshrined in his Will, she having passed away shortly after her only son, Bertram, was born.

I feel therefore that it is my duty to inform my nephew of his father's misfortune in person, and indeed his new accommodations here in Shropshire, at the earliest opportunity. I should be grateful in these circumstances if you were able to receive me at 2 p.m. on 8th inst.

Yours & co. & co.

– *Travers*

Sir Willoughby Travers, Bt.

'Well, well,' muttered Upjohn to no-one in particular, in fact to no-one at all. It was the 8th that day and the letter had only just arrived in the morning post. He had indeed read the news of Sir Bertram's demise and had been waiting for some guidance about young Wooster from the India Office. He hadn't realised the boy was motherless. At the start of term, the boy's first term, he recalled that young Bertram had been delivered by an aunt, and rather an impatient one at that. Mrs. Gregory or some such. He would look it all up in the register before the uncle arrived.

Upjohn hoped for two things in a boy at Malvern House: to be good at games and good at study; if not both, then either. He felt he hardly knew young Wooster. He taught the boy Scripture Knowledge, at which he was middling, but apart from that Wooster was just another name shouted out at Assembly. He had heard Wooster could sing and Mrs. Mackintosh wanted him in the choir for next term. It followed that he might be musical, but the India Office subventions never ran to extras considered frivolous. Come summer term he might be good at cricket, 'But I doubt it,' he said to the same thin air.

Sir Willoughby Travers ... Willoughby Travers ...

where had he heard that name before? He opened his study door and yelled, with full force, 'Faaaag!' Thirty seconds later a dozen Junior Lows stood looking up, waiting in front of him. Further scuffling announced a latecomer, rushing through the tiled corridor. 'Ah, Fink-Nottle, you last again? Go find Mr. Hargreaves for me. Now, Fink-Nottle, now.'

Alan Hargreaves was Upjohn's secret weapon when it came to affairs current, artistic, literary or worldly. He was also the English Grammar, English Literature, Latin and Ancient History teacher, and cricket coach. Young Wooster was one of his charges.

'Young Wooster,' the headmaster asked. 'How's he getting on?'

'Likeable enough. Cheery lad, headmaster,' replied Hargreaves. 'I'd say he's mentally negligible, especially at Latin. He's no trouble though. Runs well in break. Is anything wrong?'

'Read this.' Hargreaves read and returned the letter. 'Sir Willoughby Travers. Well, well. There can't be two of them.'

'Ah, I knew you'd know.' said Upjohn. 'So how come he rings a bell?'

'He wants to publish his memoirs, sent an early draft to Riggs and Ballinger. Someone there tipped off *The Times*. Pulls no punches. Lords Emsworth and Worplesdon scandalised, actively and passively. Young Wooster's father and Sir Stanley Gervase-Gervase too if I'm not wrong. It's going to cause quite a ruckus among the upper orders if it ever sees the light of day.'

At 2 p.m. Sir Willoughby Travers was shown into the Rev. Aubrey Upjohn's office. The two men could hardly have been more different. The headmaster wore the mean, pince-nez look of a shallow life led dispiritedly, whereas his visitor carried his weight before him and most of his life behind him. The former wary to the point of chariness, the latter carefree to the point of wantonness; the one wan and waning, the other florid and becoming florider.

'Thank you for your letter,' said Upjohn, as Travers sank into the red armchair, 'I've called for tea.'

'Welcome it will be too. It's a long way from Shropshire, even breaking the journey in London,' replied Travers. After further small talk, he said, 'I made the boy's parents a promise I intend to keep. Never met the boy. Lived in India all his life. Except for a month in a summer school in Hampshire. That's right, won a prize for flower arranging, or some such. I don't travel if I can avoid it. Does he know?'

'Not as far as I know. I don't see how he could. We don't allow them newspapers and read all incoming letters.'

'Probably just as well,' replied Travers.

'I didn't know about his mother,' said Upjohn. 'Or that he had siblings, until I read your letter.'

'Kathleen, my youngest sister. She died eight weeks after Bertram was born. Gave him to a native wet nurse on day one, took the next steamer back to Tilbury, caught something or other on the way home and died at her aunt's in Norfolk. She was only young, twenty-nine.'

'So who brought him up?' asked Upjohn.

'The wet nurse to start with. Sir Bertram gave her a full-time job as the boy's nanny when Kathleen died. That's how the boy learnt to speak Marathi. Later he brought out an English nanny, Hogg, when he thought the boy was becoming a bit of a Kim.'

'Marathi, really?' said Upjohn musing, before adding, 'He doesn't seem to shine at Latin.'

'Odd that,' noted Willoughby. 'You'd have thought one lingo was much the same as another.'

'And his siblings. What is to become of them?'

'Just a sister, Florentine, ten years older. Pretty filly by all accounts. Engaged to an Indian Army officer. Scholfield. Captain in the 129th Duke of Connaught's Own Baluchis.

Haven't met him. Or her actually. I'll have to foot the bill. For the wedding, do you see? They can have it at Easeby. Shall we send for him?'

'Scholfield?'

'No, Wooster, my nephew.'

'Ah yes, sorry, got a bit lost there,' said Upjohn, walking to his office door. 'Faaaag!' he shouted. Then to Sir Willoughby, 'He'll be here soon, second to last normally.'

From inside, Bertram's uncle heard: 'Wooster, it's you I want. In the study with you, please.'

Then: 'I don't believe you have met. Wooster, this is your uncle, Sir Willoughby Travers. He has something to tell you. Shake his hand and sit down, boy.'

Wooster looked around. It was normally bad news to be in here. Uncle Willoughby was sitting in the red armchair the boys bent over to be caned. The head kept the cane on the mantelpiece behind the chair and Wooster saw it there in the mirror. The boys called him 'Whipper' for his enthusiastic use of it. So far Bertie had been spared; first termers were exempt unless they were unusually foul.

Sir Willoughby said, 'There is no other way to tell you this, my boy, but to tell you it bluntly. Your father, my brother-in-law, has died. About ten days ago. Of consumption, they say. There was a funeral in Bombay of course. A memorial service in London later. I'm sorry.'

Bertram could only look at the ground. He felt his eyes well, but no tears came. He hardly knew his father; he was told many times that he was a great man. 'What about Bahnwari?

And Florry?' he asked softly.

'Who are they?' asked Uncle Willoughby.

'My ayah and sister.'

'Well, Florentine will stay in Bombay at Governor's House. For now, until she is married. The Indian woman, I don't know. Do you want her here?'

'Yes,' Bertie whispered, adding, 'So I'm not going back there next summer?'

Upjohn shuffled forward and remarked, 'Perhaps now would be a good time to tell Wooster about your wardship.'

Sir Willoughby then told his new ward about the change of circumstances. How he would now be his uncle's ward and guardian, how they would live at Easeby, how after this term he would go there for his holiday and not to his Aunt Agatha's as planned. How he would spend time with all his aunts and uncles from Boxing Day, for the Easeby shoot, until New Year's Eve, for the Easeby Ball. How his Uncle George's fiancée would help the Easeby butler Oakshott settle the boy into life there and how the two of them, Uncle Willoughby and Bertie, would rub along famously from now on.

'What's her name?' whispered Bertram.

'The fiancée? Maud, Maud Wilberforce.'

'That's my middle name,' said Bertram, looking up.

'By Jove so it is,' said the uncle. 'It's in my book, how your father's horse won the Calcutta Derby the day before you were christened. Wilberforce. Named you after it! Capital, capital! So, we'll all get along swimmingly, no doubt about that.'

'A thought occurs,' ventured Upjohn. 'The end of term is in ten days, there are no exams for Wooster. Since you are here Sir Willoughby, would you like to take him with you now? I'm sure in twenty minutes or so he could be ready.'

'Well, I could I suppose. Why not? I'm in Mayfair tonight with a down train tomorrow. Yes.'

'Please sir,' said Wooster, 'can I stay? I'm in the nativity play and all my friends are here and in it too.'

'But you must think of your uncle's convenience,' said Upjohn.

'No, no,' said Sir Willoughby, 'if the boy's in a play, "the show must go on" as they say in the circus. Many a happy hour have I spent in the music halls and vaudevilles. If I could be here myself I would. No, we'll stick to the plan, end of term and all that.'

⁓⁓⁓⁓

The first time, the only time, Bertie cried for his father was on Christmas Day. Growing up in India, Christmas was always the time when he saw his father and spent a few days with him too. They spent Christmas in the West Country cottage in the grounds of Governor's House, right on the Indian Ocean, where forty years later Jawaharlal Nehru and the Vicereine, Edwina,

Viscountess of Mountbatten would come to tryst. In the House there were always fawning servants and silent meals, dressing up and behaving like an adult. In the cottage his father dressed locally, as did Bertie, and only Bahnwari and his father's batman would be there with them. Around them were Christmas cards from family in England, with scenes of snow and folk well wrapped against the cold. He would ask his father about snow and cold. One day, he promised Bertie, they would have Christmas in England, in the New Forest in Hampshire where he had lived before India. How long? Bertie wondered. His father thought a year or so. For Bertie there were presents – presents from his father and his aide-de-camps and their wives, presents from the Indian contractors, presents from relatives back 'home', even though he was at home.

This Christmas Day at Easeby there were no presents but there was snow and plenty of it. Log fires in the great rooms and halls, coal fires in his bedroom. Easeby Hall was almost as big as Governor's House, except that instead of a hundred servants there were four. As far as Bertie could tell, Oakshott was in charge; he was kind but grumpy and he paid Bertie little heed and Bertie repaid him in kind. Mrs. Martin seemed to run the house; she was kind and swept him up in her ample arms and tickled him. Mrs. Carstairs was the cook. She played with him in the kitchen, and young Tulip, the West Indian maid, fooled with him whenever he fancied fooling. He had heard the gardeners' names but had not met them yet. His namesake, Maud Wilberforce, had only arrived there the same day as he had.

From Uncle Willoughby, Bertie just heard a few

14

cheery passings-by in the halls. Bertie found a train set in a drawing room, the tracks running all around the walls, stations and signals and steam engines. There was no-one to show him how it worked, no one to start it, just a big, lonely and cold drawing room. That's when Bertie cried.

There was no time off for the household staff that Christmas Day, because of all the great preparations for Boxing Day. Mrs. Martin, who loved a full house of guests, said, 'That's when the fleet gets in, mark my words my boy.' The next day the fleet arrived in the form of all the relations he had heard about but, apart from Aunt Agatha, had never met. There was Aunt Julia and Gussie Mannering-Phipps, Uncle Tom and Aunt Dahlia, Uncle George and Maud once more, Aunt Emily and her young twins Eustace and Claude, and cousin Algernon. It would be years before he could say where each fitted in, but in they did fit.

After elevenses on Boxing Day, the men and dogs all went shooting. Uncle Willoughby told Bertie to join him and the other guns and Bertie never left his side all day. It was the first time he had ever been cold, actually shivering cold. Bertie loved the snow and the mud, the dogs, and the constant *bang! bang! thud! thud!* of the guns and their kills. He enjoyed being a man among men with the packed lunches, liked the way the beaters called him Master Wooster and not sahib. Later, after returning to the house, he enjoyed the large tea with cake and sandwiches, liked the hot bath he ran himself, the clean clothes he found himself, liked the surprise of Uncle Willoughby calling in to say goodnight and liked the deep sleep of a day well lived.

The next five days passed in a whirl. The aunts and uncles and cousins stayed. Neighbours called around. There were outings to the church, to the village, country walks, dogs, wellington boots and long table lunches. The head coachman, Pendlebury, was told to swap horses for horse power and was made to drive Uncle Willoughby in the new Rolls-Royce 30 hp, but he clunked and clattered and even Bertie could tell he was a hopeless motorman. In Pendlebury's presence, Aunt Agatha demanded that Uncle Willoughby find a proper motor chauffeur. Bertie was embarrassed for Pendlebury. The aunts and uncles and cousins preferred to ride in one of the char-à-bancs.

If Christmas Day was spent preparing for the Boxing Day shoot, New Year's Eve was spent preparing for that night's ball. Extra staff were hired from the village and farms. Bertie loved seeing the dining hall with two long tables decorated with silver and candles and red cloth draped everywhere. A stage was set for the band and dozens of seats were placed around the sides of the ballroom. At Malvern House there was adequate electricity, unlike in Governors' House, but here in the ballroom the new electric lights seemed excessive. He also noticed the finery wasn't as fine as it was in India. The New Year's Eve Ball at Governor's House was an outpouring of opulence and revelry, with guests waited on by hundreds of finely dressed foot servants. At Easeby the party was more black and white, more hearty and earnest, less fantastical, without pizzazz or panache. Bertie and the other children were put to bed early in the evening, partly so the nannies and nurses could join the other servants to make sure the ball swam along successfully. Their charges stayed up as late as they could, visiting each other's rooms, but well before midnight tiredness triumphed over determination and sleep took them through the night.

The following morning, as he walked towards the breakfast room, Bertie overheard the following conversation:

'But Willoughby you can't keep him here. Think of the boy.' It sounded like Aunt Emily.

Then Aunt Agatha spoke up. 'She's right, Willoughby. What kind of life can you give him here? You're hardly here yourself. Even after the nannies come from Bombay, whenever that is, it won't work. No. You must give him to Emily. He'll have Eustace and Claude to play with. And there's a proper nanny. A real household.'

'But the twins are so much younger than Bertie.' It was Uncle Willoughby speaking now. 'Besides.'

'Besides what?' snarled Aunt Agatha.

'Besides, Agatha, I made my sister a promise. And I like the boy.'

'But you don't know the boy,' said Aunt Emily, 'you've only met him a few times. It's not right.'

'I went to his school. I took him shooting.' Then he remarked, 'He reminds me of me, if you must know.'

'Now, you're just being plain selfish,' insisted Aunt Agatha. 'It's not about you, Willoughby. You must see sense. I insist the boy leaves with Emily and the twins after lunch.'

'But really....' Uncle Willoughby started.

17

'No!' snapped Aunt Agatha, 'It's been decided. Now call for the wretched boy. We'll tell him as a family. We leave at noon, so he'd better start packing.'

In the hall Bertie turned around and on silent tiptoes ran along the stone floors, pushed past the swing doors and with full feet sprinted along the quarry tiles to the kitchen.

'Where's Tulip?' he asked breathlessly.

'Why, in her room. Why?' asked Mrs. Carstairs.

Without replying Bertie leaped up the stairs, each floor being darker and colder than the one below. Without knocking, he pushed open her door. He told her what he had heard downstairs and how she must hide him. 'They'll never come looking here!' Tulip agreed, they wouldn't. Then letting go of his hands, she whispered, 'I must get down to work and start my day.'

Tulip was worried. She had never done anything like this before. She certainly didn't want any trouble with Mr. Oakshott. She liked her job at Easeby far too much for that. She even more certainly didn't want any trouble with the police. She liked her unofficial arrangement of being in England far too much for that too. She found Oakshott and on finding Oakshott she spilled the beans.

Oakshott was none too fond of the plan afoot either, but as he knew young Wooster was hiding, he had to tell his employer. He, too, had overheard the aunts' demands and Sir Willoughby's replies.

Oakshott entered the breakfast room with a folded note on a silver salver. With a discreet 'a-hem', he offered it to Sir Willoughby. On it he had written: *A private word with you outside please sir*.

'Please excuse me,' said Sir Willoughby to his guests

as he rose from the table and walked into the hall: 'What is it, Oakshott?'

'A situation of some delicacy has arisen, sir.'

'Yes, tell all.'

Oakshott told all.

'By Jove, that's a sticky wicket,' said Sir Willoughby.

'Bit of a googly for the aunts though, what? We can't hide him here forever. Much as I'd like to. What to do? What to do?'

'If I may suggest a course of action, sir?'

'Suggest away, Oakshott, suggest away. The ears are flapping like never before.'

'The plan does require a degree of subterfuge, sir.'

'Subterfuge to your heart's desire, Oakshott. Needs must and all that. Who's in on the game?'

'You, sir, and I, Miss Maud if she's willing, Mrs. Martin and Pendlebury, sir.'

'Maud's a good sport. Is she up yet?'

'She is an habituée of the night, sir, and has lunch for breakfast. My stratagem involves Mrs. Martin awakening her presently. An unwelcome intrusion but as you say, needs must, sir.'

⁓

'Where is he?' asked Aunt Dahlia.

'Oakshott?' asked Sir Willoughby.

'No, Willoughby, the boy, Bertram.'

'Oakshott!' called Sir Willoughby.

Oakshott glided into the room as only the best know how. 'Sir?'

'Have you seen Master Bertram this morning? Ask him to drift down if you do.'

'I fear that won't be possible, sir. Master Bertram is currently at St. Joseph's Infirmary in Oswestry.'

Amidst the sharp intake of auntly breath and tut-tuts of astonishment, Willoughby was first to ask: 'Good heavens, tell all.'

'Soon after midnight sir, Master Bertram felt unwell and awoke Mrs. Martin. She diagnosed dyspepsia. As usual Miss Maud was awake and heard the disturbance. She offered to take Master Bertram to Oswestry, sir, if Mrs. Martin would awake Pendlebury to drive them in your Royce.'

'Then, we will go there immediately to see him,' said Aunt Emily.

'I'm afraid Oswestry is twenty miles each way in the wrong direction and your train leaves for London at 1:20 p.m. Miss Maud has made telephonic communication from the infirmary and she expects to be back here at noon.'

'That's when we leave,' said Aunt Agatha.

'Precisely, madam. She should be back in time to say her farewells.'

'She? You mean they, don't you Oakshott?'

'Unfortunately not, madam. She reports that Master Bertram has gastroenteritis and will need to be kept there for at least three nights, maybe longer.'

'Goodness, term starts in a week,' said Sir Willoughby.

'Precisely, sir. I'm sure a few days here with Mrs. Martin will complete his recovery.'

⌀⌀⌀

At noon, the aunts were standing outside the main entrance, watching the gardeners and footmen load up two char-à-bancs with their trunks and portmanteaux. The sound of squishing gravel turned all heads as the Rolls-Royce 30 hp slid silently alongside them.

'So pleased to have caught you,' said Maud from the passenger's seat. She proceeded to give the aunts a possibly too-lurid account of Bertie's orifical motions. She confirmed the enforced rest for the boy at the Oswestry Infirmary, sympathised with them about the inconvenience of its location and promised to stay with him while he completed his recuperation.

With the aunts safely on board and the wheels turning, Sir Willoughby, Oakshott, Mrs. Martin and Mrs. Carstairs waved them goodbye. The only person missing was Tulip. She was looking out at the scene from her top-floor window. Beside her, standing on tiptoe to see over the sill, was Bertram.

'Capital ruse, Oakshott,' said Sir Willoughby.

'I endeavour to give satisfaction, sir.'

◦◦◦◦

A week later, the staff were waving goodbye again. This time in the char-à-banc were three souls: Sir Willoughby, Miss Maud and Master Bertram. They were on their way to Malvern House. They waved back, none more enthusiastically than Bertram. He had found a home and some Anglo-Saxon playmates, and even though the dread of school loomed, he smiled his widest smile. He belonged.

CHAPTER 2

Eton Rag

December 1914

Bertie could tell something was wrong. At lunch in his house, Hawtrey's, the top table was completely silent. Old Parry, his House Master, looked even graver and greyer than normal. Next to him, M'Dame, Miss Atkins, was red-eyed and even paler and more po-faced than normal. To their left and right Munro-Geddes, the House Captain, and Barrington, the House Captain of Games, were ashen and picking and poking, far from eating, the boiled horsemeat and two veg. The silence was catching. By the end of pudding the room was completely muffled. After lunch, as Munro-Geddes prepared to read Notices, as he did every day, Bertie guessed there was bad news; but not as bad as it was.

Munro-Geddes stood up and read, haltingly, from a sheet of paper:

'The school is taking its full share in the War, in the defence of the Empire. It is estimated that there are already more than 1,400 Old Etonians at the front. The roll of honour contains 160 names. Every day both these numbers increase. Today, one of these numbers, has a name well known to boys in this house.' M'Dame started sobbing openly. Munro-Geddes's voice was cracking: 'Barrington's predecessor as House Captain of Games, Silvester Andrew Garland Drummond, has been killed in action.' The dining room was quieter than silent, stiller than held breath.

Now the House Master Parry, Old Parry, stood up and took the notice from his House Captain. 'Sit down now, Munro-Geddes. I will read this today.

'Drummond was well known to all of us at Hawtrey's, except for you new boys this Michaelmas half. He was not just our House Captain of Games, but without doubt the most capped and coloured boy in all the school. As a Dry Bob, he played in the cricket eleven, where he was a tremendous hitter, and captained the rugby fifteen with remarkable élan. He was a whip of the Beagles, a member of the Eton Society, won the Inter-House Racquets Cup, and was President of the Library in this house. He was a good long distance runner and was third in the school steeplechase. It may suffice to say that in junior and senior sports he wore our house colours in a variety of sports for all five seasons he was a boy here. His positive attitude set the moral tone of the school.

'His place was secured at Cambridge and there is no doubt a sparkling life and career, inheriting the family bank and peerage, lay in front of him.

'Instead of Cambridge, after leaving school he joined the 1st Life Guards. Reports confirm his bravery and dedication to duty; skills he learned well on the playing fields and ball courts here. He went with his regiment to the war and saw some very severe fighting. His commanding officer has written to his parents who have shared this commendation with us: "He was killed on November 15th, leading his squadron in action, three-quarters of a mile south of Zillebeke. He had driven the German Imperial Guard out of their trenches and was following them up, when a wounded German, left behind by his retreating comrades, seeing him right in front, and that he was an officer, shot him dead through the heart at point blank range. He is a terrible loss to us and the regiment. He was splendid out here, always cheerful and never losing his head; even under the most trying circumstances I never saw him whinge, he was always just the same. I don't believe he had any nerves at all. He was a great credit to you and to us and to all who knew him. A most remarkable light has been snuffed out so soon after it was lit."'

Old Parry paused momentarily to wipe his large nose, before adding, 'Six months ago, at the end of the summer half, he was sitting where Barrington is now. It now falls to Barrington to write his obituary for this week's *Eton Chronicle*.

'These are difficult times for everyone at Eton, the Head, house masters, beaks, dames, boys and staff. Young men are dying for king and country. We have shouldered our share, more than our share I dare say. We have lost Drummond, the first new leaver from Hawtrey to fall. There will be others. From last half, along with Drummond, we have Stevens, Winterbourne, Gore-Brown, Bland and Waterhouse all serving on the front. Lord Kitchener's claim that it would all be over by Christmas cannot be upheld.

'In death, life must go on. I will not read the team notices today but pin them up on the board. There will now be five minutes silence to remember Drummond. Then we will file out quietly.'

❀

24

That afternoon Bertie wrote his first song. Well, his first tune, accompanied by humming, the lyric would come later. For now all he could rhyme with Drummond was summoned. He sat at a piano in one of the music rooms upstairs in School Hall and practised scales. The sadness of D minor came naturally and then he made a small error, a variation in the scales, and from that a melody and from that a tune. He found himself playing it loudly, in anger, then imperceptibly more slowly and quietly.

Soon the fingers were working on their own and Bertie's thoughts turned to Drummond. When Bertie was a new boy Drummond had been his fag-master. Drummond had three fags and shared the chores out evenly among them. He also protected them from bullying, and helped with sports, introducing Bertie to racquets and tennis. Bertie knew not why, but he made Drummond laugh. But then lots of the life and liberties at Eton made Bertie laugh. Yes, Ovid and Virgil had to be endured, verses, Latin grammar, prose and construction were lessons that passed, Homer was horrid, Divinity dragged on mercilessly; but the music and racquets, the friends and leaves, the huddles and pranks, and his sunny way with the world just about outshone the storm clouds of the Classics.

Back at Hawtrey in time for tea and Latin construction, Bertie found a letter in his pigeonhole. It was from home.

❦

Easeby Park
Easeby-on-Severn
Shropshire

25

B. Wooster, Esq.
Hawtrey House
Eton College
Windsor
Berkshire

4th December 1914

Dear Bertie,

Thank you for your letter of 13th November and congratulations on the house racquets result and the successful Musical Society soirée.

I write to you with mixed news. Mrs. Martin's younger son, David, has been killed in Belgium. Like most boys around here he was serving with The King's Shropshire Light Infantry. The war is taking its toll. Mrs. M is being stoic, of course, and we are rallying around her. He was only nineteen and showed promise as a gardener under Wheatcroft. The Wheatcrofts have two boys serving at the Front.

Better news, although, in the circs negligibly so. I have now heard back from Lady Maxwell-Gumbleton in Gibraltar and they would be delighted to accept your invitation for 'Jumbo' to spend New Year's with us and to return with you for the Lent half from here. She will book his passage on an All-Red steamer to Tilbury and advise us of his arrival time.

Now I write to you on a more serious matter. An old friend of mine, and indeed of your father's, Viscount Whottleshire, has his eldest son at school: Lancelot Pellew-Bastard, Pellew-Bastard being the family name. One day he will inherit the title of Whottleshire. Young

Lancelot is in Warre House, is friendless and being ragged terribly on account of his surname, or possibly both names, or possibly even all three names. His pater needs to stay aloof but I don't see why I should.

Bertie, can you seek him out and befriend him? The virtue of brotherhood has been a guiding principle in my life, sticking up for each other and all the rest of it. You could call it my Code and you could do worse than have a Code in your life.

Until we meet again shortly, your affectionate uncle, & Co. & Co.

– *Willoughby*

'Eeks,' thought Bertie, folding the letter in his tailcoat pocket, 'what to do about this?' He had heard of a new squit in Warre's called Bastard. All the fourth formers were saying poor sap, why didn't his people choose another name? Imagine agreeing to becoming Mrs. Bastard? Do you take this man...? Why not just trade under Pellew? At least make it Ba-stard, as per the Froggies would say, anything but jolly old Bastard. Poor bastard being called Bastard. Bertie couldn't remember seeing him.

But wait, Bingo! His old mucker Bingo Little is in Warre's. And Catsmeat. It all came back now; it was Bingo who told Bertie about the benighted Bastard. About how the Warre House Captain, and Bastard's fagmaster, Spode, who was supposed to protect him as his fag, had gone out of his way to have sport with him, bullying him, over-fagging him and encouraging the other sixth formers to do the same.

Bertie caught up with Bingo and Catsmeat on top of

the wall overlooking College Field, watching some of the Tugs playing the Wall Game. He unburdened the gist of his uncle's letter onto them both.

'That's not the worst of it, Woosy,' said Bingo.

'Yesterday Spode sent Bastard to buy cigars in the tobacconist in the High Street. Completely out of bounds. We think Spode arranged for him to be nailed coming out of the shop so he could give him a thrashing. Then he sent Bastard down to the barber to buy a new cane for just that. When he returned with one, Spode told him it wasn't swishy enough and sent him back to get another. Gave him a hard six in the Library last night.'

'Bastard had to say *Floreat Etona*! after each stroke,' Catsmeat reported, 'upon which Spode gleefully shouted: "Louder!" and Bastard had to say it over again. Apparently his older brother Spode used to do that when he was a fag-master.'

'Poor bastard, as it were,' said Bertie, fiddling with his top hat.

'We need to do something,' said Catsmeat, 'but what?'

'Revenge,' said Bingo, 'only Bastard mustn't get the blame.'

Flicking through his Eton Calendar, Bertie announced, 'I've got a Leave on Sunday.' I could take him out with me for the day.'

'But you don't know him, Woosy,' said Bingo.

'No, but my aunt does. Probably. My father did and uncle does, so it's likely she does.'

'Which aunt?' Bingo asked fondly, having met all four.

'Agatha,' said Bertie.

They all fell silent while that sunk in.

'Alright,' said Catsmeat suddenly cheerful again. 'That will take him out of Warre's. Then Bingo and I will prank up Spode when he's at Chapel.'

'But shouldn't you be there too?' asked Bertie.

'They won't miss us just the once. We've escaped detection at Absence enough to know the score. It's foolproof,' said Bingo.

'I've got a great idea,' said Bertie. He explained it to them. They caught his enthusiasm and could not gainsay his conclusion: 'What could possibly go wrong?'

⁓⁓

'Do hurry up, Bertie!' urged Aunt Agatha, as her nephew lagged behind Pellew-Bastard, jumping into the rear seats of the new Talbot 12 hp. Alongside her Uncle Spencer was grinding the car into first gear. 'Still getting the hang of this,' he said to no-one in particular. With a jerk, they headed off towards Datchet and lunch with Aunt Julia and her son Augustus at Beechwood, her house on the Thames.

'And how is your father, young Lancelot?' asked Uncle Spencer.

'Well, thank you, Mr. Gregson,' answered the boy politely.

'Knew him back in the Coldstream days in London, as did Bertie's parents and his Uncle Willoughby. Isn't that right, Bertie?'

Before Bertie could reply, Aunt Agatha asked Lancelot how he was enjoying Eton.

'Well, thank you, Mrs. Gregson,' the boy answered politely.

'No, he's not!' said Bertie. 'He's having a horrible

time. His fag-master, who is supposed to look after him, is the most mean, contemptible coward and cad imaginable and spends all his time bullying and beating him instead. And he's enormous.'

'And who is this boy?' asked Aunt Agatha, turning around.

'Oh, it's alright really,' said Lancelot.

'No, it's not!' said Bertie. 'His name is Spode. S-P-O-DE, Spode.'

'Spode', repeated Aunt Agatha, 'he must be one of Sidcup's younger boys? Sidcup was a Spode when I first met him.'

'I don't know,' said Bertie. 'There's no Sidcup at school.'

Uncle Gregson jerked the brakes. 'Blasted thing! Sidcup you say? Earl of Sidcup. Frightful little shit. Excuse my French. Rich as Croesus. Tight as Shylock. His eldest boy Roderick is a frightful little shit too.' Up front, gears grinded and with another j-j-judder they re-progressed towards Datchet. 'Spencer!' said Aunt Agatha to the Talbot 12 hp.

'And it's well known at school that Spode kicks Wolfgang,' said Lancelot.

'Who's Wolfgang?' asked Aunt Agatha.

'Wolfgang is Miss Atkins's dachshund. Spode says it's a German spy', replied Lancelot.

'Aunt Agatha has a dachshund, don't you Aunt Agatha?

It's called Wilhelmina.'

'*She's* called; for heaven's sake Bertie,' corrected Aunt
Agatha. Then to Lancelot: 'This Miss Atkins, who is she?'

'She's M'Dame,' interrupted Bertie. 'Looks after all the boys at Hawtrey's. She's swell.'

'Stop talking American, Bertie, you can hardly talk English.'

Soon they heaved into Beechwood, Aunt Julia's Queen Anne house on the river. Aunt Agatha held court at Aunt Julia's, as she did everywhere she went. Bertie and Lancelot skipped off along the Thames bank after lunch. Aunts and uncle were soon talking about Sidcups and Spodes, dachshunds and dames. Finally, Spencer said: 'Well Agatha, we must do something about it.' A glint crossed the auntly eye, a twitch caught the auntly lips.

'Time to take the boys back to school. Lock-up must be in an hour or so. Come along Spencer,' she said.

'They're in the garden,' said Aunt Julia.

Aunt Agatha opened the French windows: 'Do come along Bertie, we're leaving now. Don't forget Lancelot.' Then turning around to Spencer and Julia, remarked: 'Sometimes I despair of that boy. He lives in a daze. A daze of his own. Never mind, I expect he'll grow out of it.'

❦

Giving three taps on Bertie's room door, and whispering, 'Woosy, Woosy, open up,' there was Bingo.

'It's open,' said Bertie, sitting majestically at his empty burry. Shirking their Latin division, Bingo and Catsmeat poured in.

'Spode has gone bananas, Woosy,' said Bingo.

'Tell all,' said Bertie.

'The rose hip powder worked.' Bingo announced.

'Rather too well. He was up itching all night, like a bear with a sore head.'

'And fleas I wouldn't be surprised to hear,' said Bertie.

'And did he find the note under the pillow like we planned?'

'*Leave off Bastard you bastard.* Yes, he found the note all right. But now he wants all the boys to show him their handwriting.'

'Excellent,' Bertie said, clapping his hands, 'just as I planned and why we agreed I should write it left-handed. In just this eventu-al. Number one genius idea, I'm not in your house; number two genius idea, written with a southpaw, all perfectly planned.'

'Yes, but he saw it was written southpaw. Now he wants to see all boys' left-hand writing so he can find out who wrote it.

Meanwhile, he has put all the squits on floggers, one a day till the culprit gives himself up.'

'Gosh,' said Bertie, 'bit of an overreaction. All the squits on floggers. One a day. Don't like the sound of that. That will never do.'

'No, it jolly well won't,' said Catsmeat. 'It will be Bingo's and my turn in a couple of weeks.'

The three fell silent as they pondered what to do.

'There's only one thing for it,' said Bertie after a while, 'I'll have to own up or I'll be scouted as a dastardly coward. I'll say it was all me and no-one else. I'm not in his house so he can't flog me. Ergo sum whatsit.'

'No, but it can't have been you Woosy,' said Bingo, 'any more than it could have been Bastard. You are each other's alibi.'

'True, I hadn't thought of that,' said Bertie, adjusting

his turned-down collar in the mirror.

The three fell silent again as they pondered what to do, again.

'There's only one thing for it,' said Bertie, 'we'll have to raise the stakes. Defence is the best form of attack. Learned it in Latin last week. An artful dodge hoves into view. When will the man-mountain Spode absolutely be guaranteed to be out of his house next?'

'Saturday afternoon. School rugger versus Dulwich College. He's a tight head prop in the fifteen. Biggest boy on the pitch. He won't miss that. Loves it out there,' said Catsmeat.

'And, what then Woosy?' Bingo wondered.

'His room is on the top floor I presume?' asked Bertie.

The others nodded.

'Then, I shall enter his room and make him an apple-pie bed. Then leave an identical note, with the southpaw writing, under the same pillow. If I'm not mistaken that will a) drive him mad and b) drive home the old messagio.'

'But Woosy, you'll be seen in the house. Lots of boys will be there. It's a half-holiday,' Bingo cautioned.

'Then I shall go up the fire escape. I presume there is a fire escape?' said Bertie.

'Yes, all the way up the outside,' confirmed Catsmeat.

'But what about us?'

'You two will be at Sixpenny, watching Spode smashing up the good boys from Dulwich. There's your alibi. Can't have been you, when he goes bananas a second time. Make sure Bastard is with you too,' said Bertie.

Three days later, on Saturday afternoon, just after rugger kick-off, Bertie found himself at the bottom of a suspiciously rickety looking fire escape. He looked up and counted five floors. The first floor was gained easily enough, the second with the first feelings of queasiness, by the third floor he was telling himself he mustn't look down, by the fourth floor he was only looking down and on the fifth floor his head was spinning and his hands holding tight onto the railings.

Spode's room was now in front of him. The sash windows were closed; he hadn't thought of that. Of course they were, mid-winter and all that. But were they locked? He pushed up under the top pane. It gave freely enough. From inside he heard a shriek. Instinctively, he cupped his face in his hands and pressed up close to look inside. He saw a long leg on a bed sticking out from behind a curtain, a Spode leg, and on the end of it a big foot, a Spode foot, being bandaged by a woman; must be the house dame. In that split second the dame saw Bertie as clearly as Bertie saw the dame.

He recoiled, turned round, looked down, grabbed the railing tight and hooked it. Within three seconds he heard a hearty roar from the room above. 'Hey, stop!' It was Spode. Then he heard large clumps on the metal stairs above; Spode one-footed, hopping, in full descent half a floor behind him. He mustn't let Spode see him. As Bertie fled and Spode chased him down the stairs, Bertie quickened with each flight and the handicapped Spode slowed. At ground zero, Bertie turned sharp left and sprinted up Common Lane and past the Burning

Bush towards School Yard, to be lost in the milling throng walking to and from the playing fields.

'Spode's out crook,' said Bingo, when Bertie caught up with him, Catsmeat and Bastard on the touchline. 'Something up with his foot during the warm-up.'

'I know,' said Bertie.

'How do you know?' asked Catsmeat.

Bertie then told them all about his great fire escape escapade, the dame and the damaged foot, the vertigo and the vertical dash for freedom.

'Cripes,' said Catsmeat.

'Rats,' said Bingo.

'Oh dear,' said Bastard.

'What now?' asked Bertie.

∽≈∾

After Sunday lunch, Munro-Geddes rose to read Notices. After the usual announcements about Sunday evening and Monday morning, reporting on Saturday's games results with special commendations to this boy and that boy and without a word of news from the front, he said: 'Yesterday there was an attempted break-in at Warre's by a boy from school. Warre's M'Dame got a good look at him but didn't recognise him, so the thief is not from that House. The attempted robbery was targeted at the room of the school rugby fifteen prop, Spode. Spode gave chase but being injured before the Dulwich game was pulled up. But he called the police....'

Bertie felt his face redden and pulse quicken.

'... and the police told the Head. After tea today there will be a line-up of all the boys in the School Yard, so that Warre's M'Dame can identify the culprit.

I'm sure he is not from Hawtrey's but we must comply. That's all.'

That afternoon Bertie walked alone up the High Street towards Windsor. He knew he was doomed. Spode had called the police, the police had called the Head, the Head had called the dame and the dame was certain to point the finger right at the Bertram chest. He would, in short order, be: flogged by the Head, arrested by the constabulary, up before the *magistratus*, thrown out of Hawtrey, sacked from school and sent home to Easeby. All before the age of fifteen. After that the unknown. There was no way out, he was a sitting duck awaiting his turn in the headlights.

Tea came and went for the others in Hawtrey's. Bertie's stomach felt as if a lead balloon had finally found its landing ground and was now looking for a permanent hangar. The end-of-tea bell tolled and tolled for he. All the boys trooped out for the line-up, looking forward to this new adventure, chattering and chirping as usual and were soon mingling with the boys from neighbouring houses, until this mingle was joined by outlying mingles and within minutes eight hundred boys below sixth form were standing, shivering in the School Yard beneath the fine bronze statue of the school's founder, King Henry VI.

The headmaster, the later ridiculed pacifist Rev. Hon. Edward Lyttelton, stood on the steps of the chapel, dressed in his official garb and shouted for the boys to line-up in order. Bertie's number was 97; 96 more juniors were on his right and 812 more seniors on his left. At the foot of the steps stood Spode; alongside him were two officers from the Royal Berkshire Constabulary, handcuffs at the ready; and alongside them was Miss Cuthbert, the dame from Warre who had seen Bertie, his peering face framed by his cupped hands, so clearly through the glass.

With what seemed to Bertie like unnecessary ceremony, this hounder of the Woosters crossed the yard with persecutory intent and laid eyes on the first boy in the line; the one 812 places to Bertie's left. Slowly she walked down the line. The proved innocent stayed behind to witness the shaming of the guilty. For number 97 it was an eternity of slow torture; Mistress Cuthbert was agonising over the guilt or innocence of each boy as if performing a duty even more solemn than the one to hand.

700; 600; 500; 400; 300; 200 boys; down the line she passed. She was now close enough for Bertie to see her as recognisably as he had through Spode's window, applying the Spode bandage to the Spode foot. 180; 150; 120, nearer, yet still nearer. And then a distraction, a disturbance and all boys looked towards the archway adjoining Brewhouse Yard. Through it drove a powder blue Talbot 12 hp. It parked in front of Spode and the constables and behind the deliberating Miss Cuthbert.

All attention now turned to the Talbot. Out of it leaped a dachshund, then a second dachshund, then the long legs of Miss Atkins, the dame from Hawtrey, then the long skirt of Aunt Agatha.

'Who's in charge here?' she demanded, pointing her walking stick at the reverend on the steps.

'I am the headmaster,' replied Lyttelton, 'and may I ask who you are?'

'Never mind that!' barked Aunt. 'You have a

particularly vile boy here who is also a kicker of dachshunds. I know his name but not his appearance. I will leave the offended dog to find him. The dog is clearly far more intelligent than he is. You have done well to for prepare this line-up of boys for our bully hunt.' Turning to the Hawtrey dame, she urged: 'Come along now Atkins, bring your dog to bear.'

'I'm really not sure all this is necessary, Mrs. Gregson,' replied the shrinking M'Dame.

'Of course it's necessary or we would not be doing it. Bring Wolfgang along the line. Now, Atkins, now. Wilhelmina, you come too.'

Thus in quick succession to the official inspection, the unofficial one filed down the line. This latter appraisal sped along much faster than the first. Aunt Agatha led the way, followed by Wilhelmina trotting behind, followed by Miss Atkins with Wolfgang on a lead. No-one was quite sure why they were doing what they were doing, Wolfgang least of all. As she sped past Bertie he gave his aunt a beaming smile, of relief as much as welcome, but she failed to see him. Wilhelmina, though, did stop, jumped up Bertie's leg and gave him a big dachshund tail wag and friendly yelp. Aunt Agatha looked back 'Ah, it's you Bertie. Might have known you would be in the thick of it. Still, it's not you being beastly this time.' Then Miss Atkins arrived and Wolfgang recognised Bertie too, who soon had two dachshunds admiring him. Ninety-six pairs of trousers later both dogs and both dames were at the ends of the line.

Wolfgang then looked around. And froze. Then unfroze, barking madly, pulling on the lead directly at Spode. A convoy was soon on its way: Wolfgang in the fore, followed by Wilhelmina on his shoulder, followed by Miss Atkins on a lead, with the saintly aunt bringing up the rear. She was, however, the first to utter a word: 'Who are you?'

'My name is Spode,' the same answered, with as much dignity as the situation allowed.

'Arrest him!' ordered Aunt Agatha, to the two of Windsor's finest.

'What for?' asked a perplexed looking Lyttleton, now down from the top of the steps. 'Don't you know, he's a prop in the rugby fifteen.'

'I don't care if he's the whole team of England. He is guilty of cruelty to animals under the Cruelty to Animals Act of 1876. Arrest him now!' The constables duly obliged and with Aunt Agatha's walking stick prodding him in the back, Spode was led away.

Now she turned back to Lyttleton: 'I expect you to expel him too.' Then glaring at the boys gathered around: 'You can all go now. But learn your lesson. Dogs will not be kicked. Off you go.' As they dispersed excitedly, she shouted, 'Bertie! Where are you? Bertie! You can come with me. Atkins, you can go too.' Then bending down to Wolfgang and cooing most unAunt Agathaesquely, 'Who's a good boy then?'

❦

In the Talbot 12 hp Aunt Agatha told Bertie he was going to accompany her to tea at Fuller's in Windsor.

Over tea she spoke to him about matters Bastardian and dachshundian.

'After lunch with your Aunt Julia I wrote to that fool Lyttleton's sister, Lady Massinghorn, whom I know from the Women at War Committee. She found your Miss Atkins, who said her dog was indeed called Wolfgang and a dachshund. Wirehaired unfortunately but still a dachshund. Wirehair is bordering on the indiscreet, much better a smooth hair, much more *au point*. I told her to have it put down and insert a smooth hair in his stead but I doubt if she listened. Odd girl. Mind you, she would be, locked up there with all you ghastly boys.'

Bertie pointed to the next slice of chocolate cake but before he could ask, she answered.

'If you must. I always say chocolate cake must be bad for you as it tastes so good. Now where was I? Oh yes, I am honorary president of the Society for the Appreciation of Dachshunds. We have heard about these German spy scare stories before. Completely ridiculous. My dogs are thoroughbred English, more English than a lot of members of so-called society. Anyway, I told Atkins her Wolfgang was under attack as a fifth columnist and she must join in. "United we stand, divided we fall", that's our motto.'

'But how did she know it was Spode?' asked Bertie.

'She didn't, I didn't trust her not to cosy up to the Cuthbert woman and let Spode off the hook. He had to be a taught a lesson.'

'But how did you know Wolfgang would pick out Spode?'

'He's a dachshund you stupid boy, haven't you been listening to a word I'm saying?'

'But you knew it was Spode,' said Bertie.

'Of course I did, you told me. Good heavens Bertie, keep up.'

'So, what now?'

'What now is that as usual I have arranged everything according to the natural order of things. You go back to school, although I don't suppose it will do you any good. Latin and Greek are harmless enough pursuits but best left to the eager. Take my advice and just learn manners. Too much education clouds the brain and can become vulgar.

'Sidcup will bail out Spode, although the few pounds involved will upset his equilibrium. Spode will learn his lesson, before he becomes a menace to society. Wolfgang will unfortunately remain wirehaired and Wilhelmina will benefit enormously from my company. Atkins and Cuthbert will go back to daming, or whatever these dames call it. And you will see me on Boxing Day at Easeby. You'll be looking forward to that."

Yes, Aunt Agatha,' said Bertie, eyeing his third slice of Fuller's Old Favourite Chocolate Cream Layer Cake.

CHAPTER 3

The Oxford Blues

Trinity Term, May 1921

It was, everyone later agreed, a most wondrous evening; wondrous that is until Grabber mentioned Bertie's jazz band's turn the following evening. But for now everything was perfect: two hundred undergrads sitting around U-shaped tables on the Cloisters Lawn at Magdalen College, a sunny early summer evening, a hint of a breeze, wine flowing like banter, glorious surroundings, something to celebrate, good cheer, a classic bump-supper.

'Whoa!' two hundred voices chimed as one, then the shout 'Bump!' as four hundred palms slammed the tables to see whose cutlery would fly the highest. Five more Whoas, Bumps and hand slams to celebrate Magdalen's six bumps in this year's VIIIs Week followed in quick stroke. Then the President of the Junior Common Room, Oswald J. Grabber, also Secretary General of the Snafflers' Club, floundered to his feet. Bread rolls and bits of bread rolls, whole apples and apple cores arced their way over to him, without noticeable accuracy.

'Now look here, you shower of charlatans, silence!' Grabber shouted. The din died down, partially. 'Victory was ours. We rowed, we skulled, we coxed, we BUMPED, yes SIX TIMES did we bump. The first VIII with three bumps, we salute you: our captain, myself! Hurrah!

Our stroke and coach Cheesewright, our number seven Anstruther, our middle crew myself again, Pinker, Rhodes-Boyce and Porter, our bow pair: Fotherington and Baddeley. Our second VIII with one bump; our third VIII with two bumps, we salute you too. For those that did row, we salute you! Three cheers for St. Custard's! Hip, hip...' Shouts of 'Wrong school!' drew him up short. 'Three cheers for Magdalen College!' Now all stood and cheered 'Hip hip hooray! Hip hip hooray!! Hip hip hooray!!!' Then in one crescendo all together: *'Floreat Magdalena!'*

As all fell back down Grabber continued: 'Now we look forward to tomorrow night. Three years after the war and now we revive the end of VIII's Week celebration, now called the Heads of the River Burlesque. We have music, we have comedy, we have magic, we have juggling, we have ventriloquism and this year for the first time, and the first time in Oxford, we have what we have all heard so much about, we have jazz.'

'Oh God!' said Bertie.

'What's up?' asked Harold 'Ginger' Winship.

'What's up? What's up is this time tomorrow in that new big marquee on New Buildings Lawn, yours truly has to play three Dixieland jazz numbers, to wit *I Wish I Could Shimmy Like My Sister Kate, The Sheik of Araby* and *Bugle Call Rag* with an ensemble that is anything but together. Let alone rehearsed more than twice. The word hearse lies within. Oh God is what's up!'

'Who've you got in there Bertie?' asked Harold 'Stinker' Pinker, ducking a bread roll.

'What are you called, Bertie?' asked Marmaduke 'Chuffy' Chuffnell.

'We are the Magdalen All Stars,' said Bertie, 'only we aren't. All Stars. None of us are stellar and one of our number is decidedly unstellar.' Bertie looked around; 'Squawky' Phungie-Phipps-Farmer was out of earshot halfway along the table, fashioning a catapult from his pudding spoon. 'Squawky is well named,' said Bertie, 'what he does to a violin is anything but sympa to the old *oreilles*.'

'Can't you find another player?' asked Chuffy.

'Not without breaking his heart,' said Bertie. 'Thing is he's dead keen. He's been practising all day and night, down by the river, out of earshot thank heavens. Even the swans have sought solace in the shrubbery. No, it has got be him. Half the problem is his violin, won't stay in tune, sounds like the mating call of a deranged gorgon that's just lost an argument with the Cowley omnibus.'

'Well that's easy,' said the third Harold, 'Beefy' Anstruther, 'find him another one.'

'Anything but easy, my fellow blue,' explained Bertie. 'Squawky's pockets are not deep. Unlike turnips, violins don't grow on trees.'

Beefy, Chuffy, Ginger, Stinker and Bertie looked as one at the remains of a carafe of college claret. Inspiration stayed firmly *par terre*, as sunken as their spirits.

'Hang on, hang on, hang on!' said Bertie. 'The answer is obvious. Staring us in the face. The violin to end all violins is not a million miles away. And there for the borrowing I'll wager.'

Four heads closed in on the one carafe, waiting for this bright idea to spread its wings.

'Le Messie,' said Bertie, 'the world's most perfect, actually the only perfect, Stradivarius. Stuck in the Ashmolean. Not doing anyone any good. Dying to be a fiddle for a night. We borrow it for our turn, slip it back, no-one knows, none the wiser, that sort of thing.'

Mouths opened at the audaciousness of Bertie's plan. They all knew Le Messie, the Messiah, so-called because like the messiah the world had waited and waited for it to appear and it never does. When Stradivari made it in 1716, the owner locked it away and the world has been kept waiting ever since. As far as is known it has been played only once and the Ashmolean intended to keep it that way. It is now safe and sound in a hermetically sealed glass case in the new Sainsbury section; in 1921 it was in a glass bell jar on the second floor of the old West Wing.

'And,' said Bertie, now righteously enthused, 'Ginger and I can then join the Snafflers Club. As long as Jumbo writes us up as proof of the snaffling. *Où est Jumbo?*'

'Wait a moment Bertie,' said Ginger, 'what's Ginger got to do with all this? And I'm not sure I want to be a Snaffler. And Jumbo is in his set, deadlines and all that.'

Snaffling two full carafes of claret and half a Victoria Sponge cake, the five trooped off to find Jumbo. Rupert Maxwell-Gumbleton's set, his set of rooms, was on the first floor staircase of Cloisters III. He had turned his sitting room into an editor's suite from where he published *The Oxford Blues*, the new satirical student magazine aimed at, as he put it 'upsetting as many people as eight pages can upset'. This was his first of many media adventures; in later years he dropped the Gumbleton and became plain Rupert Maxwell.

'You'll never guess what, Jumbo,' said Stinker, walking straight through a side table piled high with well-ordered loose leafs, 'but Bertie and Ginger are going to snaffle Le Messie and Squawky is going to play it tomorrow night in the All Stars.'

'Fantastic,' said Jumbo, 'the Heads Burlesque is our lead story this week. But how will we know it's Le Messie and not any old Stradiwotnot?'

'Because,' said Bertie, 'you are going to come along with your camera and notepad and record the whole episode so Ginger and I can join the Snafflers' Club. Here's the plan.'

Bertie explained the plan and a minute later Ginger completed phase one, walking in holding Squawky's violin. As Bertie said: 'See? What could possibly go wrong?'

By 10 p.m. it was dark in the sky and not much lighter in the streets as six bicycles wobbled their way up the High, turned right and past Radcliffe Camera and the Bodleian Library, then left on to Broad Street. All was quiet, save for the sound of the remnants of revelry from Trinity and Balliol Colleges. A short right swerve into St. Giles and there they were, outside the Taylor Institute serving as an East Wing to the Ashmolean Museum.

INSTITUTIO announces the left column of its portico and TAYLORIANA announces itself opposite that, but inside the Taylor Institute only modern languages are read. This was supposed to be Bertie's lair in the day, there for the purpose of his reading the French modern language, but the lecture room had seldom seen him and the library records barely knew his name. Bertie at least had the key and in went Bertie, Ginger and Jumbo. They had only one torch between them, which Bertie shone as best he could, followed by Ginger holding the recently liberated Squawkyvarius in an old blue swag bag and then Jumbo, lugging his photographer detritus in a large holdall over his shoulder. All was quiet therein; the noisiest sounds were their telling each other to 'Shush!' Ginger asked if they shouldn't wait till tomorrow when they were sober, or at least more sober; Bertie told him it was already tomorrow, jazz-turn-wise.

Bertie may not have studied much French but he knew his way around the building. Up they went to the first floor by the grand staircase, along through the library shelves to the lesser north staircase and up to the second floor. Bertie's beam soon found what it was looking for: Fire Exit. They pushed through and climbed the outside metal staircase onto the roof.

'It's filthy,' said Ginger.

'Shut up!' said Jumbo.

'Come on!' said Bertie, as reluctant pigeons flapped to the skies. Across the top of the Ashmolean entrance they walked and down the corresponding metal staircase into the top floor of the West Wing.

'I bet it's locked,' whispered Ginger.

'Shut up!' whispered Jumbo.

'It's open,' whispered Bertie, as they pushed through and walked down to the second floor.

And there it was, just where it was meant to be, right in the centre of the gallery, surrounded by glass cabinets and standing proud under a glass bell jar, Le Messie himself, perhaps herself, time would tell.

'Ready with the camera, Jumbo?' asked Bertie.

'Shine the light,' said Jumbo, fumbling into his bag of tricks. One by one out they came: the flash stand, then the flash lamp, then the powder, then the sparker, then the tripod and then the press camera.

As quietly and quickly as the paraphernalia allowed, Jumbo set up his rig. Soon an unwelcome diversion: from outside arose the sound of drunken hooligans cavorting on Beaumont Street. Inside Bertie, Jumbo and Ginger realised as one what that was: Stinker, Beefy and Chuffy setting off the planned diversionary tactic, posing to be worse drunks and more degenerate hooligans than they already were. It had seemed a good idea at the time back in Jumbo's set; now the last thing the inside team needed was the outside team drawing the rossers around.

Ginger felt his way through the gallery toward the dim light from the window. He opened it and shouted down: 'Shut up you idiots, you'll bring the rossers round!'

Unfortunately the hooligans below responded in kind: 'Have you snaffled it yet, Ginger?' yelled up Beefy.

Meanwhile all was not going well in the gallery. Jumbo's powder was in the tee-frame, the camera was primed and on its tripod, Bertie had lifted off the glass bell with one hand and had Le Messie in the other, the Squawkyvarius as in situ, Ginger had fumbled his way back from the window, but the sparker wouldn't light the powder.

'Anyone got a light?' whispered Jumbo.

In the gloom Bertie gave him his cigarette lighter.

'Not meant to use these,' said Jumbo, 'get ready.'

Bertie and Ginger posed beside the lifted Stradivarius and the replacee Squawkyvarius.

'Hey, Bertie, Ginger, Jumbo, what's happening up there?!' shouted a raucous voice from the street. 'Hurry up, it's getting cold out here!'

Whoosh! went the powder, but the flash failed to follow suit.

'Damn!' said Jumbo, holding his burnt hand.

'Try again,' said Ginger.

Jumbo lit a paper taper first and tried again. Success!

Bertie and Ginger framed for posterity and this week's edition of *The Oxford Blues*, with one hand each on the Stradivarius and the other on the Squawkyvarius and the display cabinets of the Ashmolean clearly there behind them.

Now outside a new sound: the ringing bells of a police car, then another. Bertie, Ginger and Jumbo stumbled to the window, knocking over vitrines and banging into cabinets on their way. Outside they saw Beefy, Stinker and Chuffy being helped, none too civilly, into the back of a Black Maria. Inside they made a rush for the Fire Exit, the rooftop and the Taylor Institute.

As they were leaving Jumbo asked if they had the Stradiwotnot.

'Well spotted Jumbo,' said Bertie, fumbling back to retrieve it.

⌘

The Magdalen All Stars jazz turn swung along swimmingly. That afternoon they had managed to squeeze in two more rehearsals and decided to change the order, opening with *Bugle Call Rag* to ease themselves in, then the mid-tempo *I Wish I Could Shimmy Like My Sister Kate*, and finishing with a foot-stomping version of *The Sheik of Araby*.

For most of the audience it was the first time they had heard jazz played live, or even at all. Bertie's improvised piano solos in the middle eight of *I Wish I Could Shimmy Like My Sister Kate* drew a fine round of applause and Squawky's swirling introduction to *The Sheik of Araby* showed the Stradivarius at its best, and when the rhythm section picked up the beat on the thirteenth bar the marquee was fairly jumping.

An impromptu after-party sprung up in Francis 'Bicky' Bickersteth's set on the Cloisters II staircase and the boys and their fans all retired to the arms of Morpheus, well-oiled and well-praised.

⌒⌒⌒

'Bertie, Bertie, wake up, disaster!'

'Ginger? Is that you? What is it? What time is it? Where are we? Why are we?'

'No time for philosophy now, Bertie. The Messiah has gone missing'.

Bertie eased himself onto one elbow, then the other, and brought the day slowly into focus. Like this Wednesday morning, the full impact of the startling news was beginning to dawn on him. 'What do you mean gone missing?'

'What I mean is, I went to Squawky's room to relieve him of the Messiah for safe keeping till our swap back tonight and it wasn't there. He wasn't there. It's been swiped.'

'Maybe he's taken it with him,' said Bertie hopefully.

50

'Where is he?' Ginger shrugged. 'I know,' Bertie said, 'I bet he's in the lab, setting fire to Bunsen burners or whatever it is they do down there.'

And twenty minutes later they found him there in the lab, pouring the contents of one test tube into another. But while Squawky was there, the Messiah was elsewhere. Ginger posed the question of the moment.

'Oh yes Ginger,' said Squawky, 'I sold it after the turn.'

Ginger and Bertie tried to say something but only strange noises escaped. Squawky explained: Burlesque over, a very nice man in a sheepskin coat and trilby hat had approached him and said how much he enjoyed Squawky's playing and how sweet his violin sounded and would Squawky sell him said violin as a memento of the evening. Squawky asked him for how much, the very nice man in the sheepskin coat and trilby hat said £100. 'Well I only paid £10 second-hand for it, so of course I said yes.'

Back in Ginger's set, Bertie and he held a council of war. The bright idea occurred to them that things weren't quite as bad as they seemed because all they had to do was leave the Squawkyvarius where the Stradivarius should be and quite likely no one would be any the wiser, at least until they had come down from Oxford, by which time the perpetrators could have been any of thousands of other merry pranksters. All they had to do was persuade Jumbo to spike the story and no-one would ever know. Shame about missing out on the Snafflers but *tant pis*. All they had to do right now was find Jumbo.

At which point Jumbo came breezing into Ginger's set, flung a fresh copy of *The Oxford Blues* down on the table and said, 'There you are Bertie and Ginger, fame at last!' For the second time in thirty minutes Bertie's and Ginger's mouths moved but only strange noises escaped.

Ginger picked up the paper and when words escaped said, 'Cripes Bertie, we're in the soup here. Last night is all over the front page. Photograph came out well.'

'Never mind that,' said Bertie reading the front page. 'But it's meant to be coming out tomorrow, Thursday, isn't it?' asked Bertie. 'Isn't it?'

'No,' said Jumbo, 'it always comes out on a Wednesday, you know that.'

'But we haven't swapped it back yet, the Squawky-varius for the Stradivarius. We're doing that tonight.'

'But you said you were going to swap them back after the concert,' said Jumbo.

'But not *right* after the concert, just ordinary after the concert. Tonight, for example. In time for this week's edition. To get into the Snafflers.'

Bertie read it out: 'Headline, The Messiah Cometh, by Arnold Wratt, Chief Crime Reporter. Who's that?'

'Well it couldn't be me,' said Jumbo, 'so I made him up.'

Bertie read on: 'The Magdalen All Stars' triumphant jazz turn at the Head of the River Burlesque last night had a secret ingredient, the world's most reclusive Stradivarius violin, known as the Messiah.

'Liberated from, and since returned to, the Ashmolean Museum by the band's pianist Bertram Wooster and his accomplice Harold Winship, and photographed by the *Blues'* star undercover photographer, the Messiah showed every sign of enjoying his night out. Played with great gusto by science student Basil Phungie-Phipps-Farmer, the Stradivarius showed its pedigree with deep harmonious tones and sprightly rhythms.

'Now safely back on display on the second floor of the Ashmolean Museum, the Messiah will need to be more securely guarded in the future.

'The *Blues* says: "Why, Oh Why? Who let their guard down caring for a National Treasure?" At the time of going to press the Museum's directors were not available for comment.

'Next Week: we profile the guilty men who let the Messiah be stolen and profile the heroes Wooster and Winship who borrowed it to publicise a woeful lack of security for the sake of the new music fad, jazz.'

Jumbo asked if Bertie had seen the other lead story on the front page. He had not. Jumbo read it out: 'Magdalen Three in Ashmolean Riot. Three Magdalen students, Harold Pinker, Harold Anstruther and Marmaduke Chuffnell spent last night in Oxford Gaol after being charged with Causing a Public Nuisance, Being Drunk and Disorderly and Riotous Assembly.

They were caught red-handed cavorting in a flamboyant manner outside the Ashmolean Museum at 11 p.m.

'Sentencing them this morning to a fine of £5 each, the magistrate Boris Wormwood JP said they were especially culpable in view of their elevated positions in society. Pinker is reading Divinity, Anstruther is a Racquets Half-Blue and Chuffnell is a Peer of the Realm.'

'Never mind that,' said Bertie, 'we are in far deeper mire than that, about as mirey as soup can get.' He then told Jumbo about the missing Messiah.

'Ah,' said Jumbo with one eye on next week's headline, 'now that's really interesting.'

It didn't take long for their Junior Common Room President and Head Snaffler Oswald J. Grabber to swagger in.

'Chaps,' he said to the three musketeers, 'I come bearing mixed news. The Snafflers Club would be pleased if Wooster and Winship would join our band of light-fingered pranksters. But you two are also in what I call the soup. Up to the rim of the bowl. Without a spoon. I've been sent by the President himself to escort Messrs Wooster and Winship to Wellington Square.'

'Who's there?' asked Jumbo, with the other eye on the week after's headline.

'The Vice-Chancellor Lewis Farnell for one, then there's Hardinge Cosgrove, Chief Constable of the Oxfordshire Constabulary and Professor Augustus Looseleaf, Chancellor of the Ashmolean. Whose own head is not a million miles away from what I call the block.'

And so there they all were, sitting around a desk in the Vice-Chancellor's office in Wellington Square. Bertie and Ginger stood in front of them.

The Vice-Chancellor was the first to weigh in: 'There's no need to beat about the bush. Wooster and Winship, you have been caught red-handed, largely by your own love of self-aggrandisement.'

Next was Looseleaf: 'We have already had the national press call round this morning. *The Morning Post* and the Sketch, others will soon be here. But we are willing to forgive and forget if you return Le Messie immediately. Then I can tell the press it was false news. A student jape. Isn't that right, Chief Constable, no charges in exchange for the safe return?'

Then came Cosgrove: 'If you say so sir, personally I'd have all the young sirs' guts for garters and then I would apply pressure where the young sirs would notice it, sir.'

'Right-o,' said Bertie, 'one Le Messie soon to be returned to the bosom of the Ashmolean. No more said.'

Outside Bertie and Ginger agreed on many things, but one thing above all: they needed a miracle.

~∽∾

It was already dusk when Jumbo, head down laying out type face, bellowed 'Enter!'

'Mr. Maxwell-Gumbleton?'

'I am he; who are you?' Jumbo looked up to see a shallow-looking man in a sheepskin coat and trilby hat.

'My name is ... well, never mind that. I saw your paper this morning and I have something that might interest you.'

'Go on,' said Jumbo.

'The Stradivarius. The Messiah. I have it.'

Jumbo stopped doing whatever it was that he was doing. 'Go on.'

'May I sit down?' Jumbo motioned to his armchair. 'I took it home last night and played it. It was beautiful to hear, if I say so myself. Far too good for me. I am an amateur player, gifted if I say so myself. But then I only play to myself, for my own satisfaction. Then I read your paper and realised what I had done. But I know it has value, far more than I paid for it.'

'So you want to sell it back to Mr. Phungie-Phipps-

55

Farmer? For a fat profit no doubt,' said Jumbo, now all ears.

'No, not that. I want to exchange it.'

'For?'

'As I said, I am a solitary player, happiest playing beautiful music to myself. There is a signed, original music manuscript I want, an original autograph, as it's called. A lovely violin sonata. Handel's *Sonata in D Major, Opus 1 Number 13* to be precise.'

'So?'

'So it's in the Bodleian Library.'

'So are you saying you will swap Le Messie for the Handel autograph?'

'That's it. I'll be back at midnight. If you have the Handel you can have the Messiah. Can't say fairer than that.'

'And if we don't have the Handel?'

'Then you don't have the Messiah.'

With that the man in the sheepskin coat and trilby hat slipped out, pursued moments later by Jumbo, hotfooting himself to Bertie's set.

Jumbo laid out what was on offer. Bertie wasn't one of life's great thinkers but he gave it his best. He could go back to Looseleaf, spill the beans, own up to a prank gone wrong, hand himself over to the constables, become closely acquainted with the inmates of Oxford Gaol and be the brunt of national humiliation. Or he could borrow the Handel autograph and if all went well swap it for the Messiah, hand it back to Looseleaf and no more said. But if liberating the Handel went wrong too, there would be an upset Bodleian as well as an upset Ashmolean, there would be more than one

Looseleaf, more than a few local constables, a worse fate than Oxford Gaol and not just humiliation but condemnation, and not just national but international. Deep in thunk, deciding first this way and then that way, Bertie was interrupted by a knock on the door.

It was his scout, Merriweather. 'Telegram for you Mr. Wooster.'

It read: 'JUST HEARD YOUR VIOLIN DISGRACE FROM EDITOR TIMES STOP FAMILY NAME UNDONE STOP YOU ARE IMBECILE STOP ON MY WAY IMMEDIATELY STOP AUNT DAHLIA'

Bertie turned to Ginger and Jumbo: '*Ça change tout*. Who knows their way around the Bod?'

⸏⸏⸏

'I won't Bertie, I absolutely won't. And there's an end to it,' said Stinker firmly in response to Bertie's suggestion that he help them be the vandal that stole the Handel.

'But Stinker, you are our only way into the Bod. Through the Divinity School where you learn your trade,' said Ginger.

'Come on Stinker,' said Jumbo, with an eye on a held front page. 'Just let them in, they'll do the rest.'

'So all I have to do,' said Stinker, 'is unlock the door to the Divinity School?'

'And lock it back up again on our way out,' said Bertie.

'That's it, you've already told us where the Handel is. First vitrine on the left of Duke Humfrey's Library on the first floor.'

'And what if you are caught? I'll be drummed out of the clergy before I've even started.'

'We won't be caught.' said Bertie, 'It's so simple. What could possibly go wrong?'

While the three wise men were twisting Stinker's not inconsiderable arm, another meeting was happening in Grabber's suite. Aunt Dahlia's friendly editor at *The Times*, Wickham Steed, had not only warned her of *her* nephew's impending incarceration but also recommended that *his* nephew, Oswald Grabber, a kind of head boy at Magdalen College, would be a good starting point in her quest to unscramble her nephew's predicament.

Grabber was as good as his recommendation. First he rounded up Phungie-Phipps-Farmer and found out about the man in the sheepskin coat and trilby hat. Then he called an impromptu meeting of the Snafflers. Had anyone come across a local man, the trademark of whom was a sheepskin coat and trilby hat? One of them had. Roland 'Good Thinking' Carruthers had bought a second-hand cart from him at the start of Trinity Term. Did Good Thinking know from where the sheepskin-clad cart trader traded? He did. The Warren Street Stables in Cowley.

<hr>

Thus that Wednesday night two burglaries took place. At the Bodleian Library, Stinker duly climbed up the Proscholium and unlocked the Divinity School's ancient and venerable front gate and then slipped into the shadows of the Old Schools Quad. Inside Bertie's torch beam found the old stone spiral stairs up the Duke Humfrey's Library and once inside soon found the first vitrine on the left. Like last night's display in the Ashmolean, it was not locked. While Bertie held the torch, Ginger put the music manuscript in his old blue swag bag and as quietly as they had arrived they left. Out of the shadows came Stinker, the only sound was the squeaking of a very old key turning in a very old lock.

'Sounded like the Squawkyvarius,' quipped Bertie, as they walked past Radcliffe Camera. 'We are getting rather good at this. See Stinker, what did I tell you, what could possibly go wrong?'

Meanwhile, over in Cowley an equally smooth operation was taking place. Good Thinking had called round to see our friend in the sheepskin coat and trilby hat and asked for a test ride in another old cart, but this time at Magdalen later that evening. With the Warren Street Stables unmanned it was the work of a moment for Grabber and two others Snafflers to find the Messiah and bring him back to the college and into the hands of Aunt Dahlia.

Back in Jumbo's set Bertie put his hands behind his head, his feet up on desk and rocked back in the chair. 'You know Jumbo, that was a close shave in the soup back there. But all's well that ends well as Dickens so rightly has it. What time does our friend with the Messiah arrive?'

'Anytime now, Bertie. One Stradiwotnot for one Handel sonata.' He picked up the music manuscript. 'Who'd have thought they mattered so much?'

'Strange world indeed, Jumbo, strange world indeed. Anyway, better toddle back to the old bedstead, job well done, forty winks and all that.'

Bertie swapped one Cloisters staircase for another

and pushed open his door.

'Aunt Dahlia!' said Bertie, taken aback. 'This is a nice surprise. To what do I owe the hon....'

'Don't be a fool Bertie, you know why I'm here. You received my telegram?'

'Ah, that, yes, I suppose I did. But no need for concern, Aged A in a very short time all that violin nonsense will be happily behind us and happiness will return to the land, green and pleasant as it....'

'Stop waffling Bertie! Is this what you are looking for?' From beside the armchair she produced a violin.

'A violin,' said Bertie.

'I know it's a violin, you fool. It's not any old violin. It's the violin you stole, the Messiah.'

Now Jumbo burst in: 'Bertie it's the Messiah!' Then noticing Aunt Dahlia, introduced himself. 'Hello, I'm Rupert Maxwell-Gumbleton. Sorry to burst in like this,' he said, 'only it's the Messiah.'

'Don't be silly,' Aunt Dahlia said, holding up the Stradivarius, 'this is the Messiah.'

'There can't be two Messiahs,' Bertie said. 'I can account for one, but where did the other come from?'

Jumbo revealed all: instead of stealing Handel's *Sonata in D Major, Opus 1 number 13*, Bertie and Ginger had stolen Handel's *Messiah*, a far more valuable piece than the one he was meant to steal. 'They were in matching vitrines; when Stinker had said first vitrine on the left he meant first vitrine on the right. The Bodleian will soon be on the warpath as surely as the Ashmolean has been.'

'There's only one thing for it,' said Aunt Dahlia, taking control. 'Both must be returned first thing in the

60

morning. Put the *Messiah* back in the bag Mr. Maxwell-Gumbleton. And that blue bag over there Bertie, put the Messiah in that. And tomorrow morning return them.'

And thus it came to pass that as soon as both institutions opened the next morning Bertie dropped off the two blue bags with the two Messiahs: the Messiah to the Ashmolean and the *Messiah* to the Bodleian.

But that's tomorrow's trouble.

CHAPTER 4

Easeby Revisited

June 1928

Knock! Knock!

'Good morning, Jeeves.'

'Ah, good morning, sir. You are up early this morning.'

'Awake but not up, Jeeves. I broke surface five minutes ago, heard the sound of tea in its making and have been waiting with keen anticipach ever since. I see daylight. What time is it?'

'9:50, sir. I in turn am five minutes late. A disagreeable visitor was at the door.'

'What, not an aunt this early, surely?'

'Not an aunt, sir.'

'Not a friend in need, a friend indeed?'

'Neither of those, sir. A tradesman seeking settlement.'

'Oh well, settle away, I say. Chap plying his trade. To be encouraged, Jeeves. Can't beat honest endeavour.'

'Indeed not, sir.'

'Actually I awoke from a most agreeable dream.'

'Clearly no aunts therein, sir.'

'Very droll Jeeves. No, I was a bookie at Ludlow racecourse. Who is that chappie we use when we're up at Easeby?'

'You use Honest Harold & Sons. I prefer Smithey & Peachtree. Would a further pillow help with drinking the tea, sir?'

'Thank you, Jeeves. That's better. What's on today?'

'Nothing noted, sir. It's raining most determinedly outside. Perhaps some indoor sports practice. Carpet golf or tiddlywinks? I'll prepare a light blue shirt, grey flannels and black suede loafers, sir.'

Jeeves left Bertie to ruminate on life's twists and turns until the tea soaked into the old bloodstream:

'Jeeves!'

Jeeves entered. 'You called, sir?'

'It's all coming back to me now. The dream. The bookie. So there I was, Honest Harold as you say, with the runners and riders chalked up behind me. And waiting to place their bets a long line of all my friends from the Drones: Bingo, Ginger, Chuffy, Tuppy, Jumbo, Barmy, Freddie, two Freddies, three Freddies, four Freddies, Boko, Catsmeat, Horace, Stilton, Gussie, and even Oofy was about to place a bet. Any idea on the signif, Jeeves?'

'According to the analysis of the Austrian interpreter Sigmund Freud, the dream has certain clear significances, sir.

To dream of anything long, such as the queue forming in front of you, represents what is politely called the male member, especially as the dreams also feature many of the more traditional type of member, as in club members. He also postulates on possible side issues of a repressed desire to exercise authority and dominance over other males. Unlikely in your case, sir. I would suggest a more nuanced interpretation, such as that proposed by the eminent Swiss practitioner Carl Gustav Jung, that the dream refers to the female anticipation of the male member, and thus a repressed expression of your feminine side, sir. But bear in mind the more timely theories of the much lauded American....'

'Never mind all that, Jeeves. That will be all.'

Bertie finished his tea and woke up some more.

'Jeeves!'

Jeeves entered. 'You called,sir?'

'Yes, it's all coming back to me now. Last night at the Drones. Bit of a thick one. Most of the merry crew in my dream were there and we decided we should have a Drones outing, to wit a summer party at our new home Easeby. The place is not used nearly enough since Uncle Willoughby joined the great hunt in the sky. We thought a masked ball would buck us all up frightfully. When are we due there next?'

'Not until July, sir. You had thought about the last two weeks of that particular month for your Shropshire summer sojourn, as you put it so alliteratively, sir.'

'Did I? Well, we can't wait that long. We thought we should have it in June, around midsummer's day. A Midsummer Masked Ball.'

'For any particular reason, sir, apart from the aforementioned bucking up?'

'Freddie Oaker was telling us about a new German novel he is going to borrow a scene from for his next Alicia Seymour heart-sweeper. There's a masked ball in it he is going to scoop up. That gave us the idea. Step on something or other.'

'That would be *Steppenwolf* by Herman Hesse, sir. That scene is indeed most enlivening. But if I may point out, sir, masquerade balls sometimes have disastrous consequences. Romeo and Juliet met at such an occasion.'

'Oh, come along now Jeeves, stop being such a spoil sport. What's wrong with Romeo and Juliet? Young love and all that. Art thou there Juliet? That sort of thing.'

'It's an interesting point of view, sir. But you cannot gainsay the evidence in Verdi's opera, A Masked Ball, in which King Gustav III was assassinated.'

'Jeeves, you worry unnecessarily, I can guarantee you there will be no assassinations at Easeby, Gustav IV, V or VI. Talking of numbers, how many bedrooms are there?'

'Forty bedrooms and ten and a half bathrooms sir, although I'm not sure the plumbing could take simultaneous usage. Will that be enough accommodation, sir?'

'Good heavens no. There are eighty-seven members. Plus we will have to bring McGarry, only he knows how to mix the members' cocktails. Some will be in foreign climes, some recuperating at His Majesty's pleasure, so say seventy-five active coves plus a few wives, a couple of dozen fiancées and many more fiancées-in-waiting. We will have to hire a local hostelry, maybe more than one. What am I going to wear?'

'The subject of your dream will be eminently suitable for your attire, sir.'

'What's that?'

'The on-course bookmaker, sir, you already have a surfeit of suitable outfits. For the mask we can ask Bodmin's in Vigo Street to make an Australian cork hat. Your presence will then be that of an Australian on-course bookmaker. I doubt if there will be another one there, sir.'

An hour later Bertie was on the 4th hole of the 3A Berkeley Mansions Golf Course; a particularly tricky pillow bunker in the 4th hole spare bedroom that needed his full attention. At the crucial moment of swing the doorbell rang.

'Dash it Jeeves, it's hard to concentrate with all these distractions.'

Jeeves put his head round the door. 'You called, sir?'

'Never mind. The doorbell?'

'A letter, sir. By the handwriting I should say a missive from Miss Wickham.'

'You sense trouble, Jeeves?'

'I am merely considering past form, sir.'

'Let's see. Good heavens, word travels fast. That is amazing. Why only last night and now this morning.'

'Sir?'

'Word of our Easeby shindig is abroad Jeeves. She says that although her beloved Reginald is not a member of the Drones Club, could we include him and therefore her? I suppose we can make an exception for Kipper and Bobbie.'

Five minutes later Bertie emerged from the 4th hole spare bedroom with a three over par and set himself up for the long putt 5th 2-par along the hall carpet into a tumbler. 'Birdie!' he harrumphed.

'I have taken the liberty of preparing a bedroom roster, sir. I am assuming that your closest friends and their betrothed will have rooms at the Hall and the less close will stay in the hostelries. If you would care to peruse, sir?'

Bertie read the roster: '*Mr. Wooster, master bedroom.* Very sensible. *Mr. and Mrs. Little, principal double bedroom*, all right and proper. *The two Miss Stokers, principal twin bedroom*, good thinking, double them up. *First floor single rooms for Lady Wickhammersley, the Misses Travers, Craye, Byng, Bassett, Hopwood, Glossop, Wardour, Morehead, Twistleton, Winkworth, Vickers, Glendennon, Denison*, if she comes Jeeves, and don't forget to add Miss Wickham, best room for her. *Second and third floor single rooms for Messrs Glossop, Pinker, Fittleworth, Bullivant, Cheesewright, Fink-Nottle, Pendlebury-Davenport, Prosser, Maxwell-Gumbleton, Twistleton, Widgeon, Fotheringay-Phipps, Potter-Pirbright, Oaker, Mannering-Phipps, Biffen, Chuffnell and Winship.* I think we should promote Chuffy and don't forget Kipper. How many bedrooms is that Jeeves?'

'Thirty-eight, sir.'

'But you said there are forty bedrooms.'

'I have also taken the liberty of allocating the smallest two to myself and McGarry, sir, as all the staff quarters will be needed for temporary assignees.'

'Excellent, we shall have a most eventful ball, Jeeves.'

'Of that I have no doubt, sir.'

༺༒༻

The Drones' outing to Easeby didn't start terribly well. The wording on the invitation had not been particularly clear and whereas Midsummer's Day fell on a Friday, the wording also mentioned the party as being on the Saturday.

Consequently some sportsmen had arrived on the Thursday evening expecting a Friday party. Somehow between them Shrewsbury and Easeby rallied round and no-one was incommoded.

Most had planned to arrive on the Friday evening,

taking the Great Western Railway from St. Pancras to Shrewsbury Abbey and then the Potts Line to Easeby Halt. There is only one such connection a day from London and although the St. Pancras express left on time, it arrived at Shrewsbury over an hour late and everyone missed the afternoon Potts Line connection. Even with Pendlebury shuttling back and forth in the old Rolls 30 hp, Shrewsbury soon ran short of taxis and soon after that ran short of hotel rooms.

Those arriving by road didn't fare much better. The long day run up the A5 from Edgware to Shrewsbury was being tarmacked either side of Bridgnorth and progress was slow if progress was at all. Oofy Prosser was giving his brand new Rolls-Royce Twenty its first outing but as he was refusing to give anyone else a lift, had no-one with whom to share his frustrations. But thirty cars, most two-seater dropheads, made the journey north and arrived at dusk.

Those that did spend the Friday night in the Hall ran into exactly the plumbing problems that Jeeves predicted and electrical circuit problems he had not. For the Saturday, Jeeves proposed a hot water roster system and sent out to acquire every spare candle in the county. The upper corridors creaked too with the sound of distressed gentlemen attempting to dress without valets and ladies attempting the same without maids.

However, fresh days mean fresh starts and Saturday morning broke full of promise for the country house weekend. The gardeners had prepared an impromptu five-hole golf course in the immediate grounds for the gentlemen, and old Oakshott's son, Oakshott, had rounded up some horses for the ladies for a trot and maybe more around the outer grounds. They had all agreed to meet at the far end of the third green for a picnic before returning to the Hall to dress for the evening.

Even as he slipped down a cucumber sandwich Bertie felt this was too good to be true: there he was with all his chums loafed around him, picnicking from wicker and china, sitting or loafing on blankets, and old oak tree for those that preferred the shade, interspersed among said chums, various fiancées, some from the past, some from right now and no doubt some from the future, an outer ring of horses carelessly chewing the long grass and in the near distance the fine front of Easeby Hall rising from the Shropshire bounty.

It was into this scene of pastoral perfection that Bertie saw a third Rolls-Royce (for those interested a new Rolls-Royce 40/50 Phantom in dark blue with a black roof and wicker trim) arriving and then the passenger entering the Hall. Moments later the passenger reappeared through the front door accompanied by Jeeves. Bertie could just see Jeeves pointing towards the picnic and then the passenger and Jeeves waving at him.

'I'd better go,' Bertie told his friends and wandered off towards the house. The passenger set off to meet Bertie halfway. As he hoved into view Bertie noticed he was dressed for the town and not the country and closer still he seemed vaguely familiar; closer yet and Bertie placed him from their teenage years. Only with an outstretched hand did Bertie recognise him and was about to say 'What-ho Munro-Geddes,' when the passenger said: 'What-ho Wooster, remember me from school? Munro-Geddes, house captain at Hawtrey.'

'Oh rather,' said Bertie. 'Well, this is a surprise, lovely day and all that.'

'Cracking form. I suppose we can call each other Sylvester and Bertram by now. School days long ago, what?'

'Yes rather, I normally trade as Bertie. Jolly nice to see you and all the rest but to what do I owe the p?'

'Well, I have to say it's slightly delicate and discretion would need to be extended, as far as the circumstances allow.'

'Delicatessen and discretion are long Wooster traditions. Rest assured on that score.'

'I'm sure they are. You see, I am these days the Principal Private Secretary to His Royal Highness the Prince of Wales. I don't think you've met him?'

'Well I have actually, twice, but with the public around so he probably doesn't remember.'

'I see. Well you haven't been presented to him then?'

'Oh yes, both times, but never mind, I'm sure he had weightier fish to fry.'

'Well, thank you for your forbearance, and more is needed. He is staying nearby at Attingham Park with his mother's old friend, the Countess Sherburne. Between me and thee he has been sent there by his mother to keep him out of sight for a while until what we might call an incident with a married admirer subsides. He is as you would expect bored, and between old school friends I can tell you he doesn't respond well to being bored. He wanted to organise a summer scrap shoot, then heard there wasn't a spare peasant in Shropshire as you had scooped them all up to staff your masquerade ball here at Easeby. In a nutshell, as it's a masked ball

70

they would like to come, their identity as masked as their faces.'

'They you say, so there's more than one of them?'

'Yes, he would like to bring a friend, as they say.'

'Do they? Well I can't see what difference a friend would make. We must all do our bit for the cause. King and country. Pleasure to serve. Do what we can. Each in our own way, you know, all that.'

'Good man Bertie. This is where the discretion comes in. The friend I mentioned is the wife of the Canadian High Commissioner, His Excellency Cuthbert Strand. H.E. is in Ottawa on business and Mrs. Strand is staying incognito at a hotel in Shrewsbury. Like H.R.H. she is bored, she being what we might call one of life's party goers. She is thrilled at the prospect of a masquerade ball.'

'As well she might be. Can't be much fun incog in Shrewsbury.'

'Quite. Then there is the matter of accommodation. We are four.'

'Ah, four you say?'

'Yes, four. His Royal Highness, Mrs. Strand, his valet Cardew and I. Cardew can sleep in the servants' quarters and in view of the no doubt full house I can share with another gentleman, but His Royal Highness and Mrs. Strand must have their own separate rooms. It would not be such a bad thing if they were not too far apart. I'm sure you catch my drift.'

'Caught and held at first slip. We will have to re-arrange the who-sleeps-where side of life. I must throw the balls in the air to my man Jeeves.'

'I see. This Jeeves, is he what I call reliable in the discretion department?'

'Oh he's better than that Sylvester, he is Jeeves.'

⌘⌘⌘

Ten minutes later Bertie finished his H.R.H. unburdening with:

'So there you have it, Jeeves. Bit of a pickle. Lots to go wrong. Shame and scandal heading the Wooster way.'

Jeeves replied: 'I don't see a cause for concern, sir, I know Cardew from the Junior Ganymede. His nephew Matthew is a member too. He attends the Earl of Walhampton.'

'That's all very well, Jeeves, but who sleeps where? I won't even think about with whom.'

'His Royal Highness the Prince of Wales will have to have your master bedroom, sir. You could have the spare bed in Lord Chuffnell's room.'

'Well, I suppose so. And what about Mrs. Strand?'

'There are no first floor single bedrooms spare, sir, all being occupied by the ladies present. And Mr. Munro-Geddes has suggested that the Prince's and Mrs. Strand's rooms are close to hand. I suggest she shares a room with Miss Wickham, the largest and most commodious available and next to the one that was yours, soon to be the Prince's, sir.'

'Well, I suppose so. And what about Munro-Geddes and Cardew?'

'There will have to be some doubling up, sir, as you are doing. I suggest Mr. Munro-Geddes takes the spare bed in Mr. Prosser's room. There is no room for another bed in my room, so I suggest Cardew takes that and I share with the most junior Drone, Mr. Maxwell-

72

Gumbleton. If you are sure he won't object, sir.'

'Jumbo? Oh no, he's a good sport. I'll tell him myself.'

⌁

Picnicking and golfing and riding and walking over, the house party reassembled in the billiard room for tea before going upstairs to change for the ball. Across the room Bobbie Wickham waved at Bertie and was soon by his side.

'Bertie, I have a scheme and you are part of it,' she said.

'Oh,' said Bertie.

'What do you mean Oh? Don't be such an old spoilsport.

You don't even know what it is yet.'

'Oh and double oh and no doubt treble oh with brass knobs on.'

'Listen Bertie, Oofy has been perfectly beastly.'

'Yes, I grant you that is a possibility.'

'Do you know he wouldn't give me or Reginald a ride up from London yesterday? Some nonsense about wanting to be alone with his new Rolls-Royce Twenty. I think it was because he didn't have his chauffeur and was embarrassed about his driving. Anyway, it meant a day sitting bored on the train, which was late, and then a horrid horse and trap ride to here with the Littles. I saw his car when we were out riding this afternoon. Gave me an idea. I have planned my revenge.'

'Oh.'

'Stop saying oh. We are going to steal his Rolls-Royce, that will make him think twice about putting me on train and trap again.'

'What do you mean, we are going to steal his Rolls-Royce?'

'Well I can't drive so you're going to have to.'

'What about Kipper? He can drive.'

'I'm engaged to Reginald and don't want to land him into any sort of trouble. Poor Reginald. You're the only one who can do it.'

'What do you mean poor Reginald? He's perfectly capable. Anyway how are we, I mean how are you, going to do it? I doubt if he's just left the key in the car, waiting for you to steal it and drive off.'

'He hasn't, I've checked. It must be in his room.'

'Ah, that's where your plan has hit its first rock. He's not in his room alone any more. There is also Munro-Geddes. In fact they're talking to each other right now over there.'

'Who's he, this Munro-thing?'

Never mind who he is, young Roberta. Your scheme is so full of holes I don't know where to start.'

'Oh Bertie, you are useless. That beastly Prosser and Geddes-wotnot are both down here. I'll nip up, have a rifle in the room, find the key and give it to you. Then when they go up to change, you just drive it around to back of the garage and hide it. That's all. Where's the Wooster spirit?'

'I'll have you know the Wooster spirit has seen Plantagenet days and has not been found lacking in the interim. But the Plantagenets didn't expect it to steal Rolls-Royces. And, anyway, when am I meant to change?'

'I knew you'd do it Bertie. After you've stolen the car, then you can change.'

'Does Jeeves know about this?'

'Of course. You don't think I'd round you up without clearing it with him first do you?'

'What did he say?'

'He said against anyone else but Mr. Prosser he would advise against such a course of action, but that Mr. Prosser did seem to attract unhealthy feelings of retributive justice against his person. Something like that. He lost me halfway through.'

And so the second half of the plot was hatched. After the ball, as they were climbing the staircase up to their rooms, Bertie would express surprise to Oofy at seeing him still there, as he had just seen Oofy's Rolls-Royce drive off. Oofy would not take this lightly and spend at least a good part of the night on a wild goose chase around the Shropshire countryside dressed as, well whatever he was going to wear for the ball. To make sure Bertie was blameless he would knock three times on Bobbie's door after all the lights were out and hand her the key so she could put it back where she found it when Oofy was out on his goose chase. What could possibly go wrong?

❧

The masquerade ball was a great success and everyone had the gayest time imaginable. Jeeves had ordered black velvet masks for the gentlemen and gold Colombina masks for the ladies, and one of each found itself by each bedside. He found himself dressing Bertie as an on-course bookmaker and helping Bertie's new roommate, Lord Chuffnell, bear more than a passing resemblance to a recently promoted two-armed, two-eyed Lord Nelson.

'How do I look, Jeeves?' asked Bertie.

'Memorable, sir.'

'Well, that's good. And do we know what the Prince and Mrs. Strand are wearing?'

'Mr. Cardew tells me that the Prince will masquerade as a Royal Knight of the Most Ancient and Most Noble Order of the Thistle, which is of course one of his styles and titles, having borrowed a knightly mantle from Lady Sherburne's late husband's wardrobe. Mrs. Strand has spent a fruitful afternoon in the Countess's dressing room, topped up by a visit to Shale & Mason's emporium in Shrewsbury and will soon resemble Elizabeth Stuart, the Queen of Bohemia.'

'Seen anyone else?'

'Only Mr. and Mrs. Little next door, sir. I believe they are attempting Robin Hood and Maid Marion.'

'Thank you, Jeeves. I better be the first one down to welcome them. No great hurry, Chuffy. Have the band arrived?'

'Yes, sir. George Elrick and His Music Makers have arrived from Blackpool and are assembling as we speak. A ten-piece ensemble, sir, with an occasional female vocal accompanist.'

'Capital. Ready to stomp the old feet, eh Jeeves?'

'Indubitably, sir.'

Of course Munro-Geddes's plan to keep the Prince of Wales and Mrs. Strand incognito, seeing as they would anyway be masked, lasted no more than a few whispers. Five years older and five times stiffer than the Drones contingent, they were easily noticeable, as well as being personally recognisable, even masked, to many of the Easeby revellers that evening. Their presence added only a thin top layer of glitter to what was already a brilliant occasion, the feeling that to be there then, that very evening, was very heaven and that heaven was at the centre of the world. It seemed to all that as masks went up, barriers went down and inhibitions went away. In the kitchen Mrs. Carstairs and her helpers had done them proud with a wonderful array of exotic buffets, now laid out on a long row of tables in the hall. At the library entrance McGarry from the Drones Club was in charge of the drinks and knew before each Drone arrived what to mix; the ladies had to explain themselves but were not unforthcoming.

In the ballroom Bertie had put the power-cut candles to better use, the soft reflections off the chandeliers in turn glimmering off the jewellery. He had hired the band to bring the old pile down and they very nearly did. Around and around the Drones and their female followers twirled and twisted, exchanging dance partners and laughter through the night. The Prince danced with as many ladies as stamina allowed; Mrs. Strand with as many gentleman as decorum allowed. From the hall the French windows opened out to the croquet lawn, and as dusk turned to mid-summer's night the revellers drifted in and out, turning Easeby into the set of a musical costume extravaganza.

Bertie caught up with Jeeves by McGarry's side near the library. 'Seems to going swimmingly, eh Jeeves?'

'Indeed it does, sir. There is much happiness and gaiety afoot.

You are to be congratulated on your party-giving, sir.'

'That's high praise from you, Jeeves. Hard to tell who some of these coves are. Who is the Archbishop of Canterbury?'

'That will be Mr. Pinker, sir, now next to the Zombie, who is Mr. Fink-Nottle.'

'Well, well, good old Gussie. And where is Tuppy?'

'That will be Ivan the Terrible sir, currently dancing with Cleopatra, she being Miss Moorehead.'

'And how is your roommate Jumbo?'

'I don't think he minds my presence there, sir. He is a most inquisitive gentleman. He is Julius Caesar for the night.

Did you know he has just bought the *Daily Herald*?'

'Has he, by George? Hard to keep up with him.'

'Yes, sir. He also wants to be known as plain Mr. Maxwell from now on?'

'What no Gumbleton? He can't be Jumbo without being Gumbleton. And who is King Arthur?'

'That will be Mr. Cheesewright talking to Douglas Fairbanks, who is in fact Mr. Prosser. Do you recognise Albert Einstein, sir? A particularly good disguise.'

'Gussie, I should say?'

'Mr. Fink-Nottle is on the lawn sir, as Judge Jeffries. No, Albert Einstein is in fact Mr. Biffen.'

'What, Biffy as Einstein! Well, I never. What a swell party this is. So many film stars. I can see Mary Pickford, Greta Garbo and Gloria Swanson. Don't tell me, they are the Misses Glossop and Bassett and the Lady Wickhammersley?'

'Precisely, sir. And have you noticed the sisters Stoker?'

'Yes Jeeves, but who are they?'

'I believe Athena and Artemis would be a rough approximation, sir.'

'Amazing, and the other ladies have done well, I can

recognise Florence Craye and my cousin Angela, but not their disguises.'

'The former would be Boudicca and the latter a Shooting Star, if I have made the correct interpretation. Have you seen Miss Wickham, sir?'

'No, I was wondering about her.'

'If you see Queen Isabella of Castile, sir, you shall see her.'

As the evening galloped on Bertie recognised more and more of his chums: Stiffy Byng as Queen Elizabeth I, Valerie Twistleton as Nell Gwyn, Freddie Widgeon as Rudolph Valentino, Catsmeat as Shakespeare, Gertrude Winkworth as Lillian Gish, Ginger as a gangster, Kipper as Charlie Chaplin, and many more.

As midnight beckoned, the evening ended with a terrific, Roaring '20s crescendo. Bertie took over piano duties. Marion Wardour, as Marie-Antoinette for the night, took to the bandstand and with George Elrick and His Music Makers in full flow behind her, gave out a belting version of that summer's hit *I've Danced With A Man, Who's Danced With A Girl, Who's Danced With The Prince Of Wales*.

Every lady there could really say that night that they had indeed done just what they sang along to: they had danced with a man, who had danced with a girl, who had danced with the Prince of Wales. With His Royal Highness and Mrs. Strand dancing the shimmy in the centre of the floor, surrounded by eighty Drones and what Jeeves would later call 'an equivalency of females', the whole ballroom sang along as they shimmied to the tune:

I've danced with a man, who's danced with a girl, who's

danced with the Prince of Wales.

It was simply grand, he said "Topping band" and she said "Delightful, Sir"

Glory, Glory, Alleluia! I'm the luckiest of females For I've danced with a man, who's danced with a girl, who's danced with the Prince of Wales.

My word I've had a party, my word I've had a spree
Believe me or believe me not, it's all the same to me!
I'm wild with exultation, I'm dizzy with success
For I've danced with a man, I've danced with a man
Who?
Well, you'll never guess
I've danced with a man, who's danced with a girl, who's danced with the Prince of Wales.

I'm crazy with excitement, completely off the rails
And when he said to me what she said to him – the Prince remarked to her
"It was simply grand", he said "Topping band" and she said "Delightful, Sir"
Glory, Glory, Alleluia! I'm the luckiest of females;
For I've danced with a man, who's danced with a girl, who's danced with the Prince of Wales.

⁓⁓⁓

As the last car and carriage headed off into the night and the last house guests made their ways upstairs, Bertie and Jeeves were alone at the foot of the grand staircase.

'A capital evening Jeeves, absolutely capital.'

'Indeed it was, sir. As capital as you suggest.'

'There's just one more thing to do.'

'I have not forgotten, sir. You have Mr. Prosser's

Rolls-Royce key?'

'I have it here, Jeeves. You know the drill. Code is you knock three times on Miss Wickham's door, as if on some butlery errand and slip her the key.'

'Very well, sir. About tomorrow morning, not too early for your tea I thought. Perhaps eleven o'clock?'

'Steady on Jeeves. No, you're right, I better be up early.

Eleven is fine. Good night, Jeeves.'

'Good night, sir.'

With the house to himself, Jeeves went back to his original room on the second-floor, tapped three times on the door and whispered: 'Basil.'

'Come in,' said Cardew softly. Then: 'Reginald, welcome, come up for a night cap?'

'Thank you, Basil,' said Jeeves, 'just a short one I feel, as we both have missions for our masters to prevent an engulfing scandal. If I may ask, under Junior Ganymede rules of course, when the Prince and Mrs. Strand liaise anight, who visits whom and how?'

'About fifteen minutes after the guests have retired the Prince will knock three times on her door. Sometimes she welcomes him in her room. Sometimes he deploys her in his.

Why do you ask?'

'Then we don't have much to spare. We should repair to the library presently and prepare some notes. You write one for the Prince and I write for Miss Wickham to give to Mrs. Strand. On the way I'll tell you what I know. But first I'll take up your offer of a strengthener.'

Thus a few minutes later the two gentlemen's gentlemen glided along the first floor corridor. Outside the Prince's room, Cardew knocked three times and gave the Prince an envelope. Outside the ladies room, Jeeves knocked three times and gave Miss Wickham the Rolls-Royce key and an envelope addressed to Mrs. Strand. That midsummer's night the Easeby corridors remained untrod, the Easeby doors remained unopened, Edwardian liaisons remained unrequited and Windsorian reputations remained untarnished.

Walking back along the corridor Jeeves saw ten toes nestling in two strapped sandals sticking out from behind some drapes. Lucky 'tis not the real Julius Caesar, he reflected. At the same time Cardew heard three taps on the

landing window behind him. Looking back he saw a man on top of a ladder peering in.

The next morning the house woke at different times and the guests peeled off back to London or their country seats.

Like Bertie, the royal party were late risers and it was not until noon that their Rolls-Royce Phantom 40/50 pulled up outside the main entrance to collect them. As they were leaving the Prince took Bertie to one side.

'A quiet word with you Bertram, if I may. Cardew has told me everything this morning. Can you please thank your man Jeeves personally for me? He is the most splendid fellow and I'm in his debt, don't you know. And as the host you are also in his debt, as you will have realised.'

'Ah yes, right-ho,' said Bertie.

As the royal Rolls-Royce 40/50 Phantom sped off along the drive, another Rolls-Royce, Oofy's Rolls-Royce Twenty took its place. Into it piled Bobbie Wickham,

Kipper, Chuffy, Pauline Stoker, Ginger and Magnolia Glendennon. As they sped off in turn, Miss Wickham gave Jeeves a farewell smile and wave. As if on a Crewe cue the third Rolls-Royce, Uncle Willoughby's old 30 hp, arrived from Easeby Halt, Pendlebury at the wheel, ready to collect the next group of guests for the short thrill to Easeby Halt station.

Alone at last, Bertie relayed the princely gratitude and asked: 'Now come on Jeeves, what all that was about?'

'Luckily you put me in the same room as Mr. Maxwell-Gumbleton, I mean Mr. Maxwell, sir. As soon as he heard the royal visitors were staying and who they were, or rather who she was, he sensed a scoop for his newly acquired *Daily Herald*. I happened to hear him dictate a telegram and happened to intercept the reply, sir. He laid on a ladder for his photographer and was to open a window on the first floor landing. I told Cardew and he merely warned the Prince not to venture forth and I merely warned Mrs. Strand to do the same.

Luckily for us, you asked me to deliver Mr. Prosser's Rolls-Royce key to Miss Wickham in her room and she gave Mrs Strand the message. Thus you are the one to thank, sir. I was merely the messenger.'

'Now steady on with the merelys, Jeeves. Even by your standards this was a *coup de grace*. A veritable *c d g*.'

'I endeavour to give satisfaction, sir. Shall I prepare the bags for our return to London?'

'Do you know, Jeeves, I rather like it here? Let's stay for a day or two and footle about.'

'Very well, sir.'

Bertie's Easeby story had a happy ending; it also has a sequel. A year later a fly on the 3A Berkeley Mansions wall would have heard the following conversation:

'Ahem, if I may indulge your attention for a moment, sir.'

'Indulge away, Jeeves.'

'You remember the Prince of Wales from Easeby last summer?'

'Absolument.'

'And his valet Cardew?'

'Your chum from the Junior Ganymede? *Absolument* twice over.'

'Well, sir, Mr. Cardew is retiring and has suggested that I replace him. His Royal Highness is reported to have responded most enthusiastically. In fact, sir, insistently.'

'I'm not surprised after your efforts last summer. Even by your standards the Old Grey Matter was the fancied runner. And have you accepted, duty calls and all that?'

'I have indicated that my response was more likely to be positive than not, sir.'

'You have to do the right thing for king and country. I would not be found lacking if the call ever came my way.'

'In the event, sir, I'm sure you would be at the front of the queue.'

'Actually Jeeves, that rather lets me off the hook.'
'Sir?'

'I know your policy about only working for bachelors. No married couples cross the Jeeves threshold.'

'Sir?'

'Well I have been holding off telling you. We have had a good five years together, you and I, have we not?'

'We have, sir. It's been most educational.'

'But I fear we must go our ways. You to serve the Royal Family, I to start a new family. It looks like married bliss awaits me, Jeeves.'

'I'm sure it is possible sir, but you are entering *terra incognita.*'

'There comes a time, Jeeves, there comes a time. All my chums are spliced or on their way to a mother-in-law. The life of the gay bachelor is not what it was. The Drones Bar is half-empty some afternoons. London is not what it was. New York the same. The mem'sahib in waiting feels the same. No, France beckons, at least for a while.'

'A return to Roville-sur-Mer, sir?'

'*Je pense que oui*, Jeeves, *je pense que oui.*'

'It was always very gay there, sir. So I may tell the Royal Household of my acceptance, and with your approval, sir?'

'With regret and approval, Jeeves. Enough to move a man to a w and s, if you'd be so kind.'

'Right away, sir.'

⌘

Jee d Wooster were to meet three times in later life. Jeeves was soon to prove as indispensable to the Prince of Wales as he had been to Bertie. Through the abdication he became the new king's downstairs confidant and when the crown passed from Edward VIII to George VI, he was promoted to Yeoman of the

Royal Cellars and then in 1949 to Palace Steward. It was with Jeeves in this role that they first met again; but we'll come to that later.

By 1953 he was serving the new Queen Elizabeth II as Assistant to the Master of the Royal Household, and it was then that he met Bertie for the second in the Royal Enclosure at Royal Ascot.

'We had some times back then, eh Jeeves?'

'We did indeed Mr. Wooster. And are there Masters or Misses Woosters in the midst?'

'No yet, Mr. Jeeves. Not ever I suspect. Passage of time and all that. No, it's a rummy old w. No sooner seen than gone. And a Mrs. Jeeves, is there one so lucky?'

'Not yet, no. There is however an understanding with the Lady of the Chambers. I was sorry to hear about the Drones Club. A direct hit they say.'

'Sad day. Word around the campfire is that Goering had it in for us personally. Didn't like the cut of the Drones jib. Most of us washed up in Boodles or Bucks. Any quiet words from the stables?'

'I'm led to believe that an investment in Roger's Cruise in the 3:45 may not go unrewarded.'

'No sooner said than whatsit. I'm off to the bookie now. Toodle pip.'

'Good-bye Mr. Wooster.'

They met again for the third time in 1961 at the Queen's Birthday Honours ceremony in Buckingham Palace. Jeeves had become Deputy Master of the Royal Household in 1955 and then top rung, Master of the Royal Household, in 1960.

Bertie, as we shall see, tinkled the odd ivory, wrote

the odd tune and sang the odd song. On that same afternoon Sir Reginald Jeeves was knighted for Services to the Crown and Sir Bertram Wooster for Services to the Popular Entertainment Industry.

Afterwards Sir Bertram asked Sir Reginald if he had fulfilled his understanding with the Lady of the Chambers, who would now be Lady Jeeves.

'Sadly not, Sir Bertram, the lady in question ran off with a travelling salesman to Australia.'

'That's a bit rummy.'

'It was sub-optimal at the time, I agree, but I'm set in my ways now. And I like my ways. Metaphorically, I know exactly where each sock is and they are inevitably with another of their particular kind. I have a gentleman's personal gentleman to put them there while I attend to matters of a more demanding nature higher up the social scale. And you?

Will it be the same Mrs. Wooster who will now be Lady Wooster?'

'Lady Roberta, yes, same squaw as walked down the aisle.

Won't go amiss. Can't say fairer than that.'

CHAPTER 5

Roville-sur-Mer

October 1935

Taxi drivers meeting travellers off *Le Train Bleu* at Nice often confused Villa La Masquerade with Villa La Mauresque, even though Bertie always told them that the Woosters' villa rhythmed with mallard and not marmalade while the Somerset Maughams' rhymed with more-or-less and not Mustique. Simple enough, one would have thought. Thus Willie Maugham's partner, Gerald Haxton, was only half surprised when two total strangers, one bedraggled and the other well draggled, were ushered into the salon at Villa La Mauresque.

'What-ho,' said Boko Fittleworth, the bedraggled half of the equation. 'Is Bertie afoot?'

'Ah no, they've done it again, the taxi drivers,' said Gerald. 'You want the other Villa M, the Woosters are over at Roville-sur-Mer. We are at Cap Ferrat, only a mile or two away. I'll give B1 a call. Can I say who's here?'

'That would be kind, I'm George Fittleworth and this is Zenobia Hopwood. Tell him Boko and Nobby are here. Who is B1?'

'Oh, that's just what Willie and I call Bertie. So you're the Boko who wrote *Sunny Disposition* with Bertie and you must be the leading lady? Mrs. Stapledown, wasn't it?'

'That's us,' said Boko.

'We loved that show,' said Haxton. 'Oh, here's himself. Willie, didn't we just love *Sunny Disposition*?'

'Every crackle and pop,' said W. Somerset Maugham. 'We were transported. To a better place. One far, far from earth with all its grubby smudgings. You are on your way to the Bs I presume? Cruelly mislodged by the local *conducteurs*.'

'Taxi driver confused your homes,' said Nobby.

'Mauresque, Masquerade, Masquerade, Mauresque. The syllables alone give the game away,' said Willie. '*Tant pis*, as we shrug and pout in these *environs*. I'll have our driver run you down to Roville. Luggage galore I see. We're seeing you tomorrow anyway, a night on the tiles in Monte Carlo.'

'Crack on, that's news. Full dress in the casino?' asked Boko.

Gerald said: 'Well, *I'm* going to end up there. Always do. We start at *La Gironde*. Trouble on t'hill. Hitch has called a summit.'

<hr />

George Webster Fittleworth, Boko to the Drones and other worthies, had come into Bertie's life early, they being neighbours in Shropshire. In term times, they both went to Eton, but then Boko peeled off to Cambridge and made a bit more of an effort there than Bertie did at Oxford. When he moved to London, Bertie soon had him in the Drones Club, where he met Ginger Winship. Ginger was looking for a flatmate and Boko looking for a flat, so they teamed up in Albemarle Street near the club. Oftentimes, when McGarry would beg members for respite in the early hours, the feudal few would repair to the Winship/Fittleworth abode for continuation of previous revelry. At that time Boko was stepping out with Florence Craye, cue long literary discussions late into the night. They had that much in common, topsides filled to the brim with facts and theories; below decks, nothing in common at all, he looking as lumpy and scruffy as a scarecrow trying to pass himself off as Guy Fawkes, she looking as shapely and couth as a topiaried Venus in a garden at Versailles.

At Cambridge he had turned his ambition from being an author to a playwright. By 1925 he had his first West End play, *Mrs. Maurder's Mysteries*, a romantic comedy about a co-educational headmistress and a returning ex-head girl and two male teachers, one of science, the other of physical instruction. Marriage to Nobby and a career in Hollywood beckoned but he found himself hemmed in by the studio system and Zenobia, as she had been reinvented by MGM, exploited by the same system. They both felt locked out of cultural stimulation and locked into a whirlwind of insincerity.

As a token to their sanities Boko wrote another romantic comedy for the stage, partly to give Nobby a starring role. *Not As Bad As It Looks* was about two mismatched couples on honeymoon in Capri, who through flashbacks and fast forwards discover their pasts are more intertwined than their presents and their futures would become more intertwined still. Back in London in 1932, he took the script to Noël Coward's manager, Charles Cochran, who suggested turning it into a theatrical musical, with an eye to a film-musical later on. Cochran agreed to find a producer and an angel, and

Boko agreed to find a composer to write the score.

Bertie, meanwhile, had become one half of the newly married Woosters, the other half of which, previously sole trading as Roberta Wickham, had decided before their marriage that they would extend their honeymoon at the Hotel Splendide in Roville-sur-Mer to a full time residency in a villa nearby. Decamp, as they say in English and French. No spare villa being to hand they, or rather she, had one built. La Villa Masquerade was small by their neighbours' standards, with three bedrooms, one large indoors/outdoors living area and a splash-about pool, and behind it on the hill an acre of pine trees. But the view was as large as it was handsome, looking out over Cap Ferrat and Roville-sur-Mer to the west, Beaulieusur-Mer and Monaco to the east, *la mer Méditerranée* all across the south and *mont Cenis* all across the north.

Initially to keep himself amused, Bertie had taken up a weekly Friday night residency at the *Voodiste Célèbre*, a jazz club in the *maritime quartier* of Nice. They called themselves the Riviera Quintette: Bertie on piano and vocals, local horn players Didier Chilton on sax and Maurice Belgare on trumpet, and an American rhythm section of Charlie Morse on drums and Bill 'Boomer' Garnett on bass. After the first week, spent largely improvising around old standards, they all agreed they were actually quite hot. One at a time they replaced the old standards with Bertie's new tunes, so that by the time a visiting Stéphane Grappelli heard them in the winter of 1931 they were in fine, foot stompin' fettle.

Three years later Grappelli and Django Reinhardt would go on to co-found the Quintette du Hot Club de

France but for now Bertie was in and out of different bands, some his own, some other people's. In early 1932 he was booked for a month's residency at the Bag O' Nails in Kingly Street, Soho and invited the Riviera Quintette to back him up. The jazz boys of Nice didn't need asking twice.

Bertie's sets at the Bag O' Nails emptied the Drones and other clubs up to midnight and filled them up again long into the following mornings. On the second night Boko and Nobby, and Charles Cochrane and Noël Coward were in the audience. After a few of his own tunes, Grappelli said, 'And now we would like to play a medley written by our pianist tonight, Mr. Bertram Wooster.' Three tunes into the medley Boko and Cochrane clinked their glasses: they had found their composer.

Over the next three and a half weeks the Bag O' Nails became a day time studio as Boko and Bertie set about the score. Enthusiasm was infectious: Cochrane would produce the show and persuaded Noël Coward to play the lead for the first three months; Leontine Sagan soon signed up as director; by the second week the Drones millionaire Oofy Prosser finally found his calling as a theatre angel; and by the third week Cochrane felt sure enough of the musical to book the Gaiety Theatre for an opening in November 1932. At some point over the next six months *Not As Bad As It Looks* became *Sunny Disposition*, and the names of Fittleworth and Wooster would be said in the same breath.

⤜⤛

Back to the day of the Fittleworths' arrival in Roville-sur-Mer, Bobbie Wooster had other fish to fry. Her mother had announced she was coming to stay, arriving on the evening Blue Train; and on honeymoon, except on an unmarried honeymoon. Lady Wickham rather liked being Lady Wickham and while she enjoyed Ignatius ffinch's company, she decided she wouldn't enjoy Ignatius ffinch's wife's title. Bobbie suggested Lady wwickham; her mother thought her daughter had lived too long with Bertie to come up with such nonsense, but by now had learned to keep her thoughts on her son-in-law to herself.

Lady Wickham had moved on in that department somewhat since she called Bertie a gaby or even a guffin and shuddered at the mention of his name. The reality was that after Kipper Herring broke off their engagement, as a result of Bobbie putting sugar in his petrol tank in retaliation for Kipper losing her umbrella, and after Jumbo Maxwell-Gumbleton did likewise after she gave his spats to Cyril Bassington-Bassington in retaliation for his car breaking down with her in it, her daughter was rather the last girl standing, a Dronette without a Drone. At this stage, with one eye on an empty church and unemployed bridesmaids, Lady Wickham had upgraded Bertie from a gaby to a chump. As the lack of bachelors became a dearth, the chump became that chap and when the dearth became a drought that chap became Bertram. Actually that chap had proposed to her daughter a couple of times before he became Bertram, but as he put it each time 'she had declined to co-operate, and that in a manner which left no room for doubt regarding her views, laughing like a bursting paper bag and telling him not to be a silly ass'. But glance by glance, what-ho by what-ho, arm-in-arm by arm-in-arm, Bobbie's laughter had turned to affection and the affection had melted into love; her silly ass became not such a bad sort, and the good sort in turn proved to be the right man for her. By the time they were married at Skeldings Church in Hertfordshire in June 1929, mother and daughter were respectively relieved and delighted by the match.

Much to everyone's surprise, none more so than his, married life suited Bertie, too. The valet days may have gone but Bobbie had kept on her Scottish nanny, Nanny McDuff, who had been with the Wickhams since Bobbie was born. No-one ever knew if she had a first name. Nanny och-ayed and clucked around Bertie like the son she never had and the mother he never had. Tidied up after him too, ironed his clothes and boiled his eggs as if each had been Bobbie's. Bertie wanted to rename her Valette, but Nanny stayed Nanny. And married life came with a wife for free, well not exactly for free but the combined Wickham and Wooster coffers chinged along with barely a dent. And what eased Bertie most about Bobbie, his carrot topped Jezebel as he now *fondly* called her, was not just her *espièglerie*, which remained undimmed, but the way she operated completely independently from him, yet was devoted to him at the same time. And she was as much a chum as a wife and he was a happy chap and she was a happy chum. But let anyone say a word against her husband, offer a slight real or imagined, and the wife turned into a tigress protecting her retreat. Which was why, after a few verbal bruises, Lady Wickham had learned to keep her thoughts about Bertie to herself.

No, her mother's arrival was second string in Bobbie's

mind that afternoon; the main fish in her frying pan was getting her own back on Gerald Haxton. The week before Willie Maugham had thrown a party for Prince Arthur, the Duke of Connaught, the seventh child and third son of Queen Victoria, and Leonie, Lady Leslie, sister of Jennie Churchill, with whom the Prince was on good terms (having an affair). After dinner Willie Maugham took the unusual move of dismissing the staff and inviting the ladies to stay while the cigar smoke whirled around the terrace and the port did the rounds. The decanter was working its way round as it should, clockwise from Prince Arthur to Willie to Leonie to Bertie to Gerald; then it stopped and went back to Bertie again. Not only had Gerald slighted her, he had passed the port the wrong way.

Bertie, of course, righted the wrong immediately and passed it round to her behind Gerald's chair. On seeing this, Gerald gave a ham's exaggerated apology:

'*Oh*, I am *so* sorry, B2.' Bobbie hated being called B2 too, as the beastly girl Haxton very well knew. She did bristle. Around the table only Bertie knew into what murky depths of soup Gerald would soon be plunged.

⌘

Bertie rubbed along with most people, in fact rubbing along was his modus op. But this Ignatius ffinch was a queer customer. No sooner had he unpacked than he demanded to play golf.

'Do you know any decent links?' he asked, hands on hips.

'Well yes, I do, but they are at Toulon, two hours away,' replied Bertie.

'Fine, so we'll play tomorrow morning?'

'Ah, well yes, but no.'

'What do mean yes and no?'

'I said yes but no, not yes and no. Big difference.'

'I can't see any difference.'

'Well, that is because you've just arrived; be here for a while and all will be clear.'

'Clear as mud more like.'

All most rummy as an opening salvo, thought Bertie, and before cocktails. Anyway tomorrow morning he'd be ensconced with Boko, working on their new musical: another romantic comedy tentatively called *Your Shack or Mine?* Their new third arm, the angel-turned-producer-turned-impresario Oofy Prosser was mooring his yacht in the Golfe de Villefranche in a fortnight. They wanted to have all three acts in outline sketched out by then.

Then there was his mother-in-law on the prowl, this time over cocktails.

'Bertram, Roberta tells me you are going to meet Alfred Hitchcock tomorrow night.'

'Ah, yes, mother-in-law, a visit to the great man is on the cards.'

'Roberta tells me you are going to write music for him.'

'Well, strictly speaking the music is for Somerset Maugham.

It's his rewrite, don't you see? For the film of his book *Asperger*. Hitch wants a Maugham rewrite and a Wooster score.'

'Have you met him, Somerset Maugham?'

'Oh, rather,' said Bertie, 'he lives just down the road, we see him all the time.'

'Roberta never told me.'

'Ah well, women you see. Close to the chest and all that.'

'But I'm a woman.'

'So you are. Strapping one in fine form too. Ignatius wants to play golf.'

'Never mind that. I want to meet him.'

'But you came with him.'

'Not him, you imb..., Bertram. I want to meet Somerset Maugham. And Alfred Hitchcock of course. I have so much to tell them. So much they could learn from me. I have already written three plays as you very well know. Now I am finishing my fourth. It's called *Lessons She Should Have Learnt*. I'm sure Somerset Maugham could garner much from it. Then again, I often thought my *Oh Sorrow, Oh Remorse* could easily have a cinematic adaptation. I long felt only Alfred Hitchcock could do it justice. But first he has to see it. That's where you come in.'

Bertie wondered if her brief encounter with his late Aunt Agatha at their wedding had not had too profound an effect.

'Ah, only problem there, newly bestowed kith-and-kin-in-law, is that it's not my party. Hitch has invited Willie who has invited me. I'm really third string, do you see?'

'And you have invited George and Zenobia. Roberta told me.'

'Boko and Nobby? Yes they are our house guests. And they have met Hitch in Hollywood, so it's not quite the same.'

'And we are not houseguests? Where are you going?'

'*La Gironde*, in Monte Carlo.'

'What time are you meeting?'

'Oh, I don't know, for dinner. Ten-ish.' Bertie wished he had kept his trap shut as soon as it was wide open.

'Ten?! Can't you dine earlier? Ignatius likes to be in bed by ten.'

'Ah well, mustn't keep the old chap up, what?'

As if carried by a zephyr up from Roville-sur-Mer below Nanny appeared. 'Miss Roberta says dinner is ready on the terrace, your ladyship and Mr. Bertram.' Her broad brogue was a long way from Inverness, but she was as much at home here as her Miss Roberta and her Mr. Bertram.

⁓⁓⁓

Knock knock!

'Entrez!' said Bobbie. 'Hello Nanny, you're early. Aren't you? What time is it?'

'Yes, what time is it?' asked Bertie, waking from a particularly pleasant dream about waterskiing with the house spaniel, Marshmallow.

'It is early,' said Nanny, 'only nine-thirty, but Mr. Bertram has some visitors.'

'Too early. Much too early. Who are they?' asked Bobbie.

'Oh, Miss Roberta, you'll never guess. It's Mr. Hitchcock and his wife Alma Reville.'

'Well he might be the master of the unexpected, but this is juicedly early,' said Bertie, propping himself up on a pillow and taking the tea and toast tray. 'Is Willie with them?'

'No, just the two of them,' said Nanny. 'I've given them

tea. I'll tell them you will be down soon, Mr. Bertram.'

Fifteen minutes later Bertie was down with them. They had never met before. Hitchcock, only a year older than Bertie's thirty-five, but looking all of fifty, stood all the time, pacing around, his eyes never still. He was shorter and even rounder than his photographs but not yet as stately or as bald as he was to become. His wife, Alma Reville, was and looked the same age as Bertie; a waif, even if a wiry waif, her voice pitched two octaves higher than her husband's, as if at any moment she would be borne aloft by the willowy sea breeze.

'I'll come straight to the point, Mr. Wooster...' Hitchcock started before Bertie had even what-ho'd him.

'Coffee please Nanny. Would you like some? I've had my first pot of tea already. I see you've had tea too. Then I like to change to coffee. Tea starts the engines and coffee roars them along the runway, what? Please, call me Bertie,' offered Bertie.

'I'd rather not,' said Hitchcock. 'You can call me Mr. Hitchcock. This is a business call. I'll come straight to the point Mr. Wooster, this film I'm making, you know about it I'm sure.'

'The reason you're here on the jolly old Riviera? Rather, *Agent Provocateur*, based on Willie's book, *Asperger's Secret Agent*, or some such. Spiffing of you to come all this way.

Haven't read it myself. I suppose you have. You know he's frightfully clever, Willie. Anyway, we're all dining tonight, so you'll meet him then.'

'I have never met anyone mistake so many facts in one sentence,' said Hitchcock. 'The film is called *Secret Agent*. The book is called *Ashendon: Or the British Agent*.

Of course I haven't read it, not like you mean read it; I'm the director. My scriptwriter Charles Bennett has read it. I know Maugham is "frightfully clever" and of course I've met him. And we are not all meeting tonight, Alma is leaving later today. And it was I who arranged what it is that has been arranged.'

'Ah, well, the gist you know, the gist,' said Bertie.

'Let's get back to the matter in hand, Mr. Wooster.' Now less agitated, he spoke in a drone which reminded Bertie of a lawn mower. 'The score is a musical mish mash. A typical Gaumont-inspired Hubert Bath goulash, to be precise. I like to make the audience suffer as much as possible, but not through boredom. I complained to the almighty Gaumont British Picture Corporation and they have told me to use you. Then they told me they have already contracted you. Before, if you can imagine this, clearing it with me. You've read your contract with Gaumont?'

'Quick glance. Words on pages. Wafflety this and wafflety that. Gussie does all that. Awfully good with words, Gussie, reads them given half a chance.'

'Gussie?'

'Gussie. Gussie Fink-Nottle. My contract wallah. Old mucker of mine. Why do you ask?'

'Because as I said Gaumont sent the contract to you and you sent it to this Nottle without me seeing it first.'

'Oh well, I'm sure he has sorted it out. Or will do soon. Top man, Gussie.'

'That's not the point Mr. Wooster. The point is that under the terms of the contract you submit your score to Mr. Maugham, not to me.'

'Is that so bad?' asked Bertie.

'Yes. Everyone must report to me, can't you see that? You are a musician. Imagine an orchestra not reporting to the conductor. That is the situation in which I find myself. I'm here to see Mr. Maugham because his contract says he can override Mr. Bennett and here to see you because your contract says Mr. Maugham can override me.'

'Gosh, overriding everywhere. An overridden situation if ever I saw one. So what's to be done?'

'It seems to me that you don't know what's in your contract, in any detail, am I right?'

'Well, I mean...'

'Exactly. So just don't tell Mr. Maugham. Send the score straight to me. Cut Mr. Maugham out.'

'That's a bit dramatic,' said Bertie.

'Drama is life with the dull bits cut out. Can I tempt you with a generously endowed new contract?'

'We Woosters are famous for resisting temptation. Why, in Stuart times I'm led to believe that my ancestor Sir Frederick Mannering once turned down a third boiled egg at breakfast. And, rumour has it, without a kipper to compensate him. No, no, stern stuff in the Wooster blood line.'

And so Hitch tempted Bertie with writing the score for his next Gaumont film *Young and Innocent*. All he had to do in return was bypass Willie. Mr. Maugham, Hitchcock insisted, probably didn't care much about what was in the contract anyway, even if he knew about it, which he probably didn't. From what Bertie had seen so far, writing film scores was money for old rope, but he didn't need the money and already had plenty of rope. But still, it was always gung-ho to be asked. Finishing *Your Shack or Mine?* with Boko and Oofy was going to take the next few months, then he and Stéphane were booked for a gramophone recording with Decca in Hampstead, London, but that wouldn't take long. Maybe a spell writing a score for Hitchcock would keep the old bean beaning. Then he had a beanwave.

'I tell you what Mr. Hitchcock, something else entirely. Mum's the word about what follows. How about you read a play for me and write some kind words in the margins? Or at the end. "Good effort" or "Carry on" or "Shows promise" that sort of thing, I'll forget to ask Gussie to do whatever it is he is meant to be doing. Or not. If you catch my drift.'

'Have you any idea of the number of plays I look at every week?' grumped Hitchcock.

'Dozens I'm sure, but this one is special in a different way.'

'They are all special in a different way. That's what makes them all the same. So what is this one?

'It's called *Oh Sorrow, Oh Remorse.* Or maybe *Oh Remorse, Oh Sorrow*. There's definitely remorse and sorrow involved. Not a comedy I'll wager.'

'Well, I'd change the name for a start. Who is the authoress? With a title like that it has to be an authoress.'

'She is Violet Wickham.'

'We'd have to change that too. Although Violet has potential. The name starts out so promisingly, but loses the mid-word *n* just when it's getting exciting. Known to you, is she, this Violet Wickham?'

'Absolutely. Flesh and blood-in-law.'

'Let me guess. She's your mother-in-law?'

102

Alma spoke for the first time: 'This has potential, Fred. Mr. Wooster, do you want to kill her?'

'Steady on, Mrs. H,' said Bertie. 'Do you mean kill her? As in "kill her"? As in, she ceases to be? I wouldn't go that far. A bit less of a presence maybe, but falling short of total extinction.'

Alma again: 'I'm thinking of the musical genius son who was so embarrassed by his mother-in-law's new play....'

'Alma, you are by habit right about all things,' said Hitchcock, 'but in this case I think I'll take up Mr. Wooster's offer and read the play, or at least scribble in the margins. We have a deal I believe Mr. Wooster. You show due consideration to my Mr. Maugham scenario and I will oblige your Mrs. Wickham scenario.'

'Er, Lady Wickham, as it happens,' said Bertie.

'Fred, even better, are you sure we can't....' said Alma.

'No, Alma, not this time. Lady Wickham you say,' said Hitchcock, 'then I will show even greater obligation to her scenario.'

⌒⌒⌒

Stealthily would be the word to describe how the Maugham's Rolls-Royce Phantom II Park Ward landaulette glided up to the pillared entrance of *La Gironde* on rue des Iris in Monaco. While Gerald's friend and chauffeur Gaston held open the door, out popped Bobbie, Nobby, Willie, Boko, Bertie and, with a friendly wink to his liveried lover, Gerald. Willie led the way in, to be greeted with howls of delight by Mario, the maître d'hôtel.

'Monsieur Maugham. Avec Monsieur 'axton. Always a delight! But I did not know you were coming and with a party of six. Alors, I will try, try, let me see...'

'Never mind, Mario. Tonight we are the guests of Mr. Hitchcock, is he here yet?'

'*Oui mais non*. He has eaten and left. He was here at eight, just as we opened. He said he was expecting guests for dinner not for breakfast the next day. But I did not know you were his guests. I'm so sorry.'

'We know our friends by their defects rather than by their merits, Mario,' said Maugham, 'and eating dinner at lunchtime is a passable definition of a defect.'

'He said if his guests arrived he would be a Maxim's,' said Mario.

'Then to Maxim's we shall repair. Good evening, Mario,' said Willie.

'Wait,' said Gerald, 'who are those ghastly people waving at you, B2?'

'Oh no,' Bobbie replied.

'Good heavens,' said Bertie, 'it's Bobbie's mother and her fiancé.'

'At their age?' quipped Willie, 'I mean, marriage is a very good thing, but I think it's a mistake to make a habit out of it.'

Soon Lady Wickham was making a beeline for them. 'Oooh Mr. Maugham, it's such a pleasure to meet you. I am Lady Wickham, Roberta's mother. That is my fiancé Ignatius ffinch. Two small effs. But where is Mr. Hitchcock?'

'Gone, gone to the night, like a whim to a dream,' quoted Willie.

'Oh, that's so lovely,' cooed Lady Wickham.

'The ability to quote is a serviceable substitute for wit, I grant you,' replied Willie. 'But to Maxim's are we bound, in search of the elusive Hitch.'

'Then we shall join you. We have finished dinner. Just waiting for you. I have brought a play for Mr. Hitchcock to make into a film. It's far too late for Ignatius.'

And so the party of six became a party of eight, Bertie and Boko squeezed in next to Gaston up front and the Rolls rolled Roycefully down to Maxim's on the rue de la Paix. One by one, out they filed from the landaulette; Willie led the way in; more effusive greetings from the maître d'hôtel, this one Carlo; more lack of Hitch; another note from Hitch: meet me at the Casino; and so one by one out they filed out of Maxim's and up to the Hotel de Paris for a sharp stiffener before walking next door to the Casino.

These days they let any old scruff into the Casino, and many of the scruffs get no further than the rows of slot machines in the lobby, but in 1935 there was a dress code for the Casino as a whole and an even stricter one for the inner sanctum. Here a dozen roulette wheels clinked and clattered and hushed tones and discreet nods played roulette and *baccarat chemin de fer*. Men in black or white ties and women in casino gowns sat or hovered around the tables. Jewellery sparkled. Waiters, quiet as dormice, slipped between the players. Everyone seemed to smoke. Only Gerald, who had expected to play there later, was dressed for the sanctum. Thus it was Gerald who was volunteered to see if Hitch was therein; Hitch was not. Neither was he without. Hitch, like his cinematic Lady, had Vanished. Lady Wickham declared Ignatius ffinch had not been up so late for decades and the playwright and her beau vanished into the night too, albeit only as far as La Villa Masquerade.

By now tummies were rumbling. Casse-croûtes and collations soon arrived. Bobbie excused herself while the others tucked in.

'I think Hitch's behaviour is scandalous,' said Gerald.

'Impropriety is the soul of wit, but goose chases wild or tame are not to be encouraged,' agreed Willie.

'And that's not all,' said Bertie. 'Let me tell you this.'

And Bertie told them about Hitchcock's offer to remove Willie from the fray in return for a future score. And about his own counter-offer of a Hitchcock glance at his mother-in-law's no-doubt sorry offering. And about how a deal had been done, but now the play-reading half of the equation had scratched the fixture.

'Bertie, my dear,' said Willie, 'I am touched that you put our friendship above your ambition. Such as it is of course, ambition not something with which you are overly burdened. But touched I remain.' He lit a cigarette, then: 'So let me read the scene correctly. Not that I care if I'm in or out of being your music master, God knows I'm tone deaf and my tolerance for music is merely indifference. But as Hitch cannot read Lady W's play, he not being extant so to do, you are under no obligation to cut me out of his scheme?'

'Correctomundo' replied Bertie, 'as far as I can tell.

Anyway, I would never have done it. Code of the Woosters and all that. I'll read her bally play, scribble some words of wisdom in the margins and put a great big H. at the end of it.

Ah, here's Bobbie.'

'No, no,' said Willie, 'I'll read her play and put a SM

at the end of it. Bobbie, here you are. I thought you had gone back with mama and two small effs.'

'B2, B1 is a knight of the highest chivalry,' Gerald said to her, 'what he won't do for your sainted mother has yet to be discovered.'

'Oh, Gerald, I nearly forgot. Silly me,' said Bobbie in return. 'The concierge asked me to tell you: someone has left a package for you in the luggage room.'

'For me?' pouted Gerald, 'What *can* it be?' and he upped to answer his own question.

'I'm for a round of *Trente et Quarante*,' said Bertie, 'anyone care to join me? Or there's *vingt-et-un* or five card draw poker.'

Maugham stayed behind as the Woosters and the Fittleworths headed for the tables. They had just taken their seats when:

'YOU UTTER COW!' it was Gerald shouting, he and his dinner jacket soaking wet from head to toe, striding, dripping through the salon on his way to confront Bobbie. 'I accuse you, B2, of being behind this stunt. This outrage. Look at me! Everyone is looking at me!' And they were; all playing had ceased; the string quartet had stopped; a dropped chip could have been heard.

'I wish you wouldn't call me B2,' said Bobbie calmly in return, 'I've asked you enough times before.'

'So for *that*, you'd do *this*?' shouted Gerald. 'Hellcat!! She-devil!'

Now Bertie stepped forward. 'Actually Gerald, it was I who arranged for the dousing. Bobbie is as innocent as freshly fallen snow. You've got the wrong party, there, old bean.'

'Don't you old bean me, Bertie Wooster. How could

it have been you? You were with us all the time. It was Bobbie who disappeared and put that bucket of water over the luggage door. Must have been.'

'Actually, it wasn't a bucket, it was a water bomb,' said Bertie. 'See, it must have been me.'

'Children! Children!', said Willie, walking over to the conflagration, 'Enough! Gerald you can dry and brush-up and head for the roulette room. We've all had quite enough of this particular evening. Come, come, all the rest of us. Home to our homes.'

On the drive to the Villas Masquerade and Mauresque Willie said: 'Amusing and chivalrous enough, you Woosters, but Bertie how did you know Bobbie planted a water bomb?'

Bertie replied: 'They are a specialty of Nanny McDuff's. Bobbie could make a water bomb before she could walk and talk. Always carries a spare balloon in her handbag, don't you my little carrot-topped Jezebel?'

'I do,' said Bobbie. 'Surprisingly useful, surprisingly often. Are you catching all this for future use, Boko?'

'Oh, yes,' said Boko. 'Oh, yes.'

◦◦◦◦

All of which explains why Lady Wickham's play was read and annotated by Somerset Maugham and not by Alfred Hitchcock. Less well known, this explains why Maugham's *Too Many Husbands*, starring Jean Arthur and Fred MacMurray, tilted its hat to the denouement of *Oh Sorrow, Oh Remorse*. This explains also why the film score of Secret Agent was written by Gaumont's Hubert Bath and not by Bertie Wooster and why the film score of *Young and Innocent* was written by Bertie

Wooster and not by Gaumont's Hubert Bath. But most importantly of all, this explains why Gerald Haxton stopped calling Bertie 'B1', stopped calling Bobbie 'B2', and why from then on he would always pass the port decanter to his port side, even if Mrs. Wooster was sitting there.

CHAPTER 6

Naples

December 1942

Bertie couldn't quite find the word for how he felt. Dumpy? As in down in the dumps? Lumpy? As in a lump in the tummy. Stumpy? As in an innings about to close? Bored? Yes, very bored. Restless. Feckless. Zestless. He looked at his toes. Then he wriggled them.

'This little piggy went to market,' he said aloud, 'This little piggy stayed at home. This little piggy had roast beef. This little piggy had none. And this little piggy went: wee, wee, wee, all the way home!' Bored. B for bored. B for Bertie.

Ill? Still ill? Ill still? Yes, still a bit ill, but better day by day. 'Yikes, this time last month the Maker could have come and said, "Bertram, enough of this immoral coil for you my old son," and I'd have said, "Whisk me away forsooth, my good man." Hungry? Constantly. Lonely? *Bien sur*. Worried? We Woosters don't worry. "Come on Bertram,"' he announced to the other nineteen beds in the ward. A few looked his way; most just carried on gazing at the outer space that was the old green wall.

No, now he thought about it he felt foreboding, of having a great future behind him. The gay days gone; the sad days nigh. The Italian Fourth Army was coming, any day now so everyone said, although it had been any day now since he was admitted ten weeks ago. Long weeks they had been too. The Centre Hospitalier Universitaire de Nice reminded him of, of, of ... Malvern House, that was it. He knew it reminded him of somewhere. It smelt like Malvern House on the evening of the monthly swill out. It looked like Malvern House, especially the san at Malvern House, with all the beds in a row. 'Happy days, Malvern House, compared to this,' he said aloud again to the ward. Ha, then there was this Mussolini chappie everyone was banging on about. No doubt a poncey version of the Reverend Upjohn, either of them the sort of chap that would give fascism a bad name. 'No Musso fears for me, I've had the real Reverend, thank you very much,' he said aloud again to the same nineteen neighbours. Then he wondered if they thought he was going bonkers on them. 'Mustn't let the side down,' he said aloud again.

He had been admitted to Nice hospital ten weeks earlier with suspected malaria. Process of elim: he had caught it on the 19th hole at Toulon, having 'the one' after playing the last round of golf in Unoccupied France. What little food there was in the san tasted lousy; the wine rancid. The nurses were pinafored racketeers on the black market. There were no visitors: with the Germans heading south and the Italians rumoured to be heading west, Bobbie and Nanny had joined the great expat exodus over the Pyrenees to Lisbon and a ship home to Skeldings. At least he hoped they had; that was another thing, no news. He had only stayed behind to help Taxi! deliver her puppies. Not that he knew much about delivering puppies. But the gardener Jean did. Or so he said. Bertie thought he had better stay and make sure.

By 3rd November Bertie decided enough time in the san was enough time in the san. Discharge time; he had to scarper while his sanity remained. On 4th November he had come up with a scarpering plan: head for neutral territory, ergo Monaco. It was on the morning 5th November that Bertie felt like Guy Fawkes must have done when caught red-handed trying to do the decent thing.

'Where are you going, Monsieur Wooster?' asked the only passable quack in the whole bally place.

'I'm going to neutral territory, Monte Carlo, as a matter of fact,' said Bertie.

'Oh no you're not, especially in our hospital pyjamas,' said the quack, summoning two pinafored racketeers to escort Bertie back to the dorm.

However, as Bertie told himself whenever the depth of the soup bowl beckoned, we Woosters are made of vertebrae as well as brains. During afternoon nap time Bertie stole into the quack's office, stole his overcoat and hat and stole off to Monte Carlo. One hour and two border bribes later he was back in a known bosom: the Metropole Hotel in Monaco and in the care of the Swiss hotel manager, only ever known as Herr Scheck. Proper grub, decent quaff, pressed sheets and hearty snores were the order of the first night. Now all he had to do was wait for a friendly bateau to ship himself out.

⌘

While Bertie was discharging himself, half a mile away the American Consul Walter W. Orebaugh's phone rang. It was his immediate superior, Somerville Pinkney Tuck, U.S. Chargé d'Affaires in Vichy. Orebaugh later wrote:

'"Walt," Tuck said tersely, "don't ask any questions. Just do what I'm going to tell you. Take whatever staff you feel is necessary and go open a Consulate in Monaco today. Waste no time. Leave Nice as quickly as possible. We all need to go neutral. I'm off to Geneva right now." He hung up. I sat there, stunned, holding the dead receiver. Something big must be up.'

It was; the Allies were forty-eight hours away from launching Operation Torch, the invasion of French North Africa, thus declaring war on their hosts, Vichy France. Orebaugh crossed the border that same 5th November afternoon as Bertie, only while Bertie headed directly to Herr Scheck at the Metropole Hotel, the Consul had to head for the Royal Palace to present his credentials to Prince Louis II of the House of Grimaldi. The Prince was only too pleased to welcome him and all he stood for. Thus was established the first direct diplomatic connections between the two countries.

'Where would His Serene Highness suggest placing the new consulate?' asked Orebaugh. 'Why, until you find a permanent residence, the Hotel Metropole of course, our friend Herr Scheck will help you out,' replied the Prince.

War, war, rumours of war. What had been talked about for weeks, the Italian invasion of the Riviera, finally happened a week later. 'Invasion' summons up images of conflict, aggression and resistance, whereas in reality a rag-tag, underfed, ill-equipped, demoralised Fourth Army tip-toed over the border and told the rag-tag, underfed, demoralised citizens that they were now lucky enough to be part of *Italia Irredenta*. As a third of the citizens were of some sort of Italian extraction anyway, this didn't raise any great objection; equally, it didn't raise any great enthusiasm.

However, there were Fascist scores to settle and high on the list was Walter W. Orebaugh. The Consul in Nice had been instructed by Washington to give as much covert help to the French Resistance as possible; this he had done with enthusiasm. Privately, he decided to help as many Jewish refugees fleeing south as he could too. The Vichy, Italian and German secret police all knew what he was doing, but as France and America were not at war, yet, and as he had diplomatic cover there was not much they could do about it.

The Italians had to march along the *Basse Corniche* bordering France and Monaco to reach Nice and beyond. News of Orebaugh's defection was abroad and now the Italians had their gander up, the temptation to invade neutral Monaco and arrest him got the better of them. Prince Louis II complained to Pope Pius XII and Adolph Hitler but with only a mealy-mouthed reply from His Holiness and no reply at all from the Führer. Soon the Metropole was surrounded by Italian troops, the new American Consulate had armed guards on the doors, while the secret police were asking Herr Scheck about the guests.

Bertie was playing carpet golf when the knock on his door came. It was Herr Scheck.

'Mr. Wooster, I fear you are in great danger. The SIM have seen your name on the guest list.'

'Who are they?' asked Bertie.

'The *Servizio Informazioni Militare*, the Italian secret police. It is just a matter of time before they arrest you. And then when they discover who you are, your fame, there will be even more trouble for you.'

'Bit of a sticky wicket,' said Bertie.

'What does that mean?'

'When there's a damp patch near the crease, usually after rain stopped play and the ball....'

'Mr. Wooster, I was not looking for a literal translation from your version of English. I meant what does it *mean*?'

'It means I am in the soup.'

'I don't understand. I am only a humble hotelier.'

'In a spot of bother, Herr Scheck. I might be in a spot of bother. But hang on. They can't arrest me. I'm British and on neutral territory. Tell them to go away and mind their own business.'

'Unfortunately, Mr. Wooster, we live in troubled times. They have invaded our country as well as France. Britain and Italy are already at war. You will surely be arrested. And you will surely then be a prisoner of war. Your only hope is to take refuge in the American Consulate on the ground floor suite.'

'With that nice Mr. Orebaugh? I should say so, we've been dining regularly and getting along famously. Mr. Martini I call him. Not to his face of course. "Straight up" is his catchphrase. If you're sure it's really necessary.'

'I am sure, Mr. Wooster. As your Mr. Disraeli said, we must hope for the best and prepare for the worst. Please prepare, we will move you down there now.'

With Bertie now on American soil, Orebaugh and he bunkered down as best they could. They were now effectively under house arrest, albeit five-star Monaco hotel with heated swimming pool house arrest. Apart from Herr Scheck and the hotel staff, their only visitors were the husband and wife team from the Swiss Legation, Pierre and Rosemarie Lasalle. Through them messages were passed to and from Skeldings Hall. From home he heard that Bobbie and Nanny were safe and well; the Italians had sequestered La Villa Masquerade and officers were billeted there. Taxi! and her puppies were safe with the head gardener Jean, who had taken them into hiding; Lady Wickham had died and Bobbie was fending off two small effs. And news from the world at large: the Allies were progressing well in North Africa; the Germans had reached Marseilles and Toulon before the Italians; the explosions they heard a few nights before had been the French Navy scuttling their fleet. To home he relayed he was most upset to hear about Taxi! and her puppies having to go into hiding; that the Italian officers were probably quite civilised and should enjoy their stay at Villa Masquerade; that the malaria was almost gone; that the sooner the Allies stumbled across Monaco the better; and that he sent them all his love.

∽∾∽

It soon became clear that the Italians were less intent on invading Monaco than capturing Orebaugh, and by innocent extension, Wooster. The Consul later wrote: 'Here I was, I thought grimly, representing the biggest, most powerful nation in the world, counting on the miniscule police force of one of the tiniest nations on earth to protect me from an invading army'.

On 2nd December, the Italians lost patience with the diplomatic stalemate and invaded that tiny part of America on neutral soil. Orebaugh and Bertie were playing gin rummy just after lunch. From the door came repeated loud bangs and shouts of: '*Apri la porta!*'

'Consul, Colonel Fornaciari and his troop are demanding to see you.' It was Herr Scheck from behind the door.

'Tell him the Consulate is closed,' Orebaugh yelled back. 'Tell him to call back. We will open again tomorrow morning.'

Scheck replied: 'But Mr. Orebaugh, I think they must speak with you now. I don't think these men are bluffing when they say they will break the door down if you don't open it.'

'That would be highly illegal!' shouted the Consul. 'This is the Consulate of the United States of America! It is in a neutral country and is protected under international law! This is downright illegal!'

Bertie could hear a trace of humour in Herr Scheck's voice as he replied; 'Mr. Orebaugh, I don't think these men are lawyers. I think you better let them in.'

Bertie said to Orebaugh: 'Let me help.' Then walking over to the door: 'Herr Scheck, tell them to go away. Orebaugh is a Consul. I'm British, they are foreign. I'm in America. They are in Monaco, which they jolly well shouldn't be. They can huff and puff as much as they like. Tell them to behave themselves. They are not in Italy now!'

With that translated into Italian, albeit benignly, the troop broke the door down, the Colonel brandished his pistol, Orebaugh and Wooster were arrested, and a minor diplomatic squabble was lost in the barrage of war.

❦

Via Tasso 145 in the Esquilino district of central Rome

is now home to the *Museo Storico della Liberazione*, or as the subtitle on the sign outside says The Liberation Museum. Trip Advisor gives it 4.5 stars. The museum shows how the Gestapo used the building after the German invasion of Rome in September 1943. It tells the story of the Italian Resistance movement and the heroics thereof. What it rather conveniently forgets to mention is that until that time it was the headquarters of the OVRA, the *Organizzazione per la Vigilanza e la Repressione dell'Antifascismo*. OVRA had the distinction of being the example that Heinrich Himmler used to set up the SS; in fact the OVRA founding father, Arturo Bocchini, and Himmler were close collaborators until their bosses turned on each other.

Watching movies Bertie had seen how prisoners in solitary confinement scratch a mark on a wall for each day confined, then strike through the lines every fifth day. He decided to do the same. But there was a problem: had he been here for four days or three? Can't have been five. He had been separated from Orebaugh at Genoa. They both presumed the Consul would be sent to Geneva, out of harm's way.

(Presumed wrongly, Orebaugh's further adventures as an Italian PoW and with the Italian Resistance can be read in his autobiography *Guerrilla in Striped Pants: A US Diplomat Joins the Italian Resistance*.) They told them both that Wooster was to be sent to Rome for further interrogation. There was an overnight in a guard's van of a freight train, with Bertie handcuffed to a secret policeman. Scruffy little individual he was too, but Bertie kept his views to himself. So that was night 1. Day 2 started with his arrival in OVRA, a change of clothes into blue overalls, a bowl of soup and his first interview.

'He was a plump little chappie,' he later told Bobbie.

'Spoke passable English. He told me my war was over. I said it had never started, if you don't count cheering from the dress circle. I tried to help him by Italianising English words he was struggling with. You know, I said theatre, he tried theatre? blankly, I said theatro, he said ah, teatro. It's amazing how many words they've taken from the English. Name and address, date of birth, mother's maiden name. I'm not sure I ever knew, so I made something up. Wickham probably. Then he produced a folder with some press cuttings about me, so they knew most of it all along. Then another chap arrived, yabbering in Eyetie. They seemed obsessed with Hollywood. Did I know Cesar Romero? And Frank Sinatra? Well I did of course. At least I'd met them.'

So that was Day 2. They put Bertie back in a cell on his own that night, so that was Night 2. He remembered Day 3 for the footsteps outside, walking up and down the hall. He was always expecting one passing pair to stop outside, but each time they walked past. Except twice. Once the door opened, a guard looked at him for a few seconds, then left again as abruptly as he had arrived. Second time there was some grub, same soup as the day before but with some bread and suspicious looking water. That night must have been Night 3, but then the next day repeated itself as did the night, but was there another one after that? Bertie decided that if there hadn't been there might as well have been, so took off his overalls and with the buckle scratched four strikes on the brick cell wall.

He told himself out loud, 'things could have been worse'. The bed wasn't too bad, a bit narrow perhaps. Wooden with straps, a bit like that cove Mahatma Gandhi used. They called him Me-hat-me-coat at the Drones. Ah, the Drones. Happy days. Bunfight days. The blankets kept him warm, even though ideally the bugs would have found someone to bite. No sheets of course, but you can't have everything. The food might get repetitious if they kept this soup routine up much longer, but he said aloud again, 'I'm used to being in the soup and this time I am in it more than usually.' A bath would be nice, it had been a few days now. He'd ask the grub wallah next time he arrived. Batho? Didn't sound right. Aqua and scrubbing motions should do the trick.

A while later, maybe a few hours give and take, the grub wallah did arrive and Bertie tried his aqua and scrubbing routine, with a positive response: 'Ok, meester, no problem.' But no bath happened and then that was Night 5.

Day 6 started with the door opened by a different guard, this one saying 'Come Wooster!' and Bertie replying, 'Ah, a bath at last, thank you very much.' But instead Bertie found himself in front of a very smart looking officer. Lots of ribbons and stars and a clean pressed uniform. Then he saw his own clothes laid out across a chair.

'Happy Christmas Bertram Wooster,' Captain Smarty-pants announced.

'Is it, by George?' Bertie replied, 'I've rather lost track. Anyway Happy Christmas to you too. I hope you don't mind, but haven't brought you any presents.'

'Very droll. I am pleased you haven't lost your sense of humour as our guest.'

'Well I can't say it has been a pleasure, but I've had worse. I went to Eton and this is far more civilised. Pity you chaps don't still speak Latin and I'd have felt quite at home.'

'Sorry. I have not introduced myself. I am Colonel Guido Leto, *commandante of Organizzazione per la Vigilanza e la Repressione dell'Antifascismo*. OVRA for short.'

Bertie shook his hand and said, 'Hello, I am Bertram Wooster, I'm not really....'

'But Mr. Wooster, of course we know who you are. We are an Intelligence Service. We have intelligence. I understand you would like a shower? Please. Then be dressed,' he said, gesturing to Bertie's clothes, 'I have a special treatment for you.'

'Ah,' said Bertie, 'some pasta with my soup?'

'No, no, we are to meet Il Duce himself. Quick now, a shower and dressed. You will have Christmas coffee with Mussolini.'

෴

Bertie didn't like the cut of Mussolini's jib before he had even met him, agreeing with Bobbie's assessment that he was a jumped-up little popinjay looking for someone else to fight his battles. Orebaugh had told Bertie that Mussolini said he needed a thousand dead Italian soldiers in the Riviera invasion campaign to secure his place at the peace table and the subsequent carve-up of France.

So Bertie was more than slightly taken aback to be welcomed by an averagely built, open-gestured, open-necked family man. Il Duce was dressed casually in a light blue shirt, grey flannel trousers and black loafers. Bertie found himself thinking the great Duce could have been dressed by Jeeves. This paragon of English style greeted Bertie with a warm handshake and introduced himself, rather unnecessarily, as if he were Stanley and he had just bumped into Livingstone. He then introduced Bertie to his wife Rachele and their children.

Equally, Bertie was surprised to be welcomed in his home, the neo-classical palazzo Villa Torlonia on the via Nomentana, not as he had expected in the official Palazzo Venezia, home of the famous balcony. After the family left, coffee was served, not by a flunkey but by an equally casually dressed young maid. The two great men sat in armchairs, while Leto stood away by the door; otherwise they were alone.

They chatted for a while about family Christmases and Hollywood. Mussolini spoke surprisingly good, if halting, English. Did Bertie know that his *Stagecoach* had been dubbed into Italian? Bertie had to admit that although he had written the score in Hollywood in 1939, he had taken no interest in what happened to it after that. He hadn't taken much interest in it before that either: 'Just a quick score I did as a favour to John Ford, my neighbour at the time.'

Then Benito, as he insisted Bertie call him, apologised for arresting him in Monaco.

'I had been ill. Malaria, frightful pest,' said Bertie, 'and I was on neutral ground. So it was hardly convenient.'

'I understand. But you say to make an omelette you must break an egg.' He walked over to a globe by the fireplace and spun it. 'Look at this.' Bertie walked over to the globe. 'I just want to make Italy great again. Like before. Like the Roman Empire was great. Is not so much to ask?'

'But I thought Italy was already great.'

They moved back to the armchairs. 'No, no, not great. Now is better. Our politics were a disgrace. A big disgrace. A lot of bad *guidi* out there. A lot. Good men did not go into government. There was no belief. Just take, take, take. And the people, they had no purpose. The truth is they were tired of liberty. Italy wants peace, quiet, work, calm. I will give these things with love if possible and with force if necessary. But Bertram, we don't want to talk about politics on Christmas Day. Let's talk about New Year's Eve.'

'I was hoping to be in Lugano by then. Or anywhere in Switzerland.'

'One day you will, but not by then. On New Year's Day you will cross to Lugano. I want to make you an offer. A proposal. I offer. I propose.'

'Ah, well, we Woosters are known to be partial to proposals, as long as they do not involve marriage.'

'No, no marriage, Bertram. Not this time. I want you to play music and sing at a party. A New Year's Eve party. In my honour. Everything in Italy is in my honour,' he laughed. 'You will play at the home of the admiral of the *Decima Flottiglia Mezzi d'Assalto*. He is Prince Junio Valerio Scipione Ghezzo Marcantonio Borghese. You know the Borghese family? In Naples. So I propose you play piano, sing songs at my party, then next day you can go to Lugano. Switzerland in two days.'

'And if not? I mean, if I would rather not?'

'Why would you not? I make you an offer. You are my friend. My Hollywood friend. You are welcome in

123

my home. In Prince Junio's home. Welcome in Italy.'

'Well there is the small matter of war. Orebaugh said Italy declared war on Britain while I was in the san.'

'San? San? What you say san?'

'Hospital. While I was in hospital in Nice. When I had malaria. Just now. Heavens, seems like months ago already.'

'Bertram, Bertram. It is our countries that are at war, we are not at war. Orebaugh. Pah! What he knows? Orebaugh is a prisoner of war at Gubbio.'

'I thought Orebaugh was in Geneva.'

'No, I change my mind. Our German friends insist. He and the French Jews ships.'

'French Jews ships?'

'Never mind. Omelettes and eggs. Again. Orebaugh was an egg. You are an egg. Don't forget that Bertram. I can break you, just like that. But Il Duce prefers omelettes. You are a lucky man. But remember, an egg.'

'Jolly good egg, most people say.'

'Of course. You are a good egg. I am a good egg. So now you stay a house guest of Borghese. You can prepare for your concert. You want musicians? We have musicians, just tell Leto here what you need.'

Bertie stood up and walked towards Leto and the door. Turning he said: 'I don't need musicians because I'm not going to play. Anyway, it sounds more like house arrest than house guest. I'm sorry Benito, I cannot accept your offer.'

'But you cannot refuse. I made you an offer. An offer of your freedom,' said Mussolini, standing now too.

'Ah, remember your Latin *Libertas perfundet omnia luce*?'

'I'm sorry, your Latin I cannot,' said Il Duce.

'Something about freedom cannot be given, only taken. Amazing what we remember from school days. No, my point is that Taxi! has just had puppies and she has been forced into hiding. Like a refugee, an exile in her own country. That is to say although she's technically American, she thinks she's French. She *is* French, in effect. I couldn't let her down by playing at your party.'

'Wait. You are talking about a *dog*, I am right? You say puppies.'

'I am. And not just any old dog, but one my wife bought me for my thirty-fifth birthday. An American cocker spaniel, answers to the name of Taxi! And now she has five puppies.'

'So, I no understand. You will not take freedom because of a *dog*? I'll buy you another dog. Ten dogs. Every dog in Rome.'

'I don't want every dog in Rome. I want one dog, well six if you count the puppies. With me in Naples. Then with me to Switzerland. Then I'll play at your party.'

Mussolini puffed and strutted. Then he raved; but not at Bertie in English, but at Leto in Italian. Bertie could make out some of the Italian words: *'Cane ... cuccioli ... stupido ... Inglese ... Roville ... profugo ... stronzo ... Napoli ... eccentrico ... idiota ... velocemente.'* Then he could make out some of Leto's reply: *'Ridicolo ... sei cane ... sei giorni ... Napoli ... perché no nuova cane ... comprare altros.'* But Mussolini had the last word, the shouted order: *'Dono i miei ordini! Adesso! Trova i cani!'*

Then to Bertie, more calmly: 'We will try. Leto's

men will look everywhere. But let's say no dogs in a week. You are going to Switzerland. I have billions and billions of lire. That's part of the beauty of me: I am very rich. You want American dollars? How many American dollars?'

'I don't need any money.'

'Then another man's freedom. Orebaugh. I can give you Orebaugh's freedom.'

'Orebaugh can look after himself. Besides, what about the Germans?'

'I no care about the fuggin Germans,' Il Duce was shouting now. 'I want you to play and sing at my party. When I give an order,' now at full volume he turned to – and on – Leto. Bertie heard a tirade of orders and gestures and threats. From the side door a young man in full military uniform entered and waited for Mussolini to draw breath, then whispered a message to him. Il Duce turned and strode out of the room, turning to point and shout at Leto: *'Trova il cane, adesso!'* and to Bertie: *'Sabato sera, Napoli!'*

By late afternoon the by-now dusty figures of Leto and Bertie stepped out of the back of a *Regia Marina* Lancia Astura cabriolet and found themselves being greeted by a tall, impeccably dressed middle-aged man on the marble steps of a reimagined Roman villa. 'Welcome to Villa Pompeii, welcome to Naples. We are expecting you. I am Bruno Decisi, *primo maresciallo* to Principe Junio, Ammiraglio Borghese. Follow me please.'

⌇⌇⌇

One hour later Bertie heard a knock on the door, opened

it and gestured Decisi into the room. Over the officer's arm were a variety of clothes and he said: 'I have found what clothes I can that might fit you, Mr. Wooster. If I can borrow your shoes I will find some fresh ones too.'

'Borrow away,' said Bertie.

Decisi walked across the room and turned on the radio, rather too loudly for Bertie's ideal. 'And did you find the bath?' he asked, raising his voice.

'Very refreshing, thank you,' Bertie half-shouted back. And towel?'

'Yes, yes, the towel too. All very nicely, thank you.'

'Dinner will be at nine downstairs. Cocktails at a quarter-to. Prince Junio is away until tomorrow, so just you and Mr. Leto. He is leaving early. To look for your dogs.'

'You are very well informed. Excellent English too. Decisi, isn't it? Sorry, terrible with names. This Prince Junio, who is he? Do we have to have this thing so loud?'

Decisi raised his finger to his lips, then said: 'He is of the House of Borghese. His father Livio was the Prince of Sulmona. He is the second son and has the title of Patrician of Rome, Naples and Venice. He went to Harrow.'

'Oh, that's bad luck,' said Bertie.

'Yes, then the *Accademia Navale* in Livorno. Now he is an admiral. Although we all call him Prince Junio, his exact title should really be Don Junio.' Then he walked closer to Bertie and said as softly as the radio noise allowed: 'A stickler for procedure and protocol like your man Jeeves would insist on the correct form of address. Am I right?'

Bertie was flummoxed for a few seconds. 'Good heavens, you know about Jeeves? That was a lifetime ago,' Bertie whispered back.

'Since your arrest in Monaco we know a lot about you.'

'*We?*' asked Bertie. 'Who's we?'

'British intelligence.'

'*British* intelligence? You mean you're a....'

'Spy. Correct Mr. Wooster. I am a British spy. Or agent as we prefer to be known. Spy is the verb, what we do. Agent the noun. It's important to be precise. And we have a friend in common.'

'Good heavens, who's that?' asked Bertie.

'Harold Winship.'

'Ginger? Well, well, how do you know him?'

'I met him at the Marquis of Marconi's wedding. Marconi's wife is Maria Cristina Bezzi-Scali, she is my first cousin. Her father, Count Bezzi-Scali was my uncle and guardian. Like you I was raised by an uncle, although in Switzerland rather than Shropshire.'

'Extraordinary. And what was Ginger doing there?'

'Representing your country. He was a cultural attaché at the British Embassy. Marconi was practically British, the reason the British claim they invented the radio. This was also the first time either of us met Benito Mussolini.'

'Good gosh, but how so?'

'Mussolini was Marconi's best man.'

'Was he, by George? Cultural attaché, eh? So Ginger's a British beagle too.'

'I believe, Mr. Wooster, this conversation should end here. Tomorrow I will show you around the grounds, away from prying ears. We have a mission for you. You will need courage and daring. For king and country. All will be explained. Drinks at a quarter to nine, just come downstairs.'

With that he left. Bertie turned off the radio, a Marconi he now noticed, laid back on his bed, lit a restorative cigarette and said aloud to himself: 'Bertram old son, you've been in the soup before and no doubt you'll be in the soup again. But this bowl of soup has all the trademarks of a sticky wicket. And the bowling is coming from the pavilion end. Googlies the lot of them. Something about stepping up to the crease. Nation in need and all that. Wooster the opening bat. Crikey, who'd have thought?' And he thought of Aunt Agatha and her barbs, then he thought no more of her, or it.

◦◦◦◦◦

The following morning after breakfast Bruno Decisi and Bertram Wooster took an instructive tour of the Villa Pompeii's ornate gardens. With only the Lilies of the Nile for company, Decisi briefed Bertie:

'So, Borghese is admiral of the *Decima Flottiglia Mezzi d'Assalto*, which translates as the 10th Assault Vehicle Flotilla. Mostly known as *La Decima Mas* or the acronym XMAS. They use manned torpedoes to blow up allied shipping in harbours. Remarkably effective too. They have already destroyed HMS *York* in Suda Bay. Then they attacked in Alexandria and sank some more of His Majesty's warships: the *Queen Elizabeth*, the *Jervis* and the *Valiant*. Plus about a dozen steamships, freighters mostly.'

'Manned torpedoes, eh? The old egg wobbles.'

'I'm sorry?'

'The mind boggles. How do you man a torpedo? It's hard enough manning a lifeboat.'

'They, that is we, have two frogmen ride them, astride, one behind the other. They are horrible to manoeuvre which is why the Italians called them *Maiale*, which means pig. There's an electric engine and some fins and a limpet mine on a timer, which they attach to our warships. All done at night of course.'

'I can see they'd be the devil to detect.'

'Correct. Which is where you come in.'

'Me? Well I'll do my best. I'm not one of the world's great swimmers though.'

'Swimming is not what we have in mind. Stealing. How are you at stealing, Mr. Wooster?'

'Ah, yes, that's more like it. I swiped a policeman's helmet once. And a fancy fiddle. If that's any pointer to form.'

'It's a start. Look, it's important that the New Year's Eve concert goes ahead.'

'Well, I said I wouldn't play at it. To Mussolini.'

'I know, but it gives you access to the admiral's private suite, where the piano is and where his papers are. And where I can't go. We need the papers to anticipate XMAS's next moves.'

'But what about Taxi! and the puppies. I don't want to let them down.'

'There are more important matters at stake here than your dogs, Mr. Wooster.'

'It's not about the dogs. It's about my word. I gave them my word.'

'With respect, signore, you didn't really give them

your word. Not that they would understand if you had. You gave Mussolini your word. And believe me, he couldn't care less about words or honour or principle or whatever else you have in mind.'

'But how will I know which papers to steal? I don't read Italian.'

'It will be obvious. I will show you how the folders look. They are blue, light blue, with *Regia Marina* written across them, you will see. Here is what you do. Prince Junio arrives back tomorrow, partly to prepare for the New Year's Eve ball.'

'Ball?' asked Bertie, 'Mussolini said it was a party.'

'It's a ball, believe me. Can you imagine Il Duce at less than a ball?' he chuckled to himself and shook his head. 'So, Prince Junio will bring his work with him and he always keeps it in his private suite. I'm not allowed in there, although of course I go in when he is not there. But that is where the piano is. I will introduce you. You will ask to practise before the ball. He will certainly agree. He's practically as English as you are.'

'British,' said Bertie.

'British. Practically as British as you are. Then you will ask for some sheets of music. He will ask me to buy them. I will, a lot of them. Then you leave them on purpose in the study. Next day, same again, more sheets of music left in the study. And so on, so he is used to seeing them lying around. After the ball you leave directly for Lugano, but first you go back into the study to collect your sheets of music. Only you accidentally pick up the wrong papers, his folders, as well. By the time he has noticed you will be in Switzerland.'

'And what about Taxi! and the puppies?'

'Be sure that Leto and his OVRA men are scouring the Provençal hills for them now. There's a chance they may find them. But let's say they don't. Our plan must go ahead. We already suspect XMAS are planning a new attack in Gibraltar?'

'Gibraltar? That's a frightful dump. They're welcome to it.'

'Not on Gibraltar, in Gibraltar. There's an Italian freighter, the *Olterra*, interred in Algeciras next door. Spain is supposed to be neutral but lets the Axis do what they like as long as it's done quietly. We know the Italians have been stocking her up and think it's for an XMAS attack. Right now we have the *Nelson*, the *Formidable* and the *Furious* in Gibraltar. Even after they go there will be others. American warships and Liberty ships too soon.'

'We don't want them harmed.'

'No, we don't. But that's all for tomorrow. For today, you are our house guest, but under house arrest. So just make yourself at home. Tomorrow Prince Junio arrives and your mission starts.'

'Right-ho,' said Bertie, then 'Hmmm.'

⌘

It's fair to say that Bertie and Prince Junio rubbed along famously. At thirty-six Junio was six years younger than Bertie and although in many ways so dissimilar – Junio being decisive, dashing, precise and commanding, and Bertie being, well, Bertie – they shared a lot too: English schooling, easy manners, bonhomie and confidence. Comfort without and comfort within. And they found two early and extraordinary coincidences: as a child

Bertie had met Junio's grandmother, Ilona, Countess Apponyi de Nagy-Appony at Aunt Agatha's and in 1930, at a reception at the Ritz, he had met Junio's first cousin Countess Géraldine Apponyi de Nagy-Appony, in her role as Queen Consort to King Zog I of Albania. Later they dined at a small party given by the Duke of Chiswick and organised by Bertie's old mucker and the duke's nephew, Bicky Bickersteth.

Junio also sported the ideal ice-breakers: two standard poodles, a mother and daughter, called Bandita and Cheeky. The poodles' alpha male prince knew nothing about the Taxi! and puppies saga, a situation that Bertie soon rectified, starting with his spell of malaria in the san in Nice, his arrest in Monaco, solitary confinement in Rome, the meeting with Il Duce and the great spaniel stand-off. Having unburdened himself of the last month's turns of events, Bertie was not surprised to hear Junio agree with him: 'Absolutely right, if Winston Churchill tried that trick on me, with 'Dita and Cheeky holed up under cover, I wouldn't play for him either. But look, if you want to have a tinkle to pass the time of day, there's an old Joanna right there, help yourself. Sabrina and the children arrive tomorrow, but today there'll be peace and quiet. I've got some work to do,' and with that he pulled some light blue folders from his attaché case, 'and you can fool around with the keys. I'll have Decisi go into town to find you some sheet music. We can keep each other company.'

So thus they did for the next few days. Bertie was by now so used to various forms of confinement that he no longer even dreamt of taking a stroll outside. Sabrina was as charming as Junio, the children were largely of the 'seen and not heard' variety and Bertie's main hardship was avoiding the tiresome and unavoidable Decisi. At one point Junio asked Bertie what the latter thought of Decisi.

'Seems very efficient. Wonderful English,' said Bertie, nonchalantly, hopefully.

'He's Swiss Italian, speaks endless languages perfectly. I think he's a spy,' offered Junio.

'I say, steady,' said Bertie. 'Just because a chap parlays a few lingos....'

'No, I mean an OVRA spy. One of Leto's beagles, keeping an eye on me. I won't have him in here in my study.'

'Ah, you might well be right,' said Bertie. 'Frightfully good hoteliers the Swiss. There's this chap at the Metropole....'

'Herr Scheck! Know him well. Before that he was at the Imperiale in Portofino, where we spent our honeymoon.'

'And good bankers. Frightfully good bankers,' said Bertie. 'No need to tell a blue-blooded Italian that, my friend! Red-blooded one too. There's not a lira in Italy that isn't also in Switzerland.'

Prince Junio was a man of admirable habit. He rose early, went out to do something or other naval in Naples in the morning, checked on preparations for the ball at one, lunched sparsely at two, took a short nap thereafter, then worked on his folders in the study till six, and on that dot called for cocktails in the drawing room, leaving his folders scattered around the study. After cocktails he went upstairs to change for dinner, avoiding Decisi as best he could. After dinner he retired to the orangery for a cigar and nightcap, then up to bed to sleep the whole thing off.

Bertie was a man of habit too, albeit arguably of less admirable habit. He rose late, mooched around the grounds in what was left of the morning, marvelled at the preparations for the ball at one, lunched sparsely with Junio at two, took a longer nap thereafter and played piano in the study till six o'clock cocktails, leaving his music scattered around the study. After cocktails he too went upstairs to change for dinner, likewise avoiding Decisi as best he could. After dinner he joined Junio in the orangery for a cigar and nightcap, then nothing for it but to follow him up and sleep the whole thing off.

⌘

Bertie's languorous mornings were rudely disturbed by Decisi bursting unknocked into his room. It was the dawn of New Year's Eve.

'She's here! She's here!' he enthused.

'Who's here?' said Bertie. 'What time is it? Where's my tea?'

'Tea's coming. Your dog. Taxi! Leto's men found her near Roville.'

'Good golly. But what about the puppies?' asked Bertie, now more or less awake.

'The gardener insisted on keeping them. He said Madame would understand. But that Taxi! was yours. So here she is. Call her.'

He felt his way over to the door and called: 'Taxi!? Taxi!?' then hearing her feet shuffling, her nose sniffing and her tail wagging below, 'Taxi! Taxi! Come on, girl. Come to papa.'

And with that a full-sized spaniel leapt up at Bertie, who willingly fell back on the bed for some serious licking and tickling and general canine-human reunion ritual.

When Decisi judged that man and beast had quietened down sufficiently, he brought up the subject of the ball tonight.

'I've been hearing you practise for the ball tonight,' he said. 'Now that Leto has found Taxi! I need to have the programme printed. Do you know yet which songs you will be playing and singing tonight?'

'Ah yes, rather,' said Bertie, stuck mid-quandary. 'Let me gather my thoughts. I'll let you know within the hour.'

For the first time since being reunited with Taxi!, Bertie now saw his predicament clearly laid out in front him. To play or not to play, that was the question. Except it wasn't. He had given Mussolini his word and Mussolini would be there. Half a dozen songs should be enough. He already half knew what they would be, when three visitors arrived: Bandita, Cheeky and Prince Junio.

While Taxi! and the poodles sniffed each other experimentally, then wagged tails approvingly, Junio shut the door from Decisi's ears and asked Bertie quietly what he was going to do about performing this evening.

'I'll have to play of course. I gave my word,' said Bertie.

'Not of course,' said the Prince. 'You said you would play if Taxi! and the puppies were returned. But only Taxi! has been returned. It seems to me you are off the hook, if you want to be.'

'I do want to be, believe me, and let's face it, none of us ever thought the OVRA boys would find any of them. But,' Bertie paused to gather his thoughts, 'it's the spirit of my word that counts.'

'Well, you're a better man than I am, Gunga Din. There's something you don't know yet,' said Junio. 'Edoardo Alfieri will be at the ball tonight.'

'Bit of a mouthful. Who's he?' asked Bertie.

'He is a particularly nasty piece of work. He is also Minister for Press and Propaganda. If you play tonight it will be all over the world's press tomorrow. Newsreels too. Personally, I would use the puppies defence.'

'But Mussolini said it would be a private party,' said Bertie.

'Bertie, please. Don't be so innocent. As Il Duce says, there's a lot of bad *guidi* out there. There are. They work for him. They'll destroy you, or try to. Just be warned,' and with that he whistled at the poodles and all three left.

Alone with Taxi! Bertie pondered his dilemma. They took to the bed for a council of war. After a while he said to her: 'If I play, I keep my word but will be destroyed. If I don't play, I break my word and lose my honour. Destruction or honour, what's it to be old girl?'

Taxi! looked back, gave him an impromptu wag and a friendly sniff and went back to rest. 'I agree,' said Bertie, pleased someone else had made his mind up for him.

∽∼∾

The ball was a ghastly bore. Whereas pre-war the balls back home were riots of fun, abandon and gaiety, in

Naples in Fascist Italy that New Year's Eve the ball was a procession of formality, deference and obedience. The star attractions, Benito and Rachele Mussolini, only added to the heaviness. Dressed in full regalia and sporting an unusually strutty strut, he was the opposite of the relaxed family man of Christmas Day. She, too, was dressed to the nines, and all women there had to be careful to call a halt at the eight and a halfs.

It didn't take long for Alfieri to find Bertie. How very handsome Mr. Wooster looked in his white tie. How very welcome Mr. Wooster was, here in Naples and here in Italy. How much the Italians wished this horrible war was over, that Britain and Italy could be friends again. How very much he was looking forward to the concert tonight, particularly the part Mr. Wooster was going to play in it. Il Duce, with Leto at his heels, found Bertie too and congratulated themselves on the excellent efficiency of the Italian secret police. 'If an Italian dog was lost in England,' Mussolini asked, 'would the SIS have found it so quickly? I think not. And now you sing for Il Duce, that was our deal, no?' Bertie had to agree, that was the deal.

And so the night went on; and on and on. He was introduced to various dignitaries, but couldn't for the life of him remember who any of them were half a minute later. The canapé were extracts from the buffet. The wine and whisky flowed but Bertie declined: he had long since made it a rule never to drink – or back in the jazz days snort cocaine – before a show.

Show? If only! One Italian string quartet followed another. Occasionally an opera singer gave them an aria, always drowned out by the increasingly rowdy audience. A particularly inept juggler juggled, and equally useless magician magicked. Bertie was due on, alone with his voice at the piano, at 11:30 p.m. for twenty minutes. As far as he could tell it was running on time, like the trains hereabouts of late. By 11.00 p.m. he was worried, then pleased, then worried again that with no amplification and with a party-going crowd no one would hear him anyway. A declining half of him remained bored; a heightening part of him anxious. Bored and anxious is a dangerous combination. Makes a chap mischievous. With a ha!, Bertie decided to move off the songs in Decisi's programme and onto something more racy. More amusing. More rousing. More showbiz. Yes, *Ten German Bombers* would get them, or at least him, started. Then a quick Noël Coward had played him *Don't Let's Be Beastly to the Germans*; he could remember the chorus and improvise the rest. Then to finish off one of his favourites from Hollywood: Tex Grande's *Hitler's Reply to Mussolini*. That should bring the house down. Bertie could only remember the first chorus:

> *Dear Muss, the letter you wrote me*
> *Is the first laugh I've had in a year*
> *I relate to my old friend Goering*
> *And he damn near choked on his beer*

And he'd have to make them sing along with the rest. Fast forward twenty minutes and Bertie stood centre stage, arms outstretched. Surprisingly, the guests quietened down and turned to the stage. Bertie said: '*Signori e signori, mi scusi non parlando Italiano*. I'm going to play some songs in English. Sing along if you like.' Then he sat at the piano, pounded out some opening bars and sang:

There were 10 German bombers in the air,
There were 10 German bombers in the air,
There were 10 German bombers, 10 German bombers,
10 German bombers in the air.
And the RAF from England shot 1 down,
And the RAF from England shot 1 down
And the RAF from England, RAF from England,
The RAF from England shot 1 down.

At first he sang in silence. But as the verses unfolded, with each loss to the Luftwaffe a few more guests were getting the hang of it. Most of them could count from ten to one backwards in English. Most of them knew the tune to *She'll be Coming 'Round the Mountain When She Comes*. And most of them by now hated the Germans as much as Bertie did. Looking out, Bertie could see even Il Duce sing along with the rousing finale:

There were no more German bombers in the air,
There were no more German bombers in the air,
There were no more German bombers, no more
   German bombers,
No more German bombers in the air.
'Cos the RAF from England shot them down,
'Cos the RAF from England shot them down,
'Cos the RAF from England, RAF from
'The RAF, England, from England....

Boom! Bang! Crash! Whomp! Thump! Whoosh! Swoosh! Thwack! Smash! Clunk! Clatter! Clang!

Bertie's song was immediately drowned out by the explosions. Unhesitatingly, he ducked for cover under the piano. Everyone else was running across the ballroom floor, in any direction. The chandeliers fell next, just missing the fleeing throng. One by one the lights went out. Shrieks, screams and yells. Suddenly Bertie felt a hand on his elbow. It was Decisi.

'What's happening?' Bertie coughed through the dust.

'Allied bombing,' he answered. 'We knew Mussolini and half the cabinet would be here, too good an opportunity to miss.'

'But what about us? We were here too?'

'I was safe in the basement. You were the decoy, expendable. Come quickly. Friends are waiting for you.'

Bertie followed Decisi out through the dust and noise and darkness. Outside, in the confusion of screams and faltering lights and swirling dust the same Lancia Astura was waiting.

Taxi! was already on the back seat. Bertie vaulted in beside her.

'Take me to Lugano my good man and don't spare the horses,' said Bertie to the civilian driver.

'Wait! Haven't you forgotten something?' asked Decisi.

'What's that?' asked Bertie.

'Your sheet music. And some other bits of paper?'

'Oh rather, nearly forgot', said Bertie, taking a bundle of the Italian Navy's light blue folders. 'Thanks for everything.

Must fly. Toodle pip.'

'Toodle pip,' replied Decisi, shaking his head in disbelief, the cause of which for some reason Bertie couldn't quite fathom out at that very moment.

❧

A week later six Italian frogmen on three manned torpedoes left the *Olterra* to attack the three British warships *Nelson*, *Formidable* and *Furious* in Gibraltar. Armed with new intelligence, the British were waiting for them. A Royal Navy patrol boat killed one torpedo's crew with a depth charge. Another British patrol boat spotted a second manned torpedo, chased it and captured its two surrendering crewmen. The remaining manned torpedo didn't like the way the wicket was playing and returned to the *Olterra* pavilion with its crew, if not its dignity, intact.

XMAS's war efforts declined soon after that; the British seemed to know their every move, and even their codes. Important things, codes.

CHAPTER 7

London

[Author's note: In World War II, P.G. Wodehouse was captured by the Nazis and held in prisoner of war camps. In 1941, still under confinement in Germany, he was invited to make a series of radio broadcasts to his followers in the US. The broadcasts were innocent enough, gently mocking his German captors, but the fact that they were made on German radio when Germany and Great Britain were at war, was a naive misjudgement – to say the least. In London, commentators like Cassandra and politicians like Duff Cooper and Lord Shawcross stirred trouble for their own ends; as did such as should have known better like A.A. Milne. These are the references in the chorus climax at the end of the chapter. After the war the Establishment was in no hurry to put right the slandering of Wodehouse's reputation, when they had available clear evidence that he was guilty of no more than extreme naivety.]

Bertie bounded up to Bingo at the Boodles bar. 'Bingo, old bean, all bonzer in Bingoland?'

'Not really Bertie, dropped a bit of a clanger.'

'B&S, sir?' asked McGarry from behind the bar.

'I think,' Bertie paused, 'I think I'm in more of a G&T mind this morning please, McGarry. We're still out of Boodles gin I suppose?'

'Can't get it for love nor money, sir.'

'Well, Gilbey's if poss.'

'I'll have to have a look, sir. Rationing is taking its toll,' replied McGarry, disappearing into the cellar.

'It's not the same, Bertie, is it?' whispered Bingo. Bertie knew what he meant. After Herr Goering's chaps had scored a bull's eye on the Drones, most of the inmates and McGarry himself had decamped to Boodles down the slope in St. James. Most of the others were billeted at Bucks in Clifford Street. Neither had the Drones panache; not a decent bunfight or piggyback polo in sight; no floor crawl handicap stakes to be found; no water bombs and no champagne corks dart competitions. Boodles was the stuffier and Bucks was the scruffier. Bertie belonged to both, Bingo just to Boodles. 'The infernal dress code, dark suits, for a start. Still a chap needs a club, what can you do?' asked Bingo.

'You're very down in the dumps, Bingo. What's this clanger you've let slip from your grasp?'

'We are out of Gilbey's sir,' puffed McGarry from the stairwell. 'Beefeater?'

'ABB, McGarry, ABB.'

'ABB, sir?'

'Anything but Beefeater. Can't stand the stuff. Booth's?'

'Booth's we have, sir. I'm afraid the tonic's still from the soda fountain. Can't get the bottles. Club won't be dealing on the black [market] like everyone else.'

'So, Bingo?' asked Bertie.

'So what?' replied Bingo.

'So, clanger-wise, you mentioned the dropping thereof.'

'Ah, that. Big disaster. I forgot Rosie's birthday. Not

144

just any old birthday either. There's some serious flak flying around the Little household.'

'Ah, the old flakometer is whirring around, needle off the scale,' said Bertie. 'Did it end with an 0?'

'The flakometer scale?'

'No, the mem'sahib's birthday.'

'It did and started with a five.'

'Ah, yes,' said Bertie, 'the clanger and the flakometer are not unrelated, I can see clearly your predic.'

A discreet clearing of the throat behind them suggested David, the hall porter, had floated in from his front door post. 'Mr. Maxwell-Gumbleton for you, Mr. Wooster. Shall I say you are in?'

'Oh, rather' said Bertie. A few moments later the same Maxwell-Gumbleton appeared, with rather more noise and gusto than David.

'Jumbo, old bean,' said Bertie.

'Jumbo, old top,' said Bingo.

'Bobbie said you'd be here Bertie,' said Jumbo, 'How's Bingo?'

'Sore point there,' said Bertie. 'Bingo forgot Rosie's birthday.'

'Ah, women are fond of birthdays,' said Jumbo. 'Another of life's mysteries. Listen Bertie, at the *News Chronicle* we are championing the P.G. Wodehouse cause, partly to have a pop at the *Express*. And that pompous ass Duff Cooper and his Cooper's Snoopers.'

'I saw him last month actually,' said Bertie.

'What, Cooper?' asked Jumbo.

'No Plum Wodehouse. In Long Island. I was staying with Rocky Todd at Remsenburg and Plum was staying with Guy Bolton nearby. Lovely time we had too, memories and all that. Well, it was lovely until Rocky's fire-breathing dragon Aunt Isabel showed up and Plum and I both scarpered rather pronto. He seemed chirpy enough in the circs. All rather normal.'

'That's it though, Bertie,' said Jumbo, 'that's him all over. He's abnormally normal. Someone has to say boo to the goose for him. That's what we're doing. And that's where you come in. Our angle is he didn't do too much different from you. He talked, you sang. Now, he's an outcast in exile and you're a master spy-cum-war-hero in London and Broadway. Where's the justice in that? That's what our readers will want to know.'

'I did actually say that to him and he just shrugged it off,' said Bertie. 'Neither of us wanted what we have become. I'm happy to fight his corner, Jumbo, count me in. Least I can do after all he's done for me. But what can I do?'

'OK, so here's the angle on the angle. We're republishing a short story he did for *Punch* in 1939 just after the war started. It was called *The Big Push*. A kind of satire on the Hun high command discussing their invasion of Britain plans. Not that funny actually by his standards but a good enough anti-Nazi spoof at the time. Makes the current Express nonsense even more ridiculous. Anyway, I want you to sing it.'

'Sing what?'

'Sing about *The Big Push* at the Royal Variety Performance. You can get Boko to knock up some lyrics if you can knock up a tune. Well, we know you can knock up a tune. Singalong sort of thing, our readers will go for that. Not that they'll hear it.'

'Ah, back up a moment there, Jumbo. What's all

this Royal Variety Performance performance? First I've heard of it.'

'Your slot at the London Coliseum. Haven't you heard?' asked Jumbo.

'Not a dickie bird. How do you know?' asked Bertie.

'Bertie, I'm the owner of the *News Chronicle* and six other newspapers and God knows how many magazines. Of course I know. I don't report the news, I make the news. I've told you that before. But I'm amazed Oofy hasn't told you. Anyway it's true. November 7th, to answer your next question. You've got three months to write *The Big Push*.'

'Hang on a tick,' said Bingo. 'If you can get me a couple of box seats I can say that's Rosie's birthday pressy. Then we can go backstage and swan around with Bertie there.'

'Yes,' said Bertie, 'a bit of icing on the old gateau. How about that, Jumbo?'

'You'll have to ask Oofy,' said Jumbo, 'he's running the whole racket.'

'I'm sure Oofy hasn't told me' Bertie mused. 'I wouldn't forget something like this. He must think I'm telepathetic or whatever it is. Leave it to me, Bingo. Two of the finest box seats for the mem'sahib's birthday as good as in the bag.' Bingo was just proposing a now more cheerful toast when a familiar voice sounded behind them and the three musketeers became four.

'Hey-ho, you chaps!' a familiar voice sounded behind them.

'Tuppy!' they all hey-ho'd, more or less as one.

'You're looking very spruce and dapper in the DJ,' said Bertie.

'Joe Walker and I are off to the Home Guard Eastgate Platoon reunion. Most of them are on their last legs.'

'Berlin Airlift really over?' asked Jumbo.

'Oh that, yes, more or less over now. Did well out of it. Joe and I are now going into the air charter business. Well, we've got the planes. I mean they're all grounded but we still have them. Joe's got another wheeze we're doing now as well, washing machines. Twin tubs, imported from Holland. We got some chaps selling them door-to-door. Cuts out the middle wallah. Glossopmatic we're calling them. Anyone want one?'

'Nanny will have one,' said Bertie. 'Consider it sold.'

'In that case, McGarry,' announced Tuppy, 'another round on the old mess bill for us four fine gentlemen. Nothing like spending the profits before making them, what?'

∽∞∾

While Bertie was being inconvenienced by Mussolini and his *fascisti* in Naples, Herr Goering and his Luftwaffe were being equally annoying in Mayfair. Not content with a direct hit on the Drones Club, one of his doodlebugs also scored a near miss on Berkeley Mansions. The miss was still near enough to deem the old block uninhabitable and the wrecker's ball was in full swing when the next day Bertie strode into his new spread in Arlington House, just down Arlington Street from the Ritz and just across St. James's Street from Boodle's.

Bertie knew that upstairs Bobbie was having one of her infernal girls' bridge suppers. First day summer sales on the morrow were the excuse this time. No fun for him there. No fun that afternoon either at the meeting with Oofy. Prosser International now had swanky new offices in Wardour Street. Oofy was swanky enough anyway, but his new surroundings had only swanked him up further and he was now top form favourite to win the Swank Stakes whenever they were run. When Bertie arrived Oofy was on two phones at once, then told them both to hang on while he spoke with his client Bertie Wooster. 'I did!' he insisted when challenged about the Royal Variety Performance non-comm. 'You won't!' he insisted when asked about *The Big Push* finale to his set. 'They can't!' he insisted when asked for two box seats for Bingo and Rosie.

'Dash it all, Oofy', said Bertie, 'you're being uncommon unreasonable. Plum Wodehouse needs a boost from the faithful and Bingo forgot Rosie's fiftieth. We've all got to rally round.'

'Bertie, you don't understand. It's the Royal Variety Performance. King and Queen. Two princesses. Namely George and Elizabeth and Elizabeth and Margaret Rose. No politics. I'll never be asked to do another one. Be reasonable. Put yourself in my shoes. Would you let you do it if you were me?'

'Yes, I bally well would,' said Bertie. 'You don't have a code, Oofy. Chap needs a code. And what about Bingo's box seats. Nothing to do with politics. You can't tell me there are no spare box seats.'

'There are no spare box seats. There I've said it. Well, I haven't got any. The London Coliseum run all that. Have you any idea how stingy they are? Believe me, there's not a penny in this for me. I've done you proud, top billing, want to know who else is on the bill?'

'Not much,' said Bertie, 'but I can see you're going to tell me.'

'I'll call you both back,' Oofy said into the two telephones, then to Bertie: 'We've got Arthur Askey as compère, just confirmed...'

'Heaven help us.'

'Shut up, Bertie. From Hollywood, our old friend Cora Starr. The sensational, I might add, Cora Starr. Two songs from *Gentlemen Prefer Blondes,* just opened on Broadway, everyone's talking about it here, then you'll do a number with her. *Shenanigans.*'

'What is *Shenanigans* when it's at home?'

'A duet from *Madame Rix*, everyone is singing it.'

'They are?'

'They are. And you and Cora will sing it. *Shenanigans.*'

'I will?'

'You will. And Marion Wardour you know. She's in Noël's new *Ace of Clubs.*'

'Is Noël on too?'

'No, he's in the States. Vegas to be precis. What have we here?' Oofy pulled out a sheet of foolscap with names pencilled in, crossed off, rubbed out and pencilled back in again. 'Ted Ray, The Crazy Gang, Wilfred Pickles, Maurice Chevalier, Noele Gordon – singing songs from *Brigadoon* – Michael Bentine – he's an impersonator, very funny – Ted Heath and His Band, Buster Shaver and his Trio of Lilliputians, The Tiller Girls, the Seven Ashtons – Australian acrobats they are, can you imagine? – Borrah Minevitch's Harmonica Rascals – now there's variety – the Band of HM Royal Marines and the Sea Cadets. They'll round it off as usual. Plus half a dozen others. I'm working on it. You've got three songs, two you choose – nothing racy, mind – and one with Cora, whatever she wants I told her.'

'Look, saints preserve us, I'll buy the two seats. No point two in a box, can you at least reserve me two best front rows?' asked Bertie.

'No, Bertie I cannot, you don't understand, we are not dealing with normal people,' said Oofy. 'You'll have to buy them.'

That was half an hour ago; this is now. 'Hello, Bertie,' cried out four female voices of ready recognition. There was Bobbie of course, plus Rosie Little, Pauline Chuffnell and Angela Glossop.

'Hey-ho, female counterparts. How's the rubbering rubbering in?'

'Ah, Bertie, I'm pleased to see you,' said Angela.

'Not many have said that,' suggested Bobbie.

'And I you, Cousin A. So, are we all ready for hoovering up Harrods and Harvey Nichols in the morning? Summer sales and all that?'

'Later, Bertie. But listen. About Tuppy's present,' said Angela, 'I don't know what to get him.'

'Present? For old Tuppy? Why, what's he done?'

'He stopped smoking cigarettes. I said if he stopped smoking cigarettes for three months, I'd buy him a present every month. He'll have done the first month tomorrow. What am I going to buy him?'

'Ah, forget the sales, leave that to me, I know just the thing,' said Bertie.

'Thanks Bertie,' said Angela, 'Oh, I nearly forgot.

Message from Tuppy. Tell Bertie first batch washing machines defective, would she like a plane ride instead?'

'Would who like what?' asked Bobbie.

'Never mind, it's someone's surprise,' said Bertie. 'but tell Tuppy no, I can't see that particular female taking to the skies.'

'And aren't you forgetting something?' said Bobbie.

'Me?' said Bertie, 'Oh probably, happens all the time. Give me a clue.'

Bobbie gestured towards Rosie. 'Well?'

'Hello Rosie. I'm often forgetting something. But for the life of me I can't remember what it is. Let me guess. You've got a new frock on?'

'No.'

'You had your hair done?'

'Nooo.'

'You bought a new car?'

'Nooooo!'

'You bought Bingo a present?'

'No! Double, double no with brass knobs on to that one!!' said Rosie.

'Oh Bertie, you are useless sometimes,' said Bobbie. 'what happens on July 4th?'

'The day we gave the Americans their independence?'

'And?'

'And?'

'It's my birthday!' said Bobbie, then gesturing back to Rosie. 'And?'

'It's Bingo's birthday,' said Bertie, 'silly of me, clean forgot.'

At which point four females made variations on a screech owl's mating call and Bertie headed back to Boodles to tell Bingo the good news about the tickets. Sometimes he wondered how he did it.

By the time the train puffed and panted its way towards Lincoln on their way home to Skeldings, the *Royal Princess* steam engine up front was chuffing away fit to bust. Outside the first class windows Bertie could see clouds of steam and smoke. He thought, without actually thinking *per se*: there's something about a steam engine in full puff makes a chap want to follow suit. He fished out the trusty Dunhill Bruyere from one pocket and filled it with a loose shag of St. Bruno from the other. A few draws later there was as good a fug inside the cabin as there was outside it. 'What's good for the goose is good for the gander,' he said to no-one in particular, although Bobbie acknowledged the wise words with a 'Hmm'. Then she a lit a du Maurier to keep him company.

Yes, Bertie thought, it had been a stroke of genius nipping over to Dunhill's and buying Tuppy a Chestnut pipe and bag of Royal Yacht tobacco for Angela's no smoking prize present. It had happened to him in the winter of '46 in New York. He had caught a nasty bout of bronchitis and had to stop smoking gaspers for a good month or so. When he started smoking again, it was with a pipe; best change he'd ever made, gaspers to pipe. Now when Tuppy started again he'd be a pipe smoker too. That's what friends are for.

Looking out at what he could see of Cambridgeshire, damping down the wad in the bowl, relighting and refiring it, set Bertie to ruminating; well, more of a mull really. He almost felt sorry for Oofy. This Royal Variety Performance performance was like pushing

153

water uphill. All the acts, except his as it happens, were already in performance elsewhere and trying to organise joint rehearsals was proving more or less impossible. The London Coliseum was being as difficult about rehearsals as about ticketing as about advertising. In New York there was a dock strike, meaning Cora and Cunard had to leave from Boston a week later. Cora absolutely refused to take the fifteen-hour, two-stop flight. If she arrived in time, it would be a miracle.

Then there was Jumbo. He kept pestering Bertie about the Wodehouse spoof. Bertie could see his point: they had to know so they could set the presses for the next morning. While Bertie was all for helping Plum if he could, he wasn't sure this wasn't going to blow up in all their faces and make matters worse. And talking of worse, Boko had failed to come up with any lyrics; and double worse when Bertie mentioned *The Big Push* song to Oofy again he went even more ballistic than the first time.

Then there was his own part in the whole fandango. 'Two songs from the shows,' Oofy had said, then *Shenanigans* with Cora. 'Two songs from the shows' meant two songs the audience would know, not really Bertie's style. His own show songs were now too old and his latest film musical with Boko too new; Hollywood was not due to release *A Billion Dollars More* till early '50, next spring. For his own amusement he played jazz, at the Clarion Club in New York and Club Eleven in London. But the bejewelled mighty at the London Coliseum would recoil from the Hot Club type of jazz Bertie had developed from his time with Django Reinhardt, and he wasn't about to play the type of retrograde jazz they might swallow. *Shenanigans* he had now heard and learnt; it was harmless enough; at least he'd never have to play it again.

Bertie scraped out the bowl, banged it on his heel and slowly felt up another shag in his palm. Padding it down, relighting it, he returned to his mull. No, the real problem was Rosie's birthday present. He hadn't told Bingo yet, in fact he only found out yesterday. Pauline Chuffnell, in a mad splash of extravagance she could well afford, had bought a whole box at the London Coliseum. And next to the Royal Box too. And invited the whole troop along. Not Bertie of course, he would be on stage, but Bobbie, Tuppy and Cousin A, Chuffy and argh! Bingo and Rosie. He or Bingo could sell the seats Bertie had bought easily enough, but what to do for Rosie's birthday now that Pauline had outbid them?

Backstage the royals would meet all the acts. Now if he could swing it that Rosie met the royals too, that would save Bingo's skin alright. But how? Bertie had met a few royals over the years, but they in turn had met thousands of people and wouldn't know him from Adam. He didn't know any of the royals directly; of course he knew people who did know them. But then with the last draw of the pipe, a stroke of genius descended on him from... from he knew not where, only that from time to time the old egg hatched forth a good one: Jeeves.

It had been twenty years, a bit more, but last heard of Jeeves was working his magic for King George VI and the royal household. A quick trip to the Junior Ganymede should soon open up direct lines of comm. If anyone could stand Rosie in the royal line it was

Jeeves; after all he had helped Bingo out of enough murky of soups in the past. Bertie scraped out the barrel again and put the old Bruyere back in its home pocket. Outside the old puffer was slowing down, ready for the joys of Peterborough.

As Bertie closed his eyes to give the old bean a good rest, another bubble rose most inconsiderately to the surface. Nanny. Against the odds, she wanted to try a flight after all. But all the Walker Glossop planes had been grounded as thoroughly as their washing machines. Oh, dash it, why was life so complicated?

❦

'I must be mad,' said Bertie to the cold damp air at Boston airport, his breath vaporising into the fog and gloom.

'We all must be mad,' said the pilot, helpfully. 'She's the only sane one,' he said, swigging from his hip flask and nodding at Cora flat out unconscious on a stretcher. Her nurse was trying to keep warm by drawing heartily on a gasper.

On the apron honorary co-pilot Tuppy's battered old Avro Anson looked as forlorn as its surroundings. Tuppy and Joe had bought four of the old bombers from the Royal Canadian Airforce just after the war. Three had made it across the Atlantic and been flown more of less non-stop between Blackbushe and Berlin during the Airlift. The fourth one stood sulking in front of them now.

The confluence of Cora, Cunard, the New York dock strike and Newfoundland fog had landed them in this particular bowl of soup; Cora as usual being the most flavoursome ingredient. Her fame was both a constant well that needed filling and a ring fence that no member of the public must cross. The only way she crossed the Atlantic was by Cunard liners; she made sure her arrival dockside would mean that everyone on board would know she was on the ship with them, but then she would spend the whole crossing in her suite of first class cabins with her coterie so she didn't have to suffer the ship's company or passengers. This was also one of the reasons she refused to fly: having to be gawped at close-up by the great unwashed; the other reason being the sheer terror at even the thought of it.

This time was more complicated. New York's dock strike had meant Cunard had had to send *Queen Elizabeth* up to Boston to disgorge and regorge her passengers instead. Already a few days late, the Newfoundland fog would delay her further. Meanwhile in London, Oofy was sprouting bananas. *Queen Elizabeth* could not possibly arrive in time for the Performance, let alone rehearsals. Telegrams between Oofy and Cora became more and more desperate.

ATTN O.PROSSER
AM IN BOSTON STOP CUNARD FOGBOUND STOP
BETTER CANCEL STOP CORA
ATTN C. STARR
CANCEL IMPOSS STOP MUST FLY STOP
OOFY
ATTN O. PROSSER
I DONT WONT FLY STOP CORA
ATTN C. STARR

WHY UNFLY STOP OOFY
ATTN O. PROSSER
UNLIKE PASSENGERS UNLIKE SKY CORA
ATTN C. STARR
ARRANGING PRIVATE PLANE STOP LIKEWISE
NURSE PLUS KO DRUGS STOP OOFY
ATTN O. PROSSER
AGREE ONLY IF U & BERTIE IN SAME PLANE STOP
ALL DIE TOGETHER STOP CORA
ATTN C. STARR
DEAL STOP OOFY

Later that day in Bucks, Oofy told Bertie the good news.

'Now steady on, Oofy, this is all a bit rum. You're expecting me to fly out to Boston with you just so we can bundle a comatose Cora into the back of a private plane and fly her back again?'

'That's more or less the size of it, Bertie, yes. Think of it as being for king and country.'

'But dash it, I've already done my bit for king and country.'

'Well think of it as being for the great god show business.'

'I don't care about the business part of show business. That's what you do. Can't you fish me out of this?'

'Bertie, what can I do? Be reasonable. She insisted you come too. You and I on the plane with her. Going out's easy enough, they've got it down to eighteen hours going west with only two stops.'

'And coming back? How are you going to find a private plane, let alone a willing nurse with all the needles.'

'The medical side we can wave money at. Not sure yet about the plane.'

At that moment Bertie saw Tuppy breeze into the club. 'Ah, here's a man who knows his planes,' said Bertie. Oofy unloaded the scope of the difficulty.

'It's all our lucky days,' said Tuppy. 'We bought four Ansons from the Canucks but only had time to bring three over before the Berlin bunfight. So one's still there. I'll have to go ahead of you to sort out the paperwork. Short hop down to Boston, pick up you two and Cora and the nurse, refuel at Gander and Shannon and here we are. Right as rain.'

'I hate to be picky, Tuppy,' said Bertie, 'but aren't all your Ansons grounded? Hence the twin tubs.'

'Oh that,' said Tuppy, 'just hadn't had time to service them, that was all. Anyway, that's just here in England. There're not grounded in America. Of course it will be when it lands, but we'll be here by then.'

'If it lands,' said Bertie.

'It's bound to land, Bertie. Laws of physics. What goes up, what comes down, you remember that.'

And landed it had. At Gander and Shannon to refuel and fifteen hours after leaving Boston at Blackbushe, just as Tuppy had advertised. What he hadn't advertised was everything else. First, it was so cold that Oofy and Bertie wrapped themselves around each other in one of the two blankets. The nurse did the same for herself and Cora in the other blanket. Secondly, somewhere between Gander and Shannon Cora's knock-out drug had worn off and due to some mix-up at the hospital the nurse's next injection was of adrenalin not anaesthetic. Cora sat bolt upright, realised that she was aloft with a stranger for a nurse and started screaming. Thirdly, approaching the Irish coast the pilot passed out from alcohol and frostbite, leaving Tuppy at the controls. Somewhere over Ireland he staggered back and asked the terrified passengers if any of them knew what Shannon looked like. Oofy said he only knew it was on the coast. Bertie suggested he land anywhere so they could buy some more blankets and some brandy. Tuppy said he better turn round and look for Shannon again. The Irish authorities must have radioed ahead because, fourthly, on landing at Blackbushe all the souls on board were arrested and the derivetting Anson impounded; then, like its sisters, grounded.

~~~

Knock! knock! knock! 'Fifteen minutes Mr. Wooster!'

And then a little more muffled from next door: *Knock! Knock! Knock!* 'Five minutes Miss Starr.'

Knock! knock! Knock! This time it was Bertie knocking on the dressing rooms' connecting door.

'Entrez Bertie!'

He did, and looked around in amazement. While his own dressing room looked like any old hotel room, Cora's looked like Fortnum & Mason's just before Christmas. There were three vintages of Pol Roger champagne, six bouquets of flowers, none of them white, she *loathed* white flowers, canapés of every description, a bowl of Smarties with all the brown ones removed, and three shades of Kleenex: white, pink and pale blue. Of beauticians there were three: one for the hair, one for the *maquillage* and one for the nails. This last one seemed to be doubling up: hands and feet.

'How are you feeling, old poppet?'

'Calm yet flustered. Like you I guess. The agony before the applause.'

'It's a strange addiction.'

'And like it's a career move, which it is. Re-entry onto the London stage. It's been ten years since I've been in front of an audience and not a crew. Scared and scary. But I'll be fine once the singing starts. How about you?'

'Following you. Not easy. I tell myself: Bertram old bean, you play ten thousand notes in an hour at the Clarion Club and you're happy as Larry, what's a few hundred notes with a couple of songs thrown in, in ten minutes here? Easy notes too.

Then you come on for the third song and....'

'And you still haven't decided on *The Big Push* or *Shenanigans*? I'm easy, we know them both well enough.'

'No, I'm going to play it by ear. Literally, as it happens. Remember the cue, if I straighten my tie it's *The Big Push*, if not we stick with *Shenanigans*.'

'I'm more worried you'll forget the cue. Oh, Bertie, we've had some times.'

'And more to come. Chalk this one up to ... I don't know, chalking stuff up.'

Knock! Knock! Knock! 'Stage call. Miss Starr.'

'I better go.'

'You look fabulous. As always. Half the battle won. See you on stage. Remember the tie, straighten it *Shenanigans*, not straighten it *The Big Push*.'

'It's the other way round, Bertie.'

'Ah, so it is. Straighten the tie *The Big Push*.'

'Wish me luck.'

'No need. You're a star. Starr by name, star by whatsit.'

⸙

From behind the curtain, stage left, Bertie looked on as Arthur Askey went through his link routine:

'Thank you Miss Cora Starr, playmates, ladies and gentlemen. Didn't she look lovely? I almost said still look lovely. Cheeky. I should talk. A big round of applause for her if you please. Thank you, thank you.

'Hey, did you hear the one about the wife who went to the doctor? Doctor, she said, my husband's got a filthy temper. Always shoutin' and screamin' at me he is. Have you anything for it? The doctor got a bottle, filled it up with water and said next time you feel he's about to lose it, take a swig of this and swoosh it around your mouth and then spit it out. Don't swallow it. Next week she went back to the doctor and she said doctor she said it's wonderful. He's been good as gold. Can I get some more of what was in the bottle? Nothing to do with what was in the bottle the doctor said, it was just a way of getting you to keep your big mouth shut.

'Thank you, thank you, Thank you very much ladies and gentlemen. Seriously now, will you please welcome on stage our next act, just flown in from Broadway, our leading jazz pianist, Hollywood musical composer, Mussolini's nemesis and our great war hero, Mr. Bertram Wooster.'

Wincing at that last accolade as he always did, Bertie strode on stage, pulled the piano seat up and with a nod to conductor Barry Fennan in the orchestra pit for the drum and bass accompaniment, opened his set with that summer's hit, Billy Holiday's *My Foolish Heart*, but played mid-tempo. He paid tribute to Henri Betti for writing his next song, last year's French hit, the jaunty and jazzy *C'est si bon* and to himself for his stab at translating it. Then it was time to welcome Cora back on stage for both their last numbers, their duet.

As she skipped on stage, from behind the mass of white light Bertie heard the audience breaking into even heartier applause. In an instinct Bertie knew they were warm enough for some Plum. He rose to greet Cora on stage and straightened his tie, kissed her on both cheeks and stepping up to the mic, said:

'Thank you your royal highnesses and assembled throng. In my darkest days in an Italian cell alone I used to cheer myself up by remembering a short story I read in *Punch* just after the war started. It was a satire about the Nazi top brass planning their invasion of Britain and it was called *The Big Push*. When I was playing at Mussolini's New Year's Eve party I wished I had it written to music. Boko Fittleworth and I recently met the author in New York and we set about putting that right. So I present you with *The Big Push*. Music by me, lyrics by Boko, sung by Cora and all based on a short story by the inspiration to us all and the amusement of millions beside, P.G. Wodehouse.'

∽∾∽

In the box, standing and applauding with the others, Rosie felt a discreet touch on her elbow. She turned to see an impeccably dressed gentleman, who offered her his card and beckoned her out of the box. In the light of the passage she read:

Reginald Jeeves
Palace Steward
Buckingham Palace
London, SW1

'Good heavens, Jeeves. Is it really you?'

'It really is, madam, the very same. If you would like to follow me without further delay. I believe a birthday present for your enjoyment has been suggested by Mr. Little?'

'A present for my enjoyment? Oh my, and a surprise.'

'Whether the present is enjoyable or a surprise or the surprise inherently constitutes a present and is therefore enjoyable or indeed if surprise presents are necessarily enjoyable I'm not in a position to judge, madam. This way please.'

As the applause died down behind the curtain, Rosie found herself being steered into a space between Cora Starr and Maurice Chevalier. Jeeves walked over to Bertie.

'All squared, Jeeves? Just like as the old days.'

'Yes, sir, I believe the arrangements will meet with your approval. The Princess Elizabeth has proved most cooperative, an attitude facilitated by her enjoyment of the literary conjurings of Rosie M. Banks. While Her Majesty will engage with yourself and His Majesty will engage with Miss Starr, the senior Royal Highness will engage with Mrs. Little.'

'Top-ho, Jeeves, I knew you could do it.'

'I have taken a further liberty, sir.'

'Oh?'

'Yes, sir, I have arranged for the Duke of Chiswick to be invited to the cocktail party....'

'Bicky?'

'The very same, sir. The cocktail party for the performers tomorrow evening at Clarence House. The one that you and Miss Starr will also be at.'

'Splendid, I haven't seen Bicky for months.'

'Yes, sir, and Miss Starr hasn't seen him for years.'

'I say, are you dabbling in matters matrimonial, Jeeves?'

'In view of their recent status as widower and divorcee, and remembering how Mr. Bickersteth and Miss Pirbright were not opposed to each other in more carefree days, I thought a re-union might be fruitful, sir.'

'You continue to amaze, Jeeves.'

'I continue to endeavour to give satisfaction, sir.'

And with that the master of arrangements and discretion whisped off into the shadows.

At the end of the line Rosie, Cora and Bertie waited their turns. With informal precision the following three conversations took place simultaneously.

'Good evening, Mr. Wooster, thank you for entertaining us so well.'

'It was a pleasure, Your Majesty, and I hope to have the pleasure again.'

'I particularly liked your tribute to P.G. Wodehouse. About time someone spoke up for him.'

'Thank you, ma'am, I will continue to do so.'

'Well sung, Miss Starr. I hope we see more of you back on our home shores soon.'

'Thank you, Your Majesty, and I hope to be able to sing here again soon.'

'I agree with you about Wodehouse. Frightful business.

But keep that to yourself.'

'Yes, sir, all kept to myself.'

'I believe it's happy birthday, Mrs. Little and a surprise present too.'

'It is both, Your Highness.'

'I greatly enjoy your Rosie M. Banks books. Tell me, why did the heroine in *The Goodliest of Days* not accept Captain Bamford's proposal?'

'Because she was suspicious of a naval officer's commitment to her happiness, ma'am.'

'Wise words, I'm sure. Please keep writing, more and more. Oh, and well sung about Wodehouse. We all love Lord Emsworth and the life at Blandings.'

❧

The following evening a familiar scene played itself out at the bar in Boodles.

'Well played, Bertie. One in the eye for the *Express* and Cooper and the Snoopers,' said Jumbo.

'Well scored, Bertie,' said Bingo. 'I have enough credit in the Rosie flak bank now to see me through the next few months.'

'Well done, Bertie,' said Tuppy lighting his nearly new Dunhill Chestnut. 'I haven't smoked for a good two weeks now. Oh and by the way a helicopter will soon be landing at Skeldings. For Nanny, instead of the washing machine.'

'Well matched, Bertie,' said Bicky. 'Cora and I are bounding around town like a couple of teenagers.'

'The least I can do,' said Bertie. 'Chums in need, chums indeed and all that. Quite like the old days. Cheers!'

'Cheers!' and then five clinks to chums and chumminess, wherever it takes you. Eight weeks later it took them all back to Easeby Hall for the End of the Forties New Year's Ball, but that's quite another story.

CHAPTER 8

Hollywood

Christmas Week 1956

[Author's notes: Following Jeeves's 'dabbling in matters matrimonial' at the Clarence House cocktail party in the previous chapter, Francis 'Bicky' Bickersteth, now the Duke of Chiswick, has married Cora Starr. The Hollywood Blacklist was the practice of denying employment to entertainment professionals during the mid-twentieth century because they were accused by Washington of having communist or even socialist sympathies. Louella Parsons was the first and foremost Hollywood gossip columnist, revered and reviled according to taste. At her peak, the Queen of Hollywood's columns were syndicated in 400 newspapers worldwide.]

As the Woosters' airport limousine drifted through the gates of Château Chiswick, 193 Bel Air Road, Los Angeles, California, on Boxing Day in 1956, an off-pink Lincoln Continental Convertible drifted past them on its way out. The driver waved at Bobbie and sped off.

'Who's that?' asked Bertie.

'Louella Parsons,' said Bobbie. 'The Queen of Hollywood. Cora said she's staying here too while she has the builders in.'

'Oh good, let's make some tittle-tattle,' said Bertie.

'Hmm,' Bobbie replied. 'You know, now we are so

close to Hawaii, I really think we should go there next week. We could do with a break.'

'Absolutely not,' said Bertie. 'You know I can't take the tropics and I'm allergic to grass skirts. I'm sorry, but this time, no.'

An hour later Bertie Wooster and Bicky Chiswick were tee-ing off in the bar of the Bel-Air Country Club. Half an hour later they were tee-ing off for real; and that was them done for the next eighteen holes and of course the reprise at the 19th. Meanwhile back in Château Chiswick, Cora, Duchess of Chiswick and Bobbie Wooster were comparing tales from Beverly Hills and Broadway.

'You remember that Dorothy Parker I did on Broadway in '53, *Ladies in the Corridor*?' asked Cora.

'Absolutely,' said Bobbie, 'we came to the first night. At the Longacre, wasn't it? You were on top form, Cora. Great reviews.'

'That was the best part. It didn't run four months. Ha! But then Dorothy and I toured some double-headers for her civil rights campaign. Next thing you know she's blacklisted. I protested that – and now I'm blacklisted. Me, a communist? A duchess in a château! Me, not a duchess, in not a château, a communist?! Never heard anything so stupid. But I tell you in this town it's for real. There are hundreds of people blacklisted here. The studios are spineless, they just obey Washington. It's just ... absurd.'

'So you can't work in Hollywood?'

'Can't work in Hollywood. I can work in Nowheresville, Idaho and Catchanooky, Tennessee. Broadway no problem, if I can find the role. I'm an ageing beauty, Bobbie, don't forget. The roles dry up with the skin.

'So, Michael Gordon wants to direct the movie of *Ladies in the Corridor*. You'll never guess, turns out he's blacklisted too. Dorothy has done the screenplay. It's ready to go. But no go. Between us we're triple blacklisted.

'Anyway, enough of me, how about you, sweetie, how's the happs with you?'

'Whoever invented jet travel has made me one happy girl,' said Bobbie. 'We flit from London to New York, actually Skeldings to New York. London is grim, so poor. Poor in spirit, Bertie says. He's working on a new musical with Boko in New York, so that's still going strong. He's still doing jazz for fun, mostly drop-ins at the Blue Angel in Harlem. Imagine Bertie in Harlem! But they seem to take him in their stride. We like to spend August in Easeby, but now we like Long Island too. Remsenburg's the place there. There aren't enough months in the year. There aren't enough days in a month for that matter.'

'That's the opposite of us. We just stay here in Hollywood. God knows why. Well, God does know why, because Bicky likes it. Bicky likes it because it's not England.

I like it because Bicky likes it. And I like it. Been here long enough. It's just that I've been acting for so long ... and now, this.'

'So this *Ladies in the Corridor* movie, can't you do it outside the studios? Have they got a stranglehold on everything?' asked Bobbie.

'Pretty much. You have to use the Hollywood

technicians and everyone's terrified of being blacklisted if they are seen working with someone who's been blacklisted. It's a vicious circle.'

'Dorothy Parker knows all about vicious circles,' said Bobbie.

'That she does. Still, we are going to have a great New Year's Eve party. Not just 'cos you two and Louella are staying, but we'll have a house full. We've got fourteen bedrooms here. All full. Great big awning out over the lawn, three bands playing, *le tout* Hollywood coming. After all, everyone loves a duke *and* they don't mind a duchess either, I can tell you.'

'So no blacklisting of the party hosts?'

'No, no, no problem. The opposite. Everyone knows the whole thing is rubbish. In fact they all come on purpose to show solidarity. That's a safe enough gesture for them, not to be too cynical, but we've got royalty coming.

'Really? Royalty?'

'Well royalty of sorts. The Shah and Empress of Iran. They love Hollywood. He's totally starstruck. She thinks she's an actress. No black balls there, I can tell you.'

⌘

At dusk the boys returned. Bobbie was upstairs having a nap. Bertie had a shower and while they were changing for dinner, Bobbie told him all about Cora and the blacklist and about filming and not-filming *Ladies in the Corridor*.

'Hmm,' said Bertie, thinking about the absolute sitter of a putt he missed on the 14th.

171

Well, Bertie's cousins Claude and Eustace Wooster had certainly landed on their feet. In 1946, like *everybody* else, they tired of London and took off for America. In Hollywood they looked up Bertie's old mucker Claude Cattermole, then co-starring in a remake of *Pygmalion* for Metro-Goldwyn-Mayer. This Claude was easy enough playing Freddy Eynsford-Hill but in general MGM was making a pig's ear of *Pygmalion*. As Claude Cattermole told the director, Jules Dassin, the producers and scriptwriters seemed to be confusing London's Covent Garden with New York's Hell's Kitchen. Dassin, a sophisticated – and subsequently blacklisted – Frenchman knew it too and talked the studio into hiring 'class consultants' to shed some light onto the quirkier aspects of European aristocratic behaviour. But whom? Well, actor Claude happened to have staying with him twins from the higher echelons of London society, twins who would know that fish knives were never phoned for and no-one was called Norman and that this non-Norman never sat on a settee in a lounge and never went to the toilet either.

Just as principal photography on *Pygmalion* was coming to an end, the studio started shooting *The Romance of Rosy Ridge*, an American Civil War divided-community boy-girl love story. The plot called for some Old South old money Confederate angst scenes, but no-one quite knew how authentic the scriptwriter, a second generation Russian Jewish immigrant, had them played out. Who to advise? 'Don't we still have those *Pygmalion* Limeys on set?' someone may have asked. On set they still were; and thus began cousins Claude's and Eustace's careers as Class Consultants.

Fast forward nine years and a dozen movies and it was they and they alone who could advise producer Sol C. Seigel on *High Society*, a Cole Porter corny but catchy musical comedy bringing together Frank Sinatra, Bing Crosby and Grace Kelly. Off set, in 1954 Eustace had married Maizie Grey, remuneratively employed by Paramount as a human alarm clock, whom he had met when they were both working on *A Tale of Two Cities*. Two years later their daughter Candice was born and Bertie, for the fifth time in his life, was nominated as the unfortunate girl's godfather.

Bertie, Eustace, Maizie and, unbeknownst to her, Candice were sitting around the twin's Brentwood pool discussing the next week's christening ceremony when cousin Claude joined them.

'Ye gods, that Grace Kelly is a rare one!' he said.

'How come?' asked Bertie.

'Just had her on the phone. *Again*. She's seeing the Shah of Iran. *Again*. Now Bing has found out and he's threatening to blab to Louella or anyone with an empty column to fill. And according to her it's all my fault! I'm supposed to be teaching her to live up to her name. It's more like *dis*grace. Bertie, you're well out of this town, I can tell you.'

'I thought she and the Fling with Bing were all over,' said Bertie.

'It was. It is. But he's still mad about her. Who isn't, except everyone else who's ever worked with her? But she knows how to let him know what no-one is supposed to know. That what I'm supposed to do, make sure no-one knows what no-one is supposed to know. It's not even my job. My job is classing her up, not that she needs it that much. She's all "Oh, Claudie, can you help me out with a little favour?" So I fixed up the rendezvous. Nice safe space in West Hollywood. Then she just happens to leave my note with all the arrangements where Bing is bound to see it. I tell you, things I have to do.'

'And what do they do, the Shah and Grace Kelly, all alone in the nice safe space in West Hollywood?' asked Bertie.

'Your guess is as good as mine, but I don't think it's what you think it is. She's not that gross. How he gets his kicks, I don't know. How she gets hers – well, there'll be jewellery involved, that's for sure. Best not to know, he's got his own secret police, hoodlums-I-would-not-wish-to-cross.'

'You know the Shah and Empress of Iran are coming to Cora's on New Year's Eve?' asked Bertie.

'No. We'll be there, but thank heavens La Kelly is in Philadelphia for New Year's. In theory, you can never tell with that one.'

'So what's the Shah doing in Hollywood anyway?' asked Bertie.

'Can't keep him away,' said Claude. 'Starstruck. Tons of money and bored witless running Persia I guess.'

'Tons of money and bored witless,' repeated Bertie. 'Running Persia. Tons of money and bored witless. Hmm.'

⌒⌒⌒

Leaving his goddaughter-to-be to her fate, Bertie carried on doing the rounds of his Hollywood chums.

Next up was the other Claude, the actor Claude Cattermole, at home in Malibu.

Since the heady pre- and post-war years Claude's Hollywood career had taken a dip. He too had been blacklisted; not this time by Washington leaning on Hollywood but by Claude leaning on Hollywood. He had managed to upset the easily upsettable Sam Goldwyn by refusing to play a role demanded of him on location in Europe because it would have meant being away from his dying dog. There were angry exchanges of telegrams, culminating in Goldwyn's pronouncement 'You will never work in this town again.' At the time Claude thought that Goldwyn was bluffing and that he could easily manoeuvre his way out of his contract and work for another studio. Sam wasn't and Claude couldn't.

Luckily there was someone out there with no Hollywood baggage who wanted Claude, and only Claude, to play the part of Inspector Fix in a new adaptation of Jules Verne's *Around the World in 80 Days*. Mike Todd was a Broadway impresario, larger-than-life showman, hustler, gambler and serial entrepreneur. Shut out of Hollywood as a New York gentile outsider who was too big for his boots, he bought the rights to *Around the World in 80 Days* by selling his Todd-AO film format company. He then took the whole company off on a merry-go-round of 112 film locations in thirteen countries, with a cast that would come to total 69,000 people and 8,000 animals.

Todd was forty-seven at the time; typically, like all he did in life, his fiancée was rather special too, the twenty-four-year-old Elizabeth Taylor. They would marry a year later and Todd would have the distinction of being the only one of her seven husbands she didn't divorce; he died in a plane crash a year after that.

'... so that's Mike Todd,' said Claude, bringing Bertie up to date.

'Evidently quite a player,' said Bertie. 'But the budget for *Around the World* must be absolutely enormous. The budget for Liz Taylor not much smaller.'

'Well, that's the downside,' said Claude, 'he never seems to have any ready money. He missed one of my payments and I know a lot of the crew are paid late. But it always seems to work out, something always comes up in the end. There are these people in dark suits and black briefcases in the background. From Chicago they arrive. Heaven knows what's really happening. No-one knows, no-one asks. Ultimately he's a good guy. With all the blacklisting, he's pretty much everyone intelligent's lifeline.'

'And he can get things done,' said Bertie. 'A Hollywood outsider who can get things done.'

'That's it, there's no one like him. And Bertie, thank heavens for him. A Hollywood outsider who can get things done.'

⌘

All of which set Bertie thinking. Well, not so much thinking as letting little musings come and go in the old brainbox. Cora can't work because Hollywood has blacklisted her. The Shah has lots of money, loves the movies but has no connections. Mike Todd doesn't need Hollywood connections but does need lots of money. Boko and Nobby are arriving from New York tomorrow.

Boko would know Mike Todd from Broadway. If Boko could arrange for Bertie to meet Mike Todd, and cousin Claude arrange for Bertie to meet the Shah, he could tell them both about each other and about Cora, Dorothy Parker, Michael Gordon and *Ladies in the Corridor*. He might even offer to write them a score. The film would be made, Cora would be working again and Bicky would be a happy chappy. Well, it was the least he could do.

⁓

Forty-eight hours later, on 29th December, Bertie and Boko found themselves at Elizabeth Taylor's villa in North Prescott Drive, Palm Springs.

'Mike won't be five minutes,' their hostess said, 'he's on the phone to New York. Just for a change.' Then to Bertie she said, 'We've met, you know.'

'Er, yes, of course,' said Bertie, in desperation thinking how could he not remember meeting someone so mind-numbingly beautiful.

'You don't remember, do you?' said Elizabeth Taylor, eyes smiling at him.

'It will come to me in a minute, the old bean not as sharp as it was. Sorry and all that.'

'I'll give you a clue. Las Vegas.'

Bertie tried not to look too blank, but one thing he did know was that he had never been to Las Vegas in his life. Nor did he intend to.

'Er,' he started, to be rescued by the whirlwind that was Mike Todd zomping into the room.

'Gentlemen! Boko, sure I remember you buddy, who's this other guy?'

'Bertram Wooster,' said Bertie, extending his hand to

Todd, only to have it smacked playfully by Elizabeth Taylor on her way out, along with a look that settled halfway between a twinkle and a wink.

'Ain't got long, fellers, what can I do for you?' Todd agitated.

Bertie then set out the Shah of Iran's stall for him. How the ruler of Persia was bored with his day job, happened to stumble across zillionairedom, was a Hollywood nut whose wife wanted to be an actress. Bertie was about to row in Grace Kelly but decorum and a Wooster are never far apart.

Mike Todd was now all ears. 'So you're saying if I give this Shah broad a role, he'll pay for a movie?'

'I wasn't actually saying that, no,' said Bertie with his cunning hat on, 'but now you mention it, it's not a bad idea.'

Boko said, 'You remember that Dorothy Parker, *The Coast of Illyria*, we did in '50?...'

'You betcha. Grossed like hell. To start with.'

'You know Cora Starr and Michael Gordon?'

'Heard of them both, seen her in something.'

'Well, listen to this,' said Boko.

Bertie then ran through the *Ladies in the Corridor* scenario.

Todd said, 'Lousy pitch, buddy, but I got it. Dorothy Parker is, well Dorothy Parker. Cora can act, we know that. The director, we can fire if he plays up. And this Shah guy's wife, we'll see. How many ladies are there in this corridor?'

'I'm not a hund....', said Bertie.

'Doesn't matter,' Todd said, 'we can write another one in.

So?'

'So?' said Bertie.

'Yes, numb nuts, so. So when do I meet him, this Shah guy of yours?'

'Ah, well' said Bertie, 'as good luck would have it the Shah and Empress are coming to the Duke and Duchess of Chiswick's New Year's Eve party.'

'Who the hell are they?' asked Todd, standing up to leave.

'They are my hosts. And Cora Starr is the Duchess of Chiswick.'

'Jesus Christ, whoever next! Maybe Jesus Christ? Hey! The publicity guys are going to love this.'

'So can you come? To the party to meet the Shah and Empress?'

'You bet.' Then he shouted, 'Manners!'

'Ah yes, manners maketh man. One does one's best,' said Bertie.

'No, not manners, *Manners*,' shouted Todd. Just then a butler from central casting appeared from the ether and said, 'You called, sir?'

'Fix up New Year's Eve's with these guys, Manners. I gotta vamoose.'

And so Bertie told the butler the plans for the New Year's Eve party. It was almost quite like old times.

৩১৯

Bertie and Boko called in at another old friend from New York, George Caffyn, on their way back to Hollywood. It's an ill wind and all that and with so many Hollywood scriptwriters being blacklisted, Broadway writers such as George and another old friend Percy Gorringe were plying a fine trade in the vacuum. Fortified by reminiscences and improving California wine, they called in on Percy on their way home. Soon Bicky and Cora's New Year's Eve party was not just two but now six stronger.

It was dark by the time Bertie arrived back at Château Chiswick, but not as dark as the look on Bobbie's face.

'Try to explain your way out of this, Bertram Wilberforce Wooster.'

'I say old girl, what's got up your trumpet?'

'Don't you old girl me,' Bobbie almost shouted, 'what's the meaning of this?' she asked, throwing a scrunched up telegram at him.

Bertie unscrunched the telegram and read it aloud:

HOWDY TROUBLEMAKER STOP LOVELY SURPRISE TO SEE YOU AGAIN STOP LOVE TO SEE MORE OF YOU JUST LIKE BEFORE STOP YOU KNOW WHERE I LIVE STOP I AM SURE YOU WILL COME AGAIN STOP KISSES STOP

'Well, I'll be blowed,' said Bertie.

'I expect you will!' cried Bobbie. 'And who the hell is LT?'

'Liz Taylor. Elizabeth Taylor, she's an actress I met in Palm Sp....'

'I know who the bloody hell Liz bloody Taylor is!' hissed Bobbie, unmollified, 'and she clearly knows who the bloody hell you are.'

'Ah, well, yes,' said Bertie, 'there's that, you see what happened was....' and Bertie told her the story to date, about Grace Kelly and the cousins and the Shahish trysts, about the Shah and his money, about Claude Cattermole and Mike Todd the producer and Elizabeth Taylor his fiancée and about Boko and George Caffyn and Percy Gorringe and how there would be a few extra people coming to the New Year's Eve party.

'I don't believe a word of it,' said Bobbie, 'the most ridiculous concocted story I have ever heard in my whole life, just so you can go off cavorting with Liz bloody Taylor. You're old enough to be her father, it's absolutely ridiculous.'

'I say, steady' said Bertie. 'It's all true, I tell you.'

'You want tittle-tattle Bertie Wooster, I'll give you tittle-tattle!'

And with that she strode out of the room, knocked on the door of the room next door and without being asked in, and leaving the door open so Bertie could hear, said, 'Louella darling, I've just heard the most delicious story about Elizabeth Taylor.'

∽⌒∾

Even by Beverly Hills swanky mansion standards, 1330 Angelo Drive was pretty swanky. From the road it looked like a jungle with a bit of a clearing in it, none of the fancy gates that Bertie was looking for as he drove past once going north, once again going south until finally, northbound again, he poked the bonnet of Bicky's new Chevrolet Corvette (red, 4.2 litre V8, with the RPO 449 special camshaft 240 hp engine, 4-speed manual through the hole in the jungle. Inside there was more than a clearing in a jungle. Before him, high on a crest, stood a plantation mansion, surrounded by sloping, sprinkled lawns and vibrant hedgerows. Inside the mansion was His Imperial Majesty Mohammed Reza Shah Pahlavi, Shah of Iran, Light of the Aryans, Commander in Chief of the Imperial Iranian Army – and no doubt much more besides.

As the better flunkies do, a flunky appeared out of nowhere. Bertie soon noticed that this was no run of the mill flunky. He made no attempt to conceal his weapon and he spoke in a most offhand manner. 'Yeh, waddyawant?' he asked.

Bertie said, 'Please tell His Imperial Majesty that Eustace Wooster is here to see him. He was expecting my brother Claude, but Claude has had an accident and I have come in his stead.'

While Bertie's interlocutor flunked off to relay the message, Bertie thought, so far so good, bit of the old plain sailing really. It was a wizard ruse alright, bargaining his prospective godfatherhood with Eustace for a chance to impersonate him in front of the Shah; Claude didn't need much persuading to go along with it either.

Bertie was expecting the Shah to be dressed in full ceremonial uniform like an empire portrait of King George VI. Instead, an open necked, slack trousered, loafered shoe, middle-aged, dapper, swarthy little fellow with sweptback grey hair greeted him warmly.

'I'm sorry to hear about Claude,' he said, 'nothing serious I hope.'

'No, no,' said Eustace-cum-Bertie, 'just a little stumble down the stairs. But I have his clear instructions about your next meeting with Miss Kelly. Nothing in writing as ever.'

'Excellent, I was hoping that was the case. In the

usual place on Selma Drive, West Hollywood?'

'That's right, at 4:30 in the afternoon on Tuesday. She can stay for an hour.'

'Thank you, Eustace was it?'

'Yes, Eustace. While I was here I was hoping I might tell you about something else.'

'Yes?'

And so Bertie laid out his plan for Cora Starr and Mike Todd and *Ladies in the Corridor*. He then relayed that Mike Todd had indicated that Princess Soraya might have a part, if the Shah was agreeable to letting her do so. All the Shah had to do was put up the money, and not a lot of it, after all it was only a three-act, three-scene, two-hander on stage.

'That could be possible,' said the Shah. 'I know about Cora Starr of course, I know about all the actresses, but who is this Mike Tott?'

'Todd, Mike Todd. He's a producer, more famous in Broadway than here. In fact he's never produced here at all. He's making his first film now, *Around the World in 80 Days*, not in Hollywood but well, around the world. In eighty days too, I shouldn't wonder. He's quite a whirlwind. He's what the Americans call a can-do sort of chappy. His fiancée is Elizabeth Taylor.'

'You mean *the* Elizabeth Taylor? The one who just made *Giant* with Rock Hudson and James Dean?'

'The very one, pretty girl.'

'Pretty girl? She's more than pretty and more than a girl. I'd love to meet her.'

'When you say "meet her", do you mean, meet her on the same basis as you are meeting ... well someone else whose name I've quite forgotten?'

The Shah paused, then said, 'I hope you are like your brother, although you don't look like him at all. With your brother, I can say these things. I'll back Cora's film, if you will organise ... what's the word in English?'

'A rendezvous?'

'Come now, Eustace, that's French. I speak that too. Tryst is the word. If you will organise a tryst with Elizabeth Taylor, Cora has her film. Can you organise that?'

Bertie paused for a moment to let a few cogs slip into gear. 'Well, I have an entrée. I'll have a word with my cousin Bertram. Bertram Wooster, don't you see?'

❦

It usually takes three and a half hours to drive from Beverly Hills to Palm Springs, but with the worst driver in the world behind the wheel it took considerably less than that. Boko only drove once in a blue moon and when he did he treated himself royally, this time renting a brand new white and chrome, lots of chrome, fancy finned Cadillac Eldorado Biarritz convertible for the week.

'You look pale Bertie, are you alright?'

'No, I'm not alright, thank you very much. I've never nearly died so many times in three hours in my life.'

'I get confused. Left hand drive, right hand drive, clutch, no clutch. Well, I'm enjoying it, I'm off for a drive, pick you up soon.'

There was no car in Mike Todd's drive, no reply from the gate bell, no reply from the door knocker, and no-one inside the large open plan living room. Bertie wandered outside and there Liz was, breast-stroking lengths in the pool wearing just a pair of sunglasses and a smile.

'Come and join me,' she said, treading water to wave at him.

'I don't have my trunks,' said Bertie.

'I won't look, promise,' she said, turning around to swim away from him.

Bertie summed up his what-to-do. He didn't want to get wet, which itself was a bit wet; Bobbie would go bonkers if she knew, which she probably never would; Cora is a chum in need, which itself means jumping in; it's not every day you skinny-dip with Elizabeth Taylor, which may or may not be all it's cracked up to be. His shirt came off easily enough, which could only mean his trousers next; she was now finishing her length, which on her turning would bring him, by now Harry Starkers, into view; the moment was now or never, which saw Bertie take a breath, hold his nose, and jump feet first, as Nanny would have insisted, into the pool.

'You see, that wasn't so bad, was it?' she said swimming over to him. 'In Vegas you said you'd never forget me, but you have. Haven't you?'

'No, no, of course not', said Bertie. 'Remember it like yesterday. That's why I'm here.'

'I thought so,' she said, putting her arms around his neck and giving him a lingering smackeroo on the lips.

Bertie put his arms around her waist and did his best to return the smackeroo without it becoming a snogeroo; he had this uncomfortable sense that Bobbie was hiding in the bushes with a pair of binoculars; or worse a camera. Then he thought: if he didn't remember Las Vegas at all, basically because he had never been there, there was a good chance she didn't remember it too well either.

'Liz darling, you remember in Vegas you said you'd do anything for me?'

'I did? If you say so. I thought we'd tried every variation under the sun in that suite of yours.'

'Yes, yes, of course we did. Exhausting, I mean exhilarating. Tremendously bracing at the time as I recall. No, this time I have in mind something external to our nuptial delights, as my old valet would have said.'

'What's he got to with it?' she said, kissing Bertie's neck and letting her fingers run down his bare behind.

'Oh, nothing,' said Bertie, 'nothing at all. Listen, you remember what Boko and I were taking about with Mike yesterday? About that film and the Shah of Iran?'

'Am I in the film?', she asked, pulling away.

'You might be,' said Bertie, 'but the point is, there's a price to pay.'

'There's always a price to pay,' she said, now at close quarters again. 'What's it this time?'

'You have to meet this Shah chappy. Alone.'

'And?'

'And what?'

'And what then?'

'Ah, yes I see what you mean. Might be a bit tricky. No, no, nothing untoward I can assure you. Then he gives you some jewellery.'

'That's it?' She pulled away again to look Bertie straight in the eye. 'I see him alone and he gives me jewellery?'

'I think so.'

'You *think* so?'

186

'Well, yes. Actually I don't know. But he seems like a decent enough sort of shah, as these things go. And, more importantly, if you'll do it, he'll fund Mike's film. As you say, that's the price to pay.'

'Well,' she whispered in his ear, 'first, you've got a price to pay.'

'I have? What's that?' asked Bertie.

She took his hand and led him out of the pool and, dripping wet, into the house.

'Are we going to discuss the missile crisis?' asked Bertie, hopefully.

'Oh, I'm sure you won't have a missile crisis,' she replied, helpfully.

Later, when they both relayed their own versions of what happened next, details of the accounts varied but the staple facts remained stable. Everything happened almost immediately and very quickly: there was the sound of tearing, the sense of rushing, a great commotion, some squealing, some squeaking, an orgiastic ruckus – all climaxing in sounds of a large *splosh!*, then a medium *splash!*, followed by a lesser *slosh!* and finally some defeated *burbles!* and the unmistakable sight of a brand new white and chrome, lots of chrome, fancy finned Cadillac Eldorado Biarritz convertible in the swimming pool – and floating free from it one Boko Fittleworth. 'Sorry about that,' he gurgled, 'no clutch pedal and the other two pedals got confused.'

❦

Château Chiswick looked just like a château should for the New Year's Eve's party. Cora had left the insides untouched so guests could mingle with her objets d'art and décor or just enjoy a tête-à-tête on the chaises longues and sofas. Outside, an enormous awning covered the lawn and the surrounding ornamental garden. Eighty tables filled the middle third, with a reception area and bar before it and a dance floor and stage beyond it.

Bicky was as pleased to greet his visiting friends as he was to greet the Hollywood *grands fromages* he hardly knew. Lots of friends were there, Bertie and Bobbie of course, Claude and Eustace Wooster, Percy and Madeleine Gorringe, Boko and Nobby Fittleworth from New York, Claude Cattermole and his new paramour Greta Thyssen, George Caffyn and his bon ami Miles Messenger. As he stood in line, Bertie came over to say hello.

'Bicky old bean, I have a plan.'

'Oh no, Bertie, not one of your plans. I'm supposed to be standing here greeting people. And with your plans I always end up in the soup.'

'No soup this time, guaranteed. I need your help, just for a few minutes. It's for the common good.'

'What common good? I don't believe in such a thing.'

'Cora's film. I need to have the library empty for a secret rendezvous.'

'Not your madcap scheme with the Shah of Iran and Elizabeth Taylor?'

'The very same. And it's not madcap, it's eminently sensible. Practical even. Come on, Bicky, stop being a stick-in-the-mud. They are both here,' and indeed they were, sitting with their parties at different tables, 'they just need to meet alone for a minute or two for the first time.'

'Oh, alright, but where?'

'That's where you come in. In the library. I just checked with cousin Claude, but Louella Parsons is in there with someone else. You have to tell her to leave, make up some story or other.'

'Oh, Lord, what's Claude got to do with it? Anything to do with Claude always goes wrong.'

'He's going to take the Shah in there and I'm going to take Liz Taylor in there, as they both know both of us. They both know the plan too, just for a minute alone to say hello to each other and, well, to say hello.'

'Oh well, I suppose so,' said Bicky. 'Can you get Percy to stand here and greet the guests, say I've popped into the loo if anyone asks.'

A minute later Bicky did pop back, told Bertie 'mission accomplished', Louella Parsons had wandered off, no he didn't know to where, but the coast was clear, library-wise, and that Bertie and Claude could take up muster stations.

In a carefully rehearsed and executed military-style pincer movement operation, with the precisest precision and stealthy intentions, cousin Claude and Bertie took a flank each and approached their co-conspirators. So as not to arouse even a soupçon of suspicion among the guests they had even swapped roles.

Bertie ahem'd the Shah, leant forward and said, 'Your Imperial Majesty, the Duchess would like to show you a particular ornament in the library. Would you please allow me to show you the way?'

'Ah, Eustace isn't it? Yes, of course, it would be my pleasure. Excuse me ladies, gentlemen.'

Claude ahem'd Elizabeth Taylor, leant forward and said, 'Miss Taylor, the Duchess would like to show you a particular ornament in the library. Would you please allow me to show you the way?'

'Oh, yes. Haven't we met somewhere before?' Then to Mike Todd and the others at the table, 'Back in a moment.' In the library, there was a degree of awkwardness. The Shah and Bertie arrived first and stood by the fireplace, the former straightening his already straight tie and tugging down his already tugged-down dinner jacket, the latter rubbing his hands, looking at his watch, then rubbing his hands again. Moments later the other Mr. Wooster and Miss Taylor arrived. Bertie made the introductions.

'Your Imperial Majesty, may I present Miss Elizabeth Taylor? Miss Taylor, may I present His Imperial Majesty the Shah of Iran?'

'Thank you Eustace, hello Claude.' said the Shah.

'Who's Eustace?' asked Elizabeth Taylor. 'This is Bertie Wooster.'

The very same Bertie Wooster looked flummoxed for a second, then Claude said, 'Ah yes, Eustace is his nickname.

Borrowed it from my other brother, don't you know? His real name is Bertram, but Bertie, everyone calls him Bertie.'

'Bertie?' asked the Shah.

'I mean Eustace,' said Claude. 'Yes, Eustace. And Bertie. Same same. Anyway, between us Bertie, Eustace and I must leave you two alone for now,' with which the two first cousins left the prospective trystees alone with each other.

It was lucky they were halfway back to the marquee and didn't see or hear Louella Parsons barge in through the same door and catch the two trystees alone with each other, as apart from anything else they were now much closer. In fact he was holding her hand as if about to kiss it, as is the American-Persian wont.

Elizabeth Taylor was the first to rush past Louella, hissing, 'This is *not* what you think. And don't you *dare* write a word about this!' The Shah was next past her, formally, 'I can explain everything. Nothing improper has occurred, I can assure you, madam.'

Bertie and Claude were just telling Bicky, who was still greeting guests near the entrance, how well the plan had gone and thanking him for getting rid of Louella, when three figures were seen striding purposely towards them. The closer they came, the clearer it became that it was Bertie onto whom they were striding. Claude thought this was a good time to mingle somewhere less confrontational and disappeared into the melée inside.

Elizabeth Taylor arrived first, 'Bertie, you louse, if this is some sort of sting, you're going to regret it. You might think Mike's just another producer, but he's got another side, friends from Chicago, *capisce?*' Out of the corner of his eye, Bertie saw Mike Todd, stand up, throw down his napkin and march over towards them.

The Shah arrived next, 'Eustace, I have to say I'm disappointed. You are not, after all, like your brother. This could be very embarrassing. The State Department will no doubt be in touch, and I will have to request the CIA for assistance. I'm sure you understand the implications.' Out of the corner of his other eye, he noticed that the Empress Soraya, alerted to the contretemps, was walking over to join them.

Mike Todd wasn't one to waste words, 'Look here, Wooster, I didn't like you from the get-go. Your damn stupid scheme to screw this Shah guy out of money for your film. I don't know what's goin' on here, but I don't like it.'

'Would you mind repeating that?' asked the Shah.

'Sure will,' began Todd, 'This Wooster ... oh, hello lady.'

The Empress Soraya was by now with them too, 'Mr. Wooster, I see my husband the Emperor is upset. It must be something you have done. Please explain to us all what is happening?'

Louella was now heading their way too and just as Bertie was preparing for her to join the impromptu party, she veered off to join Bobbie in what looked like an urgent confabulation by the marquee entrance.

⌘

'What's going on?' Bobbie asked Louella.

Louella told her about the secret scene in the study, leading to the angry scene at the entrance.

'Oh dear,' Bobbie said, 'looks like Bertie's in the soup again. But...'

'But what?' asked Louella.

'But I see it all now. Bertie was telling the truth after all.'

'Telling the truth about what? Come on, Bobbie, join in.'

'Sorry, I was just thinking it through. Bertie was telling the truth about Grace Kelly.'

'What about Grace Kelly?'

'About her and the Shah of Iran over there. They were "seeing" each other.'

'Now *that's* what I call a story. *That's* a scoop and a half.'

'But if you use it Bertie will be in even deeper soup.'

'I won't use it yet, but I'll let the studio know I know, that way I get leverage on other stories. That's the way it works.'

'Well that's a relief. Thanks. Now we have women's work to do.'

'Such as?'

'You'll see. What's the time?'

'11:30.'

'Half an hour. Better get our skates on.'

∽≫≪∾

On stage, band leader Vaughn Monroe took hold of the mic. 'Your majesties, your graces, my lord s, ladies and gentlemen, please charge your glasses and prepare for *lift off*. 1957 here we come! Hold on to your hats! Hold on to your neighbour's hat! Are you ready? Here we go! All together now! *Ten! Nine! Eight! Seven! Six! Five! Four! Three! Two! One! HAPPY NEW YEAR!'*

Amid all the kisses and back-slaps and toasting and merriment, Cora sought out Bertie and gave him one enormous kiss on the left cheek, and an even more enormous kiss on the right cheek and a great big smacker, almost a smackeroo, on the lips. 'Oh Bertie, my hero, you did it! *Ladies in the Corridor*. It's in the bag. They've all agreed. And they are all here. Oh Bertie, how clever you are. How can I ever thank you enough? How *did you do it?'*

'Ah well, you see,' said her hero as unflummoxed and unfussed and unfraught as he could manage on the spur of the moment, on the cusp of the ... whatever cusps do whenever they stumble onto whatever it is the stumble onto, 'We Woosters must keep our secrets. Along with our codes. Mum's the jolly old word on this one, I can tell you.'

⌘

Upstairs two hours later in the Wooster love nest, Bertie thought he needed an explanation.

'Alright, my red-haired vixen queen, schemer of a thousand schemes, how did you do it?'

'The Bertram soup extraction scheme or the Cora blacklist buster scheme?'

'Both, or either.'

'Louella had a chat to the Shah, said she wanted to interview him. Blackmail him really. Shah, she said, unless you provide Mike Todd with the finance for Cora's film, the Empress Soraya and the rest of the world, just might get to know about Grace Kelly – and Elizabeth Taylor.

'And I had a chat with Elizabeth Taylor, how I might just tell Mike Todd and the world about you two unless she agreed to make him produce the film.'

'But there's nothing between Liz and me,' insisted Bertie.

'Of course there's not, do you think Elizabeth Taylor would let a chump like you anywhere near her?'

'Well thanks,' said Bertie. 'You know I've been thinking...'

'Oh dear,' said Bobbie, 'not again.'

'Yes, after all this kerfuffle I think you are right, we could do with a week in Hawaii. I'll book the tickets tomorrow. Oh, it's a holiday, the day after, then.'

'No need,' said Bobbie, joining him in bed, 'I've already booked them.'

CHAPTER 9

Rishikesh, India

December 1963

'I am having bad news for you, Mr. Prosser,' said Colonel Singh. He rubbed his hands together against the cold.

'For the umpteenth time, I am not Mr. Prosser. My name is Bertram Wooster. Mr. Prosser is my manager. We are not remotely alike in any way. We've been through all this!'

The man's hand slammed down hard on the table between them. 'Do not be taking us for fools, Mr. Prosser. We are not hoodlums, we are professional dacoits. Your name was on your business card,' he shouted. 'Prosser is your name. We have spoken to this Mr. Wooster you claim to be. Yes, we have. In fact it cannot be you as we have spoken to Sir Bertram Wooster, not the plain mister you pretend to be. We have spoken to him in London. This is the bad news I am having for you. He will not pay kidnap ransom. He said you can go to hell, if you must know. Now we must kill you, to discourage the others.'

'To encourage the others,' Bertie corrected him. 'Why am I correcting you?' he asked no-one in particular. 'Look, Colonel Singh, or whatever your name is, a simple telephone call to Mr. Prosser or Wooster or whatever you call him will sort this whole kidnap business out.'

'No phone lines are here,' said Colonel Singh.

'No phone lines? But it's 1963,' pleaded Bertie.

'No phone lines. It might be 1963 in mother country but here in Himalayas it's not yet 1963. Telegrams only are here. We are telegramming to our hoodlum in Delhi and he is calling the number on your card from there. Then he telegrams us back.'

'Well, how much are you asking for me? If it's not too impolite to ask. Maybe I can buy me.'

'One crore rupees. At black market exchange rates that is one lakh dollars worth.'

'And what's a lakh dollar when it's at home?'

'One hundred thousand dollars is asking price. Cash of course.'

'You make me sound like a souvenir in the bazaar,' suggested Bertie, standing up. He noticed it was snowing outside.

'Sit down! That is what you are. A souvenir. We are not unreasonable men, Mr. Prosser. If Mr. Wooster won't buy you, maybe you must buy yourself as you suggest. What is your opening bid?'

'Look, I only have travellers' cheques on me. Well, back in the ashram. A thousand pounds. You are welcome to them. And I'll kill that Oofy Prosser when I see him.'

'No, we will kill Mr. Prosser before you, Mr. Prosser. You are having until dawn. That's when we will kill you.' The colonel nodded to the man by the door in a private's pullover to lead Bertie back to his room.

Bertie lay back on the *charpoy*. If he had to die, this was at least a comfortable place to do so. A Himalayan bungalow on stilts with a veranda. All good Indian words, he thought.

Ah, what he needed was some *dhotis* to tie together, then he could shimmy down and make a run for it. He looked around. No *dhotis*. Not even any pyjamas. Not even a pashmina. Lots of Indian words, no Indian goods. A one-bar electric heater did its best in a corner. Bertie sat close to it and ruminated.

'This, my dear Bertram,' he said to himself, 'is a particularly thick bowl of mulligatawny into which you have landed yourself. But how?'

Bertie thought back over the last week, looking for clues that would help him survive beyond dawn.

⌘

'Bertie, your tits keep falling out!' roared Bingo.

'Ha, blinking ha, Bingo,' said Bertie, 'I've never felt like such an ass in all my life.'

'At least you're not the horse's arse. Who are you anyway?'

'You know who I am: Widow Twankey. Whoever talked me into this mess?' asked Bertie, shoving his left grapefruit tit back into the panto dame's costume. 'Oofy Prosser, as usual,' he said, answering his own question.

'Now, now, Bertie,' said Oofy. 'Once more, cast. Act 2, Scene 1. From the top.'

'You're enjoying this, aren't you?' Bertie asked him. 'Throwing your weight around like a major-domo.'

'Yes, I am, thanks. For once in my showbiz life, enjoying myself a lot. I own the theatre,' he waved expansively at his newly acquired New Theatre Royal in Lincoln. 'I own the rights,' he waved the script of Aladdin at the cast. 'I own the crew and I own the cast,' he gestured towards the stage, 'at least until 10th

January. Now Widow Bertie Twankey, enter stage left, trip over the carpet as best you can and – script from the top. Action!'

Quite how Bertie ended up as Widow Twankey in pantomime in Lincoln for the Christmas season of 1963 was a bit of a panto in itself. To recap, Bertie stumbled into being the singing and playing compère of *Sunday Night at the London Palladium* in 1960, a stumbling helped by the fact that his manager, Oofy Prosser, owned both the London Palladium theatre and a chunk of the ATV franchise who produced it for ITV. This in turn meant that the Woosters had to relocate to England and they chose, well Bobbie chose, her family home, Skeldings, in Lincolnshire, keeping Bertie's home of Easeby for summer holidays. Bertie's more public profile soon attracted the satire of the newly launched Private Eye, who renamed him QWERTY Toffster, on account of his dexterity with the piano keyboard and his being an unashamed toff, in an era when toffs were open to ridicule. But Bertie was what we now call WYSIWYG (What You See Is What You Get) and the public loved him for it.

Then in the autumn of 1961 Bertie slipped on some leaves at Skeldings, clobbered his back and was recommended to see the osteopath Stephen Ward. Ward was an artist and socialite as well as muscle basher, and halfway into his treatment Bertie was not too surprised to find him one weekend at Cliveden, the Astors' pile above the Thames in Berkshire. The Woosters, along with a dozen members of what became known as the Establishment, were the Astors' house guests; Ward had rented the Astors' riverside cottage and his guests included Christine Keeler and Mandy Rice-Davies. Around the pool the house and cottage guests mingled and the mingling led later to the mangling of another guest, John Profumo, and indirectly the Prime Minister Harold Macmillan and his government.

The reason Bertie had agreed to demean himself at Oofy's panto in Lincoln, the reason for the returned favour, was that it was Oofy who fished Bertie out of the Profumo soup. When Ward's Wimpole Mews house was double-booked for matters extra-curricular, he asked his by-now-friend Bertie for the loan of the Arlington House flat we have already visited. In all innocence, and as Bertie would, Bertie said something like 'yes of course old bean,' not knowing that a bloodhound from the *News of the World* was following the Naval Attaché from the London Russian Embassy, Yevgeny Ivanov, to a liaison with one of Ward's charges, the model Christine Keeler; following him in fact all the way to Bertie's flat. Bertie was fingered and was about to be exposed as running a house of ill repute. It seemed only a matter of time before MI5 would want to know what Bertie knew about the Russian connection too.

Fleet Street was a small club and Jumbo Maxwell-Gumbleton heard about the story while it was still in his rival's edit and called Bertie immediately. While Bertie was still flummoxing, Jumbo called Oofy. They both knew immediately how to kill the story dead: Oofy threatened to withdraw the £3 million a year the various arms of Prosser Media spent in the rivals' paper a year. The following year the same Prosser Media bought the New Theatre Royal in Lincoln. It needed a refurb which Oofy gave it. It also needed filling. Bertie lived near Lincoln. *Sunday Night at the London Palladium* was off season. Panto would soon be in season. Bertie owed Oofy a favour. Presto! Bertie would make a grand Widow Twankey; in fact, in true panto style, Sir Bertie would make an even grander Widow Twankey.

∽∾∾

Back home at Skeldings that evening the house party assembled for dinner. Bingo and Rosie Little were staying till Christmas; Oofy just through to the opening night; a surprise guest was there too: Stiffy Pinker had called Bobbie at first light from Somerset and said she was on her way. 'With Harold?' Bobbie had asked. 'Without Harold, that's why I'm coming,' Stiffy had replied.

'Well Stiffy, what have you done with Stinker?' asked Bertie, agog for news as they all tucked into Mrs. Hoskins's vegetable potage.

'He's in India, Bertie. He's been kidnapped by a yogic sect. The Spiritual Regeneration Movement they call themselves. One minute he's the new Bishop of Bath and Wells, crozier in hand, flock all bated breath, the next he's propping up some ashram in the Himalayas. The International Academy of Meditation, can you credit it? I blame the so-called Reverend Rupert Bingham.'

'Beefy Bingham? Surely not,' said Bertie. 'He can't even tie his own shoelaces, or at least couldn't last time I saw him. Which congregation is he terrorising now?'

'That's it, Bertie, he's not. He inherited the O&P shipping fortune and gave up the calling. Went on a world cruise and came back a Buddhist, or some such. Joined a foreign flock. Then back here he met this Maharishi Mahesh Yogi fellow and fell in with him. Started meditating all over the place. Next thing he invites Harold along to a meeting, then Harold starts meditating all over the place. These people are a real menace I can tell you, Bertie, just sitting there meditating all over the place.'

'So how come he's in India?' asked Bobbie.

'Well that's it. This Maharishi, he looks like a spaniel at a toga party, his headquarters are in the Himalayas, place called Rishikesh. Beefy got up a party to go there and practise more meditating at the feet of the master. That was three weeks ago and yesterday I got this telegram from Harold,' she said, giving it to Bobbie.

'FROM PINKER RISHIKESH INDIA

TO PINKER WELLS UK

'DEAREST STEPHANIE', Bobbie read.

'So far so good,' said Bertie, 'he hasn't forgotten your name or anything like that.'

'Oh, do shut up, Bertie,' said Stiffy. 'Carry on.'

COSMIC CONSCIOUSNESS HAS FOUND ME HERE IN RISHIKESH STOP MUST STAY HERE WHILE COSMIC PRESENCE WITHOUT AND INDIVIDUAL PRESENCE WITHIN HAVE FOUND HARMONY WITH EACH OTHER STOP I PRAY FOR YOUR PATIENCE STOP PATIENCE IS AN ACT OF CONSTANCY, JUST AS CONSTANCY IS AN ASPECT OF THE ABSOLUTE STOP YOUR LOVING HUSBAND COMMA HAROLD Bobbie passed the telegram to Bingo. 'What can it all mean?'

Bingo read it, lips moving, then said, 'Cosmic, Rishikesh, patience, constancy, aspect, absolute. Oh dear, Stinker's gone all loopy on us.'

'I tell you what it means,' said Stiffy. 'It means Bertie has to go and rescue him. Drag him back home, screaming if necessary.'

'I say, steady on, Stiffy,' Bertie interrupted, mid-slurp of the soup. 'You can't expect me to go all the way to India just because Stinker has gone off his rocker. And it will be freezing up there at this time of year. Heavens knows what I might catch.'

'But you're his oldest friend Bertie, you and Bingo,' Stiffy replied. 'If you don't go and bring him back we may never see him again.'

'I know,' said Rosie brightly, 'why don't you both go, Bingo and Bertie. They say two heads are better than one.'

'Not in this case,' said Bobbie. 'Heaven help the Indians.

But it's a good idea, the boys can keep an eye on each other.

Can't you, boys?'

'Hang on, hang on, hang on.' It was Oofy. 'Haven't you all forgotten something? There is a play to consider. You can't just go swanning off to India in the middle of rehearsals.'

'It's not a play, it's a panto,' said Stiffy. 'Bertie can learn his lines on the plane. Probably before take-off. Can't you, Bertie dear? Dear Bertie.'

And what about the radio programme?' asked Oofy. This was another one of Oofy's bright ideas, to build on Bertie's success with *Sunday Night* and ITV by keeping a foot in at the BBC. Oofy had proposed to them that Bertie host a new radio quiz show Prosser Media had concocted about modern manners, *More Tea, Vicar?*, with Humphrey Lyttleton, Willie Rushton, Hattie Jacques and Dora Bryan. As Oofy now reminded them:

'It is due to pilot next week, my head's on the block with this one, BBC-wise.'

'Oh, Oofy, the boss's head is never on the block,' said Bobbie. 'It's one of your shows too. It's only a date, I'm sure you can move it around.'

'Also Oofy,' said Bertie, 'Stinker is a friend in need and that trumps More Tea, Vicar? or any of your other schemes.'

'But I'm a friend in need,' said Oofy.

'No, you're not, you're Oofy,' said Bingo.

'In that case when you meet this Maharajah chap...'

'It's Maharishi, Oofy,' said Stiffy.

'In that case when you meet this Maharishi chappie, give him my card,' Oofy flipped a card over to Bertie, 'and tell him I'm first dibs on any film rights. And don't forget I own your image rights too. If he suddenly whisks out a cine camera.'

'It's settled, then,' announced Stiffy. 'Bertie and Bingo are off to India. And won't come back without Stinker. And that's not a question. Is it, boys?'

❦

Try as he might, Bertie just couldn't get the hang of this meditating lark. The previous morning, his first morning there, Bingo and he and half a dozen other initiates had been welcomed by the mysterious Maharishi. Rather in spite of himself, Bertie found himself warming to Stiffy's spaniel in a toga. The guru was small and cuddly, mid-forties at a guess, with kind and deep eyes, held a certain aura about him, and the more seriously all those around him took him, the more he seemed to find the whole thing a tremendous joke. Bertie couldn't quite put his finger on it, but he felt safe and curious.

There had been a simple initiation ceremony and they had all been given layers of orange cotton *dhotis* and *kurtas* and pashminas along with thick yak wool *faran*, these latter all enveloping tent-like overcoats under which each kept his own censer of burning charcoal. Then, privately, they had each been given their own mantras and told to keep the mantras secret and never say the sound out loud. Bertie's was *Om Namah Shivaya*. He had no idea what it meant and as no-one could hear it anyway he soon changed it to *Mum-bo Jum-bo*. He never knew what Bingo's mantra was, as Bingo kept his secret. In fact, as Bertie shifted his bottom around the floor trying to find a less uncomfortable position, he had a quick peek through an illicit eyelid and saw that Bingo was rock steady and seemed to be annoyingly adept at this Transcendental Meditation caper right off the opening ball.

Bertie tried the mantra again, but it was no good. His mind kept racing around the world: thoughts of London and New York, Hollywood, Bobbie, Stiffy, the panto, Delhi and the flight up to Dehradun in the old Vickers Viscount, the even older Morris taxi ride from there to here. Then he thought of Widow Twankey and Stephen Ward and Stinker. Where was he? Must be in another hall, the place was big enough. He felt a new pain in his bottom. His legs had not been crossed for years and his knees were cross at being crossed now. Then his eyes stung when he opened them: he had never been mad about incense and now he was fogbound in it. That and the charcoal fumes from the censers. He lifted himself up on his fists and stole another look around. There was Bingo, still still as a rock. Around him men and women of all shapes and complexions and ages, all robed in that same sort of orangey ochre colour, all deep in stillness and an all pervading tranquillity, and around this happy band of *sannyasin* ... well, blow me down! It couldn't be! Bertie looked closer. It couldn't be! Bertie shut his eyes in disbelief. He shook his head, as if to shake the illusion free. He tried again. One clandestine eyelid first, then the other. He looked closer, blinking as if to refocus. Now there was no doubt about it. Try as he might Bertie could not convince himself that his eyes deceived him. Sitting across the floor, now the first one to twitch in discomfort like Bertie, was his old mucker and family lawyer Augustus Fink-Nottle. Gussie Fink-Nottle that ever was. As if sensing an astral intrusion, Gussie too opened an illicit eye and looked around. He saw Bertie but, without seeming surprised, gave him a wink and a finger wave and went back to meditating, or seeming to.

After what seemed an age of agitation to his racing mind and aching body, a bell rang and all the meditators stood silently, clasped their hands together and chorused *Namaste!* and shuffled off for a cup of *chai*. Bertie couldn't wait to tell Bingo about his new discovery.

'Gussie is here!' he amazed.

'Gussie?' Bingo was suitably surprised. 'Gussie? Gussie Fink-Nottle or Gussie Mannering-Phipps?'

'The former. Augustus Fink-Nottle. There,' Bertie nodded towards him. They sidled over.

'Gussie, what on earth are you doing here?' hushed Bertie.

'Same as you two. Come to rescue Stinker. Don't make it look like we know each other,' he whispered. 'Pretend we've never met.'

'But, but...,' Bertie was lost for words.

'You know I'm a lawyer,' Gussie said under his breath to the floor. 'You know that because I'm your lawyer. And yours too, Bingo, for that matter. But the firm Flannel, Fink-Nottle and Phudge represents the Church of England too. They want their bishop back. They've sent me here personally to unkidnap him.'

'So he *has* been kidnapped?' asked Bingo.

'No, but the C of E think he has. On the contrary, he's as happy as Larry here.'

'Have you spoken to him yet? Where is he?' asked Bertie.

'No, but I've seen him alright. He's in a different dorm,' Gussie explained, 'we're all in with the beginners. He meditates in a different hall too.'

'Must have been promoted,' said Bingo.

'Closer to heaven, and all that,' said Bertie.

⌇⌇⌇

That evening, after lights out, the Three Musketeers wrapped up warmly and stole into Stinker's dormitory. With only the faltering light from the butter lamps to guide them, they looked around until they found the large hunk of dishevelled priesthood that could only be the Right Reverend the Lord Bishop Harold Pinker of Bath and Wells.

'Stinker! Wake up, it's us!' whispered Bertie.

The large hunk stretched and knocked over the bedside candlestick. 'Well, that hasn't changed,' said Bingo.

'Who's there? Who's us?' asked the aroused *sannyasin*, by now up on one elbow.

If Bertie was surprised to see Gussie in Rishikesh, Stinker was triple surprised to see them both plus Bingo by his bedside. By the time he had come to, he had kicked over two stools and banged into the *charpoy* next to his and then the one next to that. Outside in the moonlight the four of them held an impromptu expatriate huddle.

Unfortunately for the new arrivals, far from being kidnapped, Stinker backed up Gussie's impression: he was not just a willing volunteer but a religious soul whose whole calling, and therefore his life, had been turned upside down. Now he had seen the error of his ways: all those years worshipping God, who hadn't invented Man after all, but had in fact been invented by Man in dark, illiterate nomadic days to explain to himself the Inexplicable. Instead he had now seen, as he explained with awestruck awe, that 'we were all rays of the same sun and each one of us as much a god as God'. After five minutes of enthused monologue along these lines, Bertie called a halt.

'Yes, yes, Stinker, that's all very well, but can't you spout forth accordingly back home? I'm sure the great ungodly in Bath and Wells will be Transcendentally Meditating like good 'uns in no time.'

But it was useless. Stinker's mind was made up. He had to Discover Himself before he could help others on the Way. They weren't to expect him back for several months. Later, Gussie suggested he might never come back at all. Then Bingo worried about what they were going to tell Stiffy. All of which led Bertie to conclude that unless the Maharishi told Stinker to spread the mantra back in Somerset, the best solution was to kidnap their wayward friend and bring him back themselves. Tomorrow morning they would seek an interview with the Maharishi and beg him to send Stinker back home as a sort of meditating missionary. If that failed, well they would jolly well have to kidnap him themselves.

⚬⚬⚬

Seeking an interview with the Maharishi was without difficulty; he kept an open house and anyone and everyone seemed to wander in and out at will.

He sat at the head of a constantly evolving circle, whose shape breathed in and out as lesser gurus, all sorts of *sannyasin, swamis, sadhus, dhobi wallahs, attar wallahs, chai wallahs, dudh wallahs, kaan-saaf wallahs and dabba wallahs*, came and went. Everyone was sitting cross-legged on a wooden floor. Flowers were everywhere; sandalwood incense too. The Maharishi seemed to be holding several conversations at once. Eventually his eyes settled on the three Englishmen.

'You have just arrived, I believe?' he asked the three Englishmen.

'Oh yes, rather,' said Bertie. 'Jolly nice it is too.'

'Splendid!' he giggled, clapping his hands. Then as he was turning away to talk to someone else, Gussie ahem'd. 'I say, sir,' he said. 'I can see you are very busy and we only came for one thing.'

'Everyone is coming here for one thing. It has many names. Peace, Happiness, Love, Fulfilment. But it is one thing, thing because no one name can describe it. Words are just signposts.'

'But we have a name,' Gussie replied. 'Stinker.'

'Stinker?' The Maharishi looked curious.

'Stinker Pinker?' Bertie contributed. The holy man looked at him kindly, but blankly. 'Sorry, Harold Pinker,' Bertie explained.

'The Bishop of Bath and Wells,' said Gussie.

By, now the hubbub around the table had died and all ears were on Gussie and the Maharishi.

'Can we take him back with us? Everyone is worried.'

'He is free to go and so is everyone else. But I can't send him back. That would be as bad as kidnapping him.' Everyone seemed to laugh at the very idea.

The Maharishi turned away from them and as he did so, Bertie remembered his promise to Oofy. 'Oh by way,' he said, placing Oofy's business card on the floor in the centre of the circle, 'if you ever want to make a film, please get in touch.'

A few hours later, in the afternoon break, Bertie was generally drifting along the bank of the River Ganges, lost in the imaginary conversation he was going to have to have with Stiffy. Two men overtook him.

'About the film, we picked up your card from this morning.' The smaller man said; the larger man stood in front of Bertie, blocking his path.

'Oh yes, rather, I can tell all about that.'

'Come with us please,' said the smaller man.

'Right-o,' said Bertie. And with that he was kidnapped.

'Mr. Prosser is on the line, sir,'

'Thanks, Sally,' said her boss. 'Oofy, always, well nearly always, a pleasure. What's up?'

'Very droll, Jumbo,' said Oofy. 'This morning I've got just two words to say to you.'

'I know, I know,' replied Jumbo. 'Buckingham and Palace.'

'Actually' said Oofy, 'you are right, but those weren't the two words I had in mind.'

'Buckingham Palace. New Year's Honours. Don't tell me, you are about to be Sir Alexander Prosser.'

'I am, how did you guess?' asked Oofy.

'I didn't guess. I know everything. Looks like we got the same phone call from SW1.'

'You don't say....'

'Sir Rupert Maxwell-Gumbleton. Yup. That's me. And that's you. Knights all round. Congrats Sir Alex.'

'Arise, Sir Rupert. Ha! But that's not why I called. Not my two words.'

'Go on,' said Jumbo.

'World Exclusive!' Oofy sounded as triumphant as he felt.

'Now those are two words I like. Even more than Sir Rupert. Go on.'

'Well, talking of knights, Bertie has been kidnapped. In India. Some weird sect up in mountain caves. They want a hundred thousand US bucks. There's a million bucks of publicity in it if we play this one right.'

'Who else knows?' asked Jumbo.

'No one,' said Oofy. 'Some guy from Delhi rang me.

I've got his number. He thinks he's kidnapped me, so I played along and said I was Bertie. First person that came to mind. Then the penny dropped. I gave Bertie my card to give them. For any rights. Anyway, they put two and two together and came up with a hundred thousand. But it's not just Bertie.'

'What do you mean?'

'Remember Stinker Pinker and Bingo Little?' and Oofy relayed the whole Stiffy rescue mission, throwing in his lack of panto rehearsal angst for good measure.

'Got it,' said Jumbo. 'So we've got three of them up there kidnapped. Bertie, Bingo and Stinker...'

'Well, it's just Bertie that's been kidnapped. The others...'

'Better news if they've all been kidnapped. Plus you're in touch with the kidnappers...'

'I've just got the phone number of some guy in Delhi, he's just the messenger.'

'Never mind that, he's part of the gang. The story's coming together now. My Editor-at-Large is just the man to sort this out. He can deal with the Indians and we'll get a damn good story. You know him too. Olly Sipperley.'

'Sippy Sipperley!'

'That's him. Top man. Let's have lunch, run through a plan.'

'Buck's at one?'

'Buck's at one.'

∽◦∾

It was dusk when Bertie had his brainwave. Gussie! Of course, Gussie had come here to unkidnap Stinker, so now Gussie could jolly well unkidnap Bertie instead. Bertie banged on the door and told the private to take him to see Colonel Singh. Bertie was careful not to reveal too much, clever this, only that his lawyer Augustus Fink-Nottle, from the highly reputable firm of Flannel, Fink-Nottle and Phudge, was also at the ashram and that if one of the soldiers slipped Gussie a note from Bertie saying soup extraction needed, Gussie would come willingly to them post haste. After all, Gussie would be missing him by now. Soon Gussie could arrange Oofy/Bertie's ransom and then they could team up with Bingo again and get on with the business of kidnapping Stinker. Bertie was about to say, 'Maybe you chaps could help us with that,' but a sixth sense told him that probably wasn't a very good idea.

⁓⁓⁓

'Bertie,' said Gussie, 'this is the stupidest idea I've ever come across. Even by your standards, this takes the biscuit. Now we are both up for sale. What are we going to do now?'

'I was rather hoping you were going tell me that,' said Bertie. 'Being my lawyer etcetera. How were you going to get Stinker out?'

'I was going to buy him out. Offer the Maharishi chappie some money. Then he would despatch Stinker back home *tout de suite*. He obviously likes the stuff. Did you see the Rolls Royces up there?'

'They are gifts apparently, from bonkers American women. He never uses them. So why can't you buy me out?'

'Because, in case you had forgotten, hearing the

words lawyer and Flannel, Fink-Nottle and Phudge they immediately assumed I was as rich as the Oofy Prosser you're supposed to be and promptly kidnapped me on arrival. I'm a prisoner just like you. No longer a free agent to pick up the cash and bandy it about.'

'There's always Bingo,' said Bertie. 'We could send him a note asking for help.'

'But then they'll kidnap him too! This one lakh dollars has already become two lakh dollars, with Bingo in here too it will be three lakh dollars. What the bloody hell is a lakh dollar anyway?'

'Ah, that I know,' said Bertie. 'A hundred thousand. Dollars in this case.'

'I can't even call the office,' said Gussie. 'Telegrams only. Imagine the telegram. I'll be a laughing stock at Flannel, Fink-Nottle and Phudge. And Stinker is still at large. We'll probably lose the C of E account.'

'Yes, sorry about that Gussie. But look on the bright side. Something will turn up. Usually does.'

⋅⋅⋅

Around the breakfast table at Skeldings, Bobbie, Rosie and Stiffy were in turn apoplectic, anxious and annoyed. They read Bingo's telegram to Rosie to themselves and aloud to each other; then one by one to themselves again. No matter how they tried to square it, the news was bad.

ARRIVED SAFELY RISHIKESH STOP STINKER SIGHTED STOP UNFORTUNATELY HAVE LOST BERTIE AND GUSSIE STOP IF CONTACT YOU PLEASE ADVISE THEM TO FIND ME STOP STILL HERE STOP LOVINGLY COMMA BINGO

'What's Gussie doing there, that what I'd like to know?' asked Stiffy.

'Which Gussie? Fink-Nottle or Mannering-Phipps?' asked Bobbie.

'Fink-Nottle is Bingo's lawyer. Is that a clue?' asked Rosie.

'A'hem.' It was Hoskins. 'Today's papers, madam.'

If Bingo's telegram had flummoxed them the headline splash across the top of the *News Chronicle* had them vanishing through the floor.

World Exclusive! Sunday Night Compère Sir Bertie
Wooster And His Lawyer Kidnapped In India.
$200,000 (£83,000) Ransom Demanded
Weird Sect Involved
News Chronicle On The Scene
By Editor-At-Large Oliver Sipperley.

'Good heavens, is that Sippy?' asked Bobbie. They all agreed it was he. 'At least we know what Gussie is doing there.'

'Except we don't. I mean know what Gussie is doing there. And what about my Harold?' asked Stiffy. They all agreed it was good news he had not been mentioned in despatches.

'I wonder if Bingo knows,' Rosie mused. They all agreed he probably didn't, unless Sippy was up there already.

'I'll kill that Bertie Wooster when I see him,' said Bobbie, the only certain sentiment largely shared by all of those around the breakfast table.

On the top floor of the MI Building in Fleet Street all lights were on as they prepared to work through the night. As usual the switchboard would be working through the night too.

'Media International, how can I help you?'

'Mr. Maxwell-Gumbleton's office, please. He's expecting my call. It's Olly Sipperley.'

A few clicks and crackles later they were connected.

'Good evening Olly. You're on speaker phone. I've got Oofy Prosser here. Where are you?'

'I'm at the Foreign Correspondents' Club in New Delhi. It's midnight here. The line's not secure so be careful. That's how all my latest copy is verbatim in the Indian press.'

'And from there all over the place. It's the biggest story in the world right now. And you are on it, good man. So, what's up?'

'I've met the so-called hoodlum here in Delhi. He's straight. Well, he's not but we can deal with him. The problem is there are no phones up in the hills, so it's all telegrams. But I've got messages to Colonel Singh, Bertie and Gussie in the bungalow and Bingo and Stinker in the ashram.'

'Who's this Colonel Singh? He's a new one,' asked Jumbo.

'Not his real name, no doubt. He's the head kidnapper. He's in the bungalow with Bertie and Gussie.'

'Ah,' said Jumbo, 'we've worked out what the hell Gussie is doing there. I've just had the Archbishop of Canterbury on the phone. Not a happy cleric. Gussie is the Fink-Nottle in Flannel, Fink-Nottle and Phudge. They are the C of E's lawyers and someone from Lambeth Palace sent him there to buy Bishop Stinker back. Now Archbishop Ramsey has found out and he's going apeshit.'

'What does he want?' asked Sippy.

'He wants nothing to do with it, basically. He wants Stinker to be handed over to the local Anglicans who are threatening to break away from the C of E. The lawyers are demanding access, so you better forward Gussie their message. It's a clerical mess. Anyway, ignore it all. I am.'

'Sippy, it's Oofy here. How's Bertie?'

'No way of knowing, he didn't telegram back any problems. Beyond being banged up of course. But this is all the easy part. The switchover is at Dehradun airport up in the hills. We give them £85,000 and they give us our four friends. I haven't worked how yet. We need to smuggle the money in and smuggle the amigos out.'

'Use my plane,' said Oofy. 'Brand new Learjet 23. Midnight run. They've got runway lights up there I suppose.'

'Let me see,' said Sippy. 'And a photographer, we need to fly one in. Wouldn't trust any of these local ones an inch with an exclusive. Better make that 85k 100k, I'll have to buy off the locals.'

'Good man, Olly,' said Jumbo. 'We'll have the cash and a staff smudger on board. Just give us the word. You'll be at this Da-doo-run-run too, I guess?'

'Dehradun. Yes, for sure and I'll fly out with them. How's it all playing back home?' asked Sippy.

'Fantastic. 300,000 extra copies a day and rising,'

Jumbo replied. 'We've got all the TV credits and downstream print exclusives lining up. You can write the book if you like. If not, let me know, they're all screaming for it. Film rights too for sure.'

'Sippy, it's Oofy here again. I need Bertie back by the 10th, can you do that?'

'I'll try. How come the 10th?'

'Because he opens as Widow Twankey that night. I'll kill him if he hasn't learned his lines, God knows he's had enough time. And there better be an airport at Lincoln.'

'Olly, it's me again,' said Jumbo. 'Phone in your copy from the hotel. No more leaks. And keep on it. Good work. Bye.'

✂

FROM SIPPERLEY NEWS CHRONICLE DELHI
TO BISHOP PINKER RICHARD LITTLE
INTERNATIONAL ACADEMY OF MEDITATION
RISHIKESH RELAY TO COLONEL SINGH, BERTRAM
WOOSTER COMMA AUGUSTUS FINK-NOTTLE AT
VITTASARI BUNGALOW RISHIKESH
INSTRUCTIONS MEET ENTRANCE CONTROL
TOWER MIDNIGHT TONIGHT STOP RANSOM CASH
AS AGREED COLONEL SINGH EXCHANGE FOUR
SOULS ABOVE STOP CONFIRM BACK

'What on earth is all this about, Bingo?' asked Stinker.

'I don't know much more than you,' Bingo replied. 'Bertie and Gussie have been gone for two days, looks like they've been kidnapped. Funny that, we came to kidnap you, in a friendly kind of way, now look what's happened. Doesn't sound too friendly at all.'

'And what's Sippy got to do with it?'

'And the *News Chronicle*? That must mean Jumbo's involved. And if Jumbo is involved, Oofy Prosser won't be far behind. Thick as thieves those two.'

'Well I'm jolly well not going,' said Stinker firmly. 'I'm just finding myself here. I'm not haring around airports and paying ransoms. This is one Bertie scheme too many.'

'Actually Stinker, it's a Stiffy scheme,' replied Bingo, before filling in all the blanks from the dinner at Skeldings. Stinker looked confused. 'Look, Stinker, why not ask the Maharishi what to do, he's supposed to be the fount of all wisdom?'

Meanwhile, over at the bungalow there was fresh excitement: a second telegram had arrived. Having read it himself, Colonel Singh gave it to Bertie. 'It's for Mr. Nottle, Mr. Prosser. If you'd be so kind. By the way, I've confirmed first telegram.'

Bertie didn't actually mean to read Gussie's telegram, but somehow he just did; and when he did, he said aloud, 'Well, knock me down with a feather.' He put this second telegram down on his bed alongside the first one and read them both again.

The first one said:

FROM SIPPERLEY NEWS CHRONICLE DELHI
TO BISHOP PINKER RICHARD LITTLE
INTERNATIONAL ACADEMY OF MEDITATION
RISHIKESH RELAY TO COLONEL SINGH, BERTRAM
WOOSTER COMMA AUGUSTUS FINK-NOTTLE AT
VITTASARI BUNGALOW RISHIKESH INSTRUCTIONS

MEET ENTRANCE CONTROL TOWER MIDNIGHT
TONIGHT STOP RANSOM CASH AS AGREED
COLONEL SINGH EXCHANGE FOUR SOULS
ABOVE STOP CONFIRM BACK

Now this new one said:

FROM PHUDGE LONDON VIA SIPPERLEY NEWS
CHRONICLE DELHI
TO COLONEL SINGH AUGUSTUS FINK-NOTTLE AT
VITTASARI BUNGALOW RISHIKESH ARCHBISHOP
CANTERBURY UNAMUSED PINKER RESCUE
SCHEME STOP YOU STAY ASHRAM STOP
ARCHBISHOP BOMBAY DISCUSS WITH MAHARISHI
NEXT WEEK STOP CONFIRM BACK

Bertie folded away both messages and lay down to have
a ponder. If he, Bertie, tells Gussie, then Gussie has to
stay and if Gussie stays then Stinker stays, which means
he'll have to fend off Stiffy. Not an easy task. Plus he
lands Bingo in the soup too. If he doesn't tell Gussie,
then Gussie is in some serious soup of his own, not just
with his lawyer partners but with the A of C himself.
For some reason he couldn't explain then or later, at
that moment a vision came to mind: he was dressed
up as Widow Twankey with Stiffy chasing him around
the dining room with a rolling pin. Then Bobbie and
Rosie picked up rolling pins and he was being chased
around and around the dining room by three very irate
women, each shouting variously: 'What have you done
with my Harold?' 'Where's my Richard?' and 'I suppose
you've lost Gussie too!'

As Bertie scrunched up the second telegram, four imperious car horn blasts came from outside the bungalow. From three windows Colonel Singh, Bertie and Gussie peered through the darkness and saw what each held to be the last thing they ever expected to see right there and then: the unmistakeably majestic sight of a Rolls-Royce Silver Cloud III. In the driver's seat was Stinker Pinker and alongside him, Bingo Little.

That was the good news; the bad news was that Stinker drove the way he walked, knocking over everything in his way and causing innocent bystanders to run for the nearest cover. The Darwinian, self-policing, India road pecking order was as confused by the Rolls-Royce Silver Cloud III as Stinker was confused by everything and anything that came within the headlamps' beam. On the way to Dehradun airport, while mayhem befell all before them and pandemonium visited all behind them, Bingo brought the three backseat passengers up to date. Stinker had consulted the Maharishi; the Maharishi had listened patiently, quietly, then suddenly burst into open laughter. He called for a pen and paper and wrote a one-sided letter and put it in an envelope. He gave the envelope to Stinker and told him: 'Give this letter to whomsoever is your captor, this so-called Colonel Singh, when he is ready to take the money. Now come with me.' Stinker and Bingo and a dozen orange clad others followed him out to the yard, then across it to what looked like stables. 'Take whichever one you are liking,' he said gesturing at a row of Rolls-Royces. 'And let it be speeding you to your Destiny.'

At the airport they were saluted though the gates and headed towards the control tower. Sippy was there as planned to meet them all with a briefcase bulging with money. On the apron a small jet with flashing lights and its ladder down awaited them.

From his pocket Stinker gave the envelope to the Colonel Singh. 'This is for you. From His Holiness Maharishi Mahesh Yogi.'

'One, two, three, four,' said Sippy to Colonel Singh, counting out the four Englishmen. 'I believe you are expecting this,' he said, offering Colonel Singh a thick, black briefcase. 'Better count it. I would.'

Colonel Singh paused while reading the letter. 'No need,' said Colonel Singh, 'you keep the money. I have something far more valuable. The car keys please, Mr. Stinker.'

∞∞∞

Bertie edged back the curtain and looked across at the front row of the New Theatre Royal. The Skeldings house party had decamped there. Alongside and behind them were all sorts of families currently roaring at the antics of Aladdin, the Police Chief and Wishee. Bertie couldn't see them, but he'd been told the standing room was full of journalists come to see The Great Escaper live and in person. Bertie let the curtain fall back. He'd been onstage a thousand times, two thousand times, but he still felt tight in his body and dread in his mind Being 'only a panto' made it worse in a way. 'Oh just ham it up if you dry up,' Oofy had said. Thanks! Bertie waited for his cue. In front of him was a supermarket trolley with Twankey Laundry on it. He heard Wishee say: 'Better, ladies and gentlemen, boys and girls, better. And now please welcome the most beautiful woman in

222

all the world. I'm sure you'll agree when you see her, please welcome Widow Twankey.' Bertie strode onto stage to wild applause.

'What's all that noise? Whoo hoo! Lovely to see you all. Look at all you good looking people at the back. Whoo hoo!

'I tell you what: a washerwoman's work is never done. Aaahhh!'

Aaahhh

'I know. I know. Look at this pile of washing. Anyway, how are you all? Are you having fun?'

Yyyeeesss

'You look a lovely lot. Just like me. Aren't I the loveliest girl in all the world?'

Nnnooo

'Well that's not very nice. I'm going to have to deal with you lot later. Is there anyone in from Skegness? Yes, a big welcome to you. Both of you. What about Grimsby? Sorry? No, that wasn't a question. I'm just sorry you live in Grimsby.

'Right! As Wishee said, I'm the Widow Twankey. I run the laundry in this part of old Peking. Yes, Peking. And let me tell you, there's a lot of peeking goes on in Peking. Not as much as in Lincoln of course.

'Talking of peeking, I was upstairs in my bathroom the other day, standing in the altogether. Yes, I know. I can see all the men in the audience getting an exciting picture of that in their heads. You ladies had better watch out when you get them home. You'll have a lot to live up to.

'Anyway.... There I was in the naughty naked nude when the window cleaner erected his ladder up to my

223

double glazing. Ooooh what a large ladder and that was before he extended it! He was giving things a quick going-over with his damp shammy when I shouted, "No hanky-panky or wanky-wanky with Widow Twankey" and his extension collapsed.

'If my husband Frankie Twankey was still alive I wouldn't have to worry about it. He was quite lanky and if there had been hanky-panky with Twankey, lanky Frankie would have given them a good spanky.'

∽∾∿

And so on. Bertie survives the opening night. The panto survives the season. The Maharishi survives and prospers. The somewhat unorthodox Bishop of Bath and Wells survives deeply in Transcendental Meditation. Stiffy Pinker survives peacefully in her domain. Sir Alexander Prosser and Sir Rupert Maxwell-Gumbleton survive a few scandals. Bingo and Rosie Little survive quite comfortably off her royalties. A forgiven Gussie Fink-Nottle survives the wrath of the Archbishop of Canterbury. Olly Sipperley survives and thrives from his best seller *Four Englishmen and a Guru*, with film rights due to ensure further survival. And Bobbie Wooster survives by wondering how her beloved Bertie survives at all.

CHAPTER 10

Mustique

December 1970

Since the early '50s Bertie had been helping Edward
Hoskins, the son of the Skeldings housekeeping and
gardening family, with his musical tuition. Edward
had a natural talent where notes where concerned
and in 1965 had been accepted for a Bachelor of Music
course at the Royal College of Music. Bertie provided
for him for the four years required there too. The RCM,
never slow to recognise a benefactor, then invited
Bertie to set up a scholarship fund for three financially
disadvantaged undergraduate students a year. By 1968
Bertie was keen to expand this further and asked Gussie
Fink-Nottle of Flannel, Fink-Nottle and Phudge to set
up a formal Wooster Young Musicians Fund to pay for
musical tuition for poor students of all ages.

Bertie's reasoning was mostly, but not entirely,
altruistic. He knew that over the following few years he
was about to come across a gigantic windfall; Bobbie and
he had both inherited and he had subsequently made
far more than they could ever need. Children were there
none, neither nephews nor nieces. A satisfying urge to
do something useful had come over him. The windfall?
In 1966 Boko and he had written a one-act piano
musical, officially for Boko's daughter's ballet and drama
school, unofficially because they were between jobs and

somewhat bored. The idea was the students would all dress as dogs and dance around the stage, a-howling and a-barking to the slightly manic score. It was so popular – and frankly so easy to compose, let alone write – that within two months Boko and Bertie had turned it into a three-act Broadway show. *King Dawg* was then taken up by Disney to be a full-length animation film, as well as being repeated all over the world as a stage show. For Boko and Bertie the '70s promised to be rung in to the tune of cash registers chinging.

However, not for the first time, there was a snag. The Labour government had promised to tax the rich 'until the pips squeak' and Bertie's royalty earnings would be taxed at 83% and his other earnings at as much as 98%. The idea of funding musical scholarships from royalties didn't make much sense if the government was going to steal the royalties first.

In New York, Bertie was bemoaning along these lines to his old friend, Atlantic Records' boss Ahmet Ertegun. Bertie had been with Atlantic for over thirty years and although jazz sales were slow by comparison with pop and rock sales, they were close to Ahmet's heart and Atlantic's heritage, and the LPs were inexpensive enough to make. To Ahmet this tax grab was now a familiar refrain from his British artistes. He had just helped solve a similar case for the Rolling Stones. Did Bertie know their financial adviser Prince Rupert Loewenstein? Yes, but only on a weddings and funerals basis: Bobbie was Rupert's wife Josephine's second cousin.

Before waiting for another wedding or funeral, a meeting was soon arranged. Rupert could not take

Bertie on as a client; he had his hands more than full untangling the Rolling Stones from their past affairs and ensuring the future ones were more or less tax-free – he later commented that the subsequent LP Exile on Main Street was the only record title with an element of tax planning in it. He did however offer various solutions all revolving around one theme: if Bertie wanted his Wooster Young Musicians Fund to go ahead, he would have to join the *Légion étrangère* of other top earning artistes, sports stars, financiers and landowners, and become a tax exile.

Rupert proposed options: Ireland, but it was a bit too wet; France, but that was a bit too familiar; Holland was a bit too flat; Singapore a bit too strict; Bermuda a bit too triangular. Then Rupert mentioned a raft of Caribbean islands. Of these he preferred Mustique. Ten years earlier one of his friends and a slight Bertie acquaintance, Colin Tennant, had bought the island for £45,000 and over the ensuing years had developed it into a tax and privacy paradise for royalty real and faux, plus the rich and infamous.

Before fully committing to tax exile status in general and Mustique in particular, the Woosters thought it would be a good idea to rent a house on the island for a few months, for as Bertie feared, 'it could all be pretty ghastly'; he meant culturally and socially. Thus we rejoin Bertie and Bobbie in December 1970, in the rented villa Gentle Breezes overlooking Britannia Bay, Mustique. All was jolly enough, but it didn't take Bertie long to be back in the soup.

⌘

It was the custom of the island-governing Mustique Company to arrange for longer-term renters like the Woosters to host a small get-to-know-you welcoming party for their immediate neighbours. In 1970 there were sixty-five villas on the island, itself a mere three miles by five, and when newcomers arrived the Company would round up the occupants of the nearest half dozen or so villas. It was a popular arrangement all round, a chance for longer-term residents to meet each other again as much as to meet the new arrivals. To the Wooster party came what they assumed was a fairly typical cross-section of island residents.

First to arrive were Michel and Isobel Carosse of the *La Carosse* French-American cosmetics company. Fit and tanned and in their late sixties or early seventies, they had recently been in the news as their son had just settled a spectacularly expensive alimony claim. Isobel was a famous patron of the arts and Michel a famous collector of the same.

They were followed by another famous figure from American business, the Texan oil explorer David Sinclair and his new, and very much trophy, wife Candice. Sinclair was famous for being richer-than-thou: in Mustique every foreigner was a multi-millionaire, but to be a billionaire had an added cachet. Young Candice was, well, young and spectacularly blonde: perhaps in her late twenties, thirty years younger than her husband. She didn't say much and maybe had not much to say, and she wore a fixed smile on her first iteration face. She looked as though she would be fun in the bed but a bed of nails out of it.

The Woosters recognised their next guests, although

curiously they had never met, the British Hollywood, Oscar-winning actor Ray Colquhoun and his long term partner Simon Stacey. Ray had been up for male lead in one of Boko and Bertie's musicals, but didn't get the role. Bertie didn't know why he didn't; casting always passed him by. Unusually, perhaps in view of the actor's leading role status, if any trousers were worn, they were worn by Simon.

The next guests were less welcome; at least he was, she they had never met. She was Princess Sunny von Tripps, a one-woman gossip column in herself, *fatale* by reputation and *bien roulée* by constant dieting. Her fiancé was ten years younger: Alexis de Méné, now in the gossip columns himself, accused of gold digging, wastrelling and gigoloing. He and Bertie had had an unpleasant altercation at Barbados airport en route to Mustique. Carib Air had overbooked the ten-seater island hopper and Bobbie having already checked in, they chose Bertie over de Méné for the last seat. As de Méné had flown down first class from Miami he demanded to have Bertie's seat. Bertie was too polite to point out he had just flown by private Learjet from New York, so could be said to outrank de Méné, aviationally. When Bertie demurred de Méné grabbed him by the lapels and suggested fisticuffs outside. Luckily a security guard intervened and de Méné had to wait for the next plane.

Next to arrive was the organiser, The Hon. Quentin Rowbotham from the Mustique Company. It was he who had arranged the Woosters' rental, this party and all else besides, including hiring the gardener Devon and maid Millie, both of whom he had already introduced.

The last guest had not only not been invited, but his arrival caused Bertie such a shock of surprise that he almost dropped his sangfroid. 'Well, blow me down if it isn't old Stilton. Top hole! It must be, what, ten years? The Drones reunion at the Savile Club. What on earth brings you here?'

'Bertie, old bean, I heard you were staying and had to pop over. You know I retired five years ago, head of "A" Division, the Royal Household's private police force really. Got a K out of it....'

'I read that. Sir Gerard D'Arcy Cheesewright, congrats, old chum.'

'Not just a K and decent enough pension but a nice little retirement earner. You soon pick up the criminal lingo in my line of work, Bertie. Anyway, I'm Princess Margaret's personal, well I wouldn't say bodyguard, don't get the wrong impression, let's say minder.'

'Is she still due tomorrow?' asked Bobbie, who had wandered over and welcomed Stilton equally warmly.

'She was, but she arrived today. Got bored at a party in Barbados en route. She sends me ahead to prepare the ground. I've been here a week. Mostly dealing with that little greaser Denbow. You met him on the way in.'

'Did we?' asked Bobbie.

'The one in uniform. He's the only one with a uniform, a kind of one-man police state. Customs, immigration, policeman – that's a joke. HRH's guest this time is David Niven, I expect you know him.'

'Yes, rather,' said Bertie.

'Oh, there's Quentin Rowbotham, young Mr. Fixit. I want to have a word with him. I've met most of the others over the years. See you chaps later.'

The party had started rather early at 5 p.m., as tropical evening parties do, owing to the sudden sunset at 6 p.m. Halfway to dusk Michel Carosse asked Bertie if he could look around the grounds; he was a keen gardener and promised not to take any cuttings. Bertie told him to help himself on both counts and thought no more of him. On his way out Michel asked Quentin Rowbotham to join him, and Bertie last saw them in conversation heading towards the croquet lawn.

Just before 6 p.m. – Cheesewright later pinned it down to 5:50 – the Sinclairs announced they were leaving. They were on the dawn flight to Barbados and needed to pack. Bertie, being the good host, offered to walk them to their Mule, one of several parked by the pool – a Mule being a mechanised buggy used in car-free Mustique. In what little time they had spent together, he had rather liked the cut of Sinclair's Texan jib, surprisingly unpretentious. His Mule was surprisingly unpretentious too: an old John Deere two-seater. Just as they were saying good-bye, Bertie was surprised to see Quentin Rowbotham leap round the corner to say goodbye too; Quentin was equally surprised to see Bertie. The Sinclairs drove away, Quentin headed back to find Michel in the garden, and Bertie went to his room to find a jacket for himself and a stole for Bobbie.

As the sun dipped, Bobbie was holding sway on the terrace. With her were Sunny von Tripps, Alexis de Méné, Ray Colquhoun, Simon Stacey and Isobel Carosse. Cheesewright was talking to the maid Millie. At this point, and later no one could remember why, Alexis de Méné announced he had left his camera in the Mule and must rush out to get it; he'd be back soon.

The policeman, overhearing, thought that rather odd: one the few rules among the Mustique-goers was no photographs and no films. Moments later Simon Stacey said he was 'just going to pop out to the loo'. Moments after that Quentin Rowbotham re-joined them, having 'just tidied up a bit outside'. Michel too re-joined the party, fresh from his garden walk.

When the scream came it wasn't really a scream at all, more a prolonged bellowed shout from Simon Stacey: 'Help! Come quickly! I'm at the pool! Help! Anyone there! Come quickly! Come to the pool! He's dead!' From their different venues the cast reassembled around the pool. In it, face down and with a harpoon in his back, floated Alexis de Méné.

Cheesewright instinctively took charge. 'Right, nobody touch anything. This is a crime scene. Let's all go back upstairs. Devon, are you there?' He was. 'Take my Mule and go and fetch Maurice Denbow. We'll be upstairs waiting for him. Off you go now.'

Upstairs the talk was of disbelief. Who saw what? Who heard whom? Who came in and when? Who left and when? When had the Sinclairs left? Sunny von Tripps was crying; Bobbie and Isobel were comforting her. Quentin Rowbotham was pleading for secrecy. Bertie was fixing those who wanted a loosener a tight one. The detective was making notes.

Ten minutes passed before Devon and Denbow returned. The one-man police state insisted on interviewing each one present individually in the kitchen. Did he want ex-Chief Superintendent Cheesewright to help him? Of course he didn't, Quentin rushed in, Cheesewright was as much a suspect as any of the others. The interviews did not last long. As the host, Bertie was first around the kitchen table.

'I hear you had a row with Monsieur de Méné at Barbados.'

'Yes, but it was nothing really and he later apologised.'

'Where were you when he was murdered?'

'I'm not sure, as I don't know when he was murdered. But most likely in my room fetching some clothes, or on my way back from it.'

'Witnesses?'

'None.'

'The spear gun. Do you know where it is it kept?'

'Yes, just inside the pool house, along with all the other swimming kit.'

'Thank you Sir Wooster, that is all.'

As the hostess, Bobbie was next to be interviewed, then Michel Carosse, then Isobel and so on until all those present, including Stilton Cheesewright, had told all to the impromptu policeman. From the kitchen Denbow emerged.

'This seems a simple enough case,' he announced expansively.

'Oh good,' said Bertie. 'Do tell.'

'Sir Wooster, I am arresting you for the murder of Alexis de Méné. I must warn you that anything you say may go against you in court.'

'Me?' said Bertie, 'but why?'

'Because he was your enemy. Because you have no alibi. And because you know where the murder weapon was kept.' From his back pocket he produced a set of handcuffs. 'Come with me. The rest of you, no-one leaves the island until I say so.'

'How's the jailbird this morning?' asked Stilton. Before Bertie could answer 'How do you think? Lousy. Hardly slept at all. There's not even a bed. Bit worried too, truth be told. I've been in the soup before, but this one looks murkier than most. I mean, any chance of a fair trial? Or are we talking kangaroos. This fellow Denbow would string me up tomorrow given half a chance. It's not as though I can swim for it. I might as well be on Alcatraz. You better put your helmet back on Stilton and get me out of this,' before Bertie could say any of this, Stilton said, 'You're in the soup this time Bertie. Murky it is too. At least I've got you out on bail. Well, it's hardly as if you can make a run for it, is it? But you've got to stay with me at Les Jolies Eaux, HRH's pad. Has he not, Mr. Denbow?' Denbow grunted in agreement.

'What, you mean I'm under house arrest?' asked Bertie.

'More or less. Bobbie can join us there. I have to keep an eye on you. Round the clock. Or our Mr. Denbow will have you back in here quick time, isn't that right?' Denbow grunted again.

'But what about HRH?' asked Bertie. 'Won't she be there?'

'She will, but in the main house. I'm in the guest cottage and that's where you'll be too. Anyway it's no problem, I've already told her all about the murder and she's keen to meet the prime suspect, you. She loves a good scandal.'

'And if there isn't one she'll soon invent one, from what I've heard,' said Bertie. 'Last thing I need is her stirring it up.'

'Not unknown. You've heard of Holmes and Watson?'

'Er, yes thank you Stilton, yes I have actually heard of Sherlock Holmes and Dr. Watson,' Bertie replied.

'Good start. I'm Holmes. You're Watson. Denbow can be Inspector Lastrade. We have not got long. I'd like this done and dusted by the time David Niven arrives.'

'Niven's a good egg, he'll vouch for me.'

'We are not looking for vouchers, Bertie. We are looking for a murderer. Now come along.'

'Where to?'

'We'll start at the Mustique Company, the centre of any spider web being woven around here. A certain Honourable Quentin Rowbotham might just be able to help us with our enquiries, as we say in the trade.'

On the short walk along to the Mustique Company's offices, Stilton explained how Mustique worked. Colin Tennant bought the island twelve years ago. He was a dreamer, but a dreamer with a difference. He actually did something about his dreams. He was also clever, in a big picture kind of way; clever enough to give Princess Margaret a plot of land as a wedding present. She loved it and had her husband's uncle, Oliver Messel, build Les Jolies Eaux on it.

That attracted more royalty, both real and self-fulfilling. But in a way, as Stilton explained it, Tennant rather shot himself in the foot. These kinds of people want electricity without power cuts, phones in their homes, drinking water and proper roads for their Mules. Not Tennant's forte, infrastructure. Pretty soon the residents got together, behind his back really, and formed the Mustique Company. Each plot owner is a shareholder. Pretty soon the island was functioning the way they liked it, not just because everything worked but because prying eyes were kept at bay. There is one bylaw against telephoto lenses, another against tape recorders. In theory the most paparazzi'd people in the world could swing stark naked from the chandeliers and get away with it; and in practice they did, up to a point.

'This Quentin Rowbotham is one of Tennant's nephews. He runs the place day-to-day, although he answers to a board, all residents of course. But he's not a resident so not a shareholder, he's employed, a renter.'

'How come?' asked Bertie.

'Don't know. Probably not rich enough. But listen. The problem we are going to face is the lack of any scientific evidence, so no autopsy, no forensics, no laboratories, no database, we're going to have to rely on good old-fashioned detective work. Have you heard of MMO?' Bertie said he hadn't. 'MMO stands for Means, Motive and Opportunity. The guilty party must have all three. Two out of three and they're innocent. So someone like Bobbie, who was up top all the time, would not have had the opportunity. So she couldn't be our murderer. With me so far?' Bertie said he was. 'Who else was on the terrace with her all the time?' Before Bertie could answer, Stilton said: 'Isobel Carosse, Princess Sunny and Ray Colquhoun. The Sinclairs had left, so no opportunity. Everyone else is a suspect. That's you, yes Bertie you, Michel Carosse, Simon Stacey, Quentin Rowbotham.'

'And you. You left them to find the maid to get more ice.'

'Well spotted Bertie. You're learning fast. Yes, and me. Much to Denbow's delight if that proves to be the case. Which it won't. Here we are.'

236

If Bertie had ever met a Fulham estate agent, Quentin Rowbotham would have reminded him of one. The Woosters had not seen him until last night at the party, all their prior dealings having been done by telex and telephone. Last night he had seemed full of insincere bonhomie; now in the office, in long trousers and wearing a tie, sitting behind a tidy desk, with a telex machine chattering away in the background and the aircon humming away to itself, with notices pinned up behind him, he had added an air of efficiency to the insincerity.

Cheesewright asked him what he knew about the victim.

'Alexis de Méné? I liked Alexis. Breath of fresh air. The air can get a bit stuffy around here. He is, well he was, the son of a wealthy Belgian industrialist. Spent a large chunk of it as we know. Down to his last few million they say. Of course nobody knows. I don't know that much more about him. He was in love with Sunny. Aren't we all?'

'So he had no direct connection to the island? Only through her?' asked Cheesewright.

'Look,' Quentin paused. 'You'll found this out soon enough, so I'll tell you. Sunny has the best plot on the island, it's called La Dama de Noche. Given to her by her prince, Klaus von Tripps. He'd bought it for a song from Colin in the early days. He died in a plane crash in Barbados on his way here. But the fact is she's spent a lot and doesn't have a much left, or at least not Mustique type of money. If they married it meant she could stay at La Dama de Noche.'

'But if they are both on the uppers, what's the point?' asked Bertie.

'Uppers is a relative term, Bertie. I wouldn't mind being on their uppers. Now I expect she'll have to sell it.'

'Through you?'

'Probably. She doesn't have to sell through us, but it makes sense, as everything has to come through us eventually. Of course this whole affair will knock back the value of all houses.'

'Murder in Mustique, I can just see the headlines,' said Bertie, thinking to himself it would make a good name for a tune too.

'It's just a matter of time before it gets out, isn't it?' said Quentin. 'It's just the type of scandal everyone here comes to avoid. The sooner it's wrapped up the better. Lucky you are here, Chief Superintendent. Denbow's does his best but he's all heart and no head. The sooner you can sort this out the better for us all.'

'Except the murderer,' said the detective. 'Who else knew she'd have to sell it if Alexis was no more?'

'Everyone. Well not literally everyone, but all the residents. We're a small island with few secrets. La Dama de Noche is prime property, maybe the prime property, lots of people would like to knock it down and build something grander. Before you ask me, that includes Michel Carosse and Ray Colquhoun.'

'I might want to buy it,' said Bertie. 'If it's ever for sale that is.'

'Thank you, Bertie,' said Stilton, 'and David Sinclair?'

'Maybe. Why not? He's the richest of them all. But his place, Yellow Bird, is pretty swanky as it is.'

'And Michel Carosse, you spent a long time with him in the garden. May I ask what you were talking about?'

'Gardens. Plants. What grows, what doesn't. He's mad keen on them. Gardens and plants.'

'And after that did you come back indoors?'

'No, I left him to say goodbye to the Sinclairs. I saw them leaving and rushed over. Bertie was there too, weren't you Bertie?'

'Yes, that's right.'

'Then I had a walk around while it was still light. Force of habit, being nosey about property.'

'And Simon Stacey, did you see him?'

'I hardly saw him all night.'

'One last thing. The murder weapon, the spear gun. Where was it?'

'I'm not sure, but ninety-nine times out of one hundred it would be in the pool house. Everyone keeps their swimming stuff in their pool houses. Yours has a sauna too, if I remember. Most of the others do too.'

Stilton and Bertie stood up to leave. 'That's all for now. Many thanks, more soon no doubt.'

As they walked back to the only car on the island, HRH's white Land Rover Series IIA four-door parked at the police station, Stilton asked Bertie what he thought.

'Well he's got the first M, no obvious second M and a clear O.'

'Precisely, my dear Watson. You are catching on. He had the means, the spear gun. The motive was a juicy house for sale I suppose, but it might be more than outweighed by no new rich and famous customers for a while. The opportunity, yes he was out and about, at large we might say. Now let's pay a visit to Greenfingers.'

'Michel Carosse?'

'The very same. Hop in.'

⤟⤟⤟

Michel Carosse certainly put his money where his heart was, horticulturally. The two-acre spread was a frenzy of tropical colour surrounding a grass field mowed to look like a lawn. Looking down on it all from the terrace, drinking one of Isobel's lovely mint coolers, Bertie felt almost overwhelmed by the abundance and the view over to Bequia.

'Everyone is talking about last night,' she said. 'It's just so terrible, to happen here of all places.'

'That's why we are here,' said Cheesewright. 'That and to admire the Carosse garden we've heard so much about.'

'Michel will be back soon, he can tell you all about it. I can tell you all about the kitchen and recipes, but the garden is his and his alone. But you can see why he wants more space. We only have two acres. He spends half the time looking over there,' she nodded to their neighbour's plot, 'with a far off look in his eyes.'

'Who's over there?' asked Bertie.

'That's La Dama de Noche. Sunny's place. Ah, I can see a Mule, he'll be here now. I'll leave you boys to it.'

Michel arrived shortly from the bar with a cold beer. Could he fix them up with one? Bertie said he'd love one, Stilton declined: 'On duty and all that.'

'Have you any clues about last night?' asked Michel. 'I presume that's why you are here. I see they have let you out, Bertie. Can't have been much fun in the cell.'

'It wasn't,' said Bertie. 'Beastly, in fact.'

'What do you think?' Michel asked looking down on his tropical paradise.

'It's wonderful,' said Bertie. 'But is it big enough for you?'

'Oh, good God yes. It's more than enough work already. The problem is not the garden but the gardeners. There just aren't enough of them. It's all very well the Mustique Company keeping the island as a rich white man's playground, and God knows I'm one of them, but the rich white men need poor black men to keep it all up to snuff, as you British say. To be blunt about it, I hope you don't mind?'

'Blunt is good,' said Cheesewright, 'it has the ring of truth about it. We coppers like truth. You spent some time with Quentin Rowbotham last night. Can I ask what you were talking about?'

'Yes, I wanted to stop de Méné's airport plan. I suppose it died with him, come to think of it. I'm sure I'm not alone in wanting it stopped. Quentin knows everybody and everything. I wanted him to help me round up resistance to it.'

'But there's already an airport,' said Bertie.

'Yes, the tiny strip and bamboo terminal we all come and go from. Alexis is fronting some PR for an executive jet charter business in Florida. They want to expand the runway so they can operate into here as well. And add a heliport. At the moment there's just the air ambulance allowed and that has to land on the runway.'

'Are the plans advanced and public knowledge?' asked Cheesewright.

'No, not really. I only heard about them from David Sinclair. God knows he can afford a Boeing, but like me he wants to keep the place off-piste, as it were.'

'And you were with Quentin all the time?'

'No, he left me to say goodbye to the Sinclairs.'

'And then what did you do?'

'I walked around the garden some more, then came back to the terrace when I heard the shouts.'

'So you were on the terrace when the body was found?'

'Yes, along with everyone else, I think. Except Simon Stacey of course. I'd be inclined to start with him.'

'How come?' asked Bertie.

'I could say because he's a nasty piece of work. Then you'd say that's not a good enough reason. So I will say because he was desperate to get his greedy little hands on La Dama de Noche.'

'Let me ask you, do you keep a spear gun here?' asked Cheesewright.

'Yes, in the pool house. Why?'

'Just curious. Bertie and I are staying at Les Jolies Eaux if anything else comes to mind. Give me a call, 101 is the number.'

Back in the Land Rover, Bertie said: 'Well, he's got MMO written all over him. And someone is not telling the truth.'

'Almost no-one is telling the truth,' said Stilton. 'Let's have lunch back at base, then let's try our new widow-that-wasn't-quite-meant-to-be, Princess Sunny von Tripps.'

❧

In the guest cottage Stilton and Bertie both had their mouths full of baguette when Princess Margaret wandered in with a handful of something clinking in a

242

glass. They stood and mumbled 'Your Royal Highness' as best they could.

'So you're our Mustique murderer are you, Mr. Wooster?'

'No, ma'am, I'm....'

'Never mind that, we've met before. I called Reggie in London. I can never remember. I meet so many people they merge into one nightmare. But I bet you can remember meeting me. People seem to. Don't know why. Maybe because

I'm unique, the daughter of a king and sister of a queen.'

'I do indeed ma'am, ' said Bertie. 'First time at the Royal Command Performance in 1949.'

'That's right, you did that extraordinary Wodehouse song.

Very brave. Then?'

'At Royal Ascot, I can't remember exactly, late '50s, early '60s?'

'It was 1957, according to Reggie. You don't have a very good memory. Better remember what you did last night though, eh Cheesy? Otherwise it's clink, clink for you.'

'Yes, ma'am,' said her minder, lighting the next in her chain of cigarettes.

'And?' she asked Bertie.

'My wife Roberta and you are both on the committee of the Royal Opera House Benevolent Fund. We met at a reception there about five years ago.'

'Funny,' she replied, 'Reggie didn't say. I'll call him now. Tell him off. Nice to know something he doesn't. Mrs. Wooster you say.'

'Lady Wooster, to be precise, ma'am.'

'Really?' And with a raised eyebrow, empty glass in one hand and full cigarette in the other, she strode off to harass old Reggie.

⌘

'Gosh,' said Bertie, 'I can see what all the fuss is about.' They were waiting for the other Princess on her wooden terrace, surrounded by carefully crafted, colour-faded driftwood, looking out over her garden and orchard, sloping down onto her private beach, overlooking Bequia five miles away. It was a kind of paradise.

Moments later Sunny wafted in, followed by her billowing tropical kaftan and her pet Scottie. 'This is one of the original houses,' she explained, 'designed by Margaret's uncle-in-law, Oliver Messel, at the same time as he did Les Jolies Eaux. He was really a stage designer, as you can see.'

'It's quite a set,' said Bertie.

'He called himself a decorator,' said Sunny. 'Now they want to pull it down and build something in concrete. Something more practical they say. I say, who cares if it leaks. I'm not here in the wet.'

'Who wants to pull it down?' asked Cheesewright.

'The Barbarians. Literally at my gates. I could sell this place for a fortune but it would break my heart. Maybe I'll take in guests now Alexis has gone.'

'So Alexis was going to...?' asked Bertie.

'Keep it exactly as it is. Exactly as I want it.'

'And did Alexis have any other plans for the island. Any developments?' asked the detective.

'Not as far as I know. What do you mean?'

'Nothing in particular. I have to ask you this, I'm

sorry. Did he have any enemies here? Anyone who is enough of an enemy to want him dead?'

'I can't think of anybody. He had a bit of a row with David Sinclair. And a row with my neighbours,' she nodded towards Ray and Simon's house next door. 'A bit short-tempered at times, as you know Bertie. I know he was so sorry about that.'

'Entirely forgiven and forgotten,' said Bertie.

'Sinclair,' asked Cheesewright, 'what was that about?'

'I don't know, he wouldn't say. He knew Candice from before, maybe David was jealous. Not an affair, I asked him that.' Sunny replied.

'I noticed they were a bit frosty at the party,' said Bertie.

'Me too. Something is puzzling me,' said Cheesewright. 'Alexis left the party to fetch his camera from the Mule. Yet there was no camera at the crime scene. Which means he was murdered on his way to the Mule. Did you find his camera in the Mule?'

'Yes, along with other things from the day. Do you want to see it?'

'Not for now, but thanks. And his will? Have you seen his will?' asked Cheesewright.

'Ha, yes and no. We were drawing up a nuptial agreement, which included looking after me in his will. That was three weeks ago in New York. We were planning to finish all that back in New York next month. You can't do anything from here. But I do know that I am not in his will at the moment.'

'Can I ask you about Quentin Rowbotham? Has he been talking to you about selling La Dama de Noche?' asked Cheesewright.

'Yes, several times. But that is what he does, he's a realtor. He says my neighbours would buy it tomorrow.'

'The Carosses?'

'Yes, them for sure and the other neighbours, Ray and Simon. Actually, Alexis had a bit of fight with Simon,' said Sunny.

'Yes, you said and I was about to ask. About buying this house?' asked Cheesewright.

'No, not all. Simon wanted him and Ray and their guests to use my private beach. Frankly, I never use it. At my age you stay out of the sun, never mind the sea and the sun together. I didn't mind, but Alexis absolutely refused. Simon said it was nothing to do with him and they had an argument. Then one day Alexis saw Simon down on the beach, bathing and swimming naked. Alexis went nuts, really. He ran down to the beach and I could see them having a fight, not for long, but an actual fight. Simon gathered his clothes and ran back to their house. I suppose after that I was surprised that Quentin invited us and those two to your party.'

'Maybe Quentin didn't know about the fight?' suggested Bertie.

'On Mustique? Impossible, everyone knows everything about everybody,' replied Sunny.

'Then we should pay them a visit too,' said Cheesewright.

'It's all so terrible,' Sunny said. 'On here, Mustique, of all places.'

~~~

As they drove up to Ray Colquhoun's villa, Bertie noticed how plain it looked. 'I can see why they wanted to buy La Dama de Noche. It's the first house we've seen here I wouldn't rent at any price.'

At the porch they were greeted by Simon Stacey. 'Ray won't be long,' he said, 'just taking his third shower of the day.'

'Actually, it's you we want to talk to,' said Cheesewright, 'Have you got a moment?'

'Yes of course. Come up topsides and we'll have some tea. Proper Fortnum's tea. Or something stronger.'

Armed with three cups of proper tea they sat on stone stools around a stone table under an umbrella. The view was down to Sunny's beach.

'Lovely beach down there,' said Bertie.

'Yes, it belongs to La Dama de Noche,' said Simon.

'Can you use it?' asked Bertie.

'No, no, it's private. Belongs to Sunny. We've no interest in it. We're not really sea people.'

'And the house, La Dama de Noche. If it was for sale, would you buy it?' Bertie asked.

'No. We're very happy here, Ray and I. Our friends love it too. I'm sure others would want Sunny's though. It's quite a spot.'

'Tell me about Alexis,' said Cheesewright.

'I hardly knew him. In fact, I think the Woosters' party was the first time we met properly.'

'Yet you followed him down to his Mule. Why was that?'

'Did I? Yes, I suppose I did, but I didn't follow him on purpose, he just happened to leave before me. He said he was going to his Mule, didn't he?'

'And you?'

'I needed a pee, that's all.'

'Tell me, do you have a spear gun here?' asked Cheesewright.

'Yes, in the pool house. Snorkels and flippers too. Never use it though. Wouldn't know which end to point.'

Bertie drained the last drop of tea. 'Thanks for that. Clever of you to find Fortnum's.'

'Yes, thanks,' said Cheesewright. 'We must seek information on pastures new. Say hello to Ray from us.'

~~~

'More lies,' said Bertie as they drove away.

'Unless they are truths, and the others are lies.'

'Confusing.'

'Let's go back to Les Jolies Eaux and sum up where we are,' said Stilton.

'Can we collect Bobbie on the way?'

'Good idea. She'll be worried.'

'I doubt that,' said Bertie, 'but she's awfully good at crosswords and puzzles and things. That's funny.'

'What's funny?'

'That Mule that just drove the other way. It was a Willys. Blue with silver sides. I recognised it because we rented one exactly like that in Barbados last year.'

'And?'

'No, it's just that it was at our housewarming. Reg number 66. And we haven't seen it since. I wonder whose it is? I can ask Denbow I suppose.'

'About time he did something useful,' said Stilton.

~~~

Back at his cottage at Les Jolies Eaux, with Bertie and Bobbie before him in the open sitting room, Stilton held court: 'So what do we know so far? At about 5 p.m. we three and all the others were at Gentle Breezes, your housewarming party. Organised by Quentin Rowbotham. Butter wouldn't melt in his mouth. On the other hand, he knew exactly where the murder weapon was and he was outside at the time of the murder. But then again, any murder on his patch would be bad, to say the least, for his business. Hard to see what he has to gain.'

'And he doesn't seem to have it in him,' said Bobbie.

'Maybe, maybe not. With you all the time on the terrace were Sunny von Tripps, Ray Colquhoun and Isobel Carosse.

Right?'

'Right,' said Bobbie.

'So you're all clear. First to leave were Michel Carosse and Quentin, ostensibly to look round the gardens. Agreed?'

Bertie and Bobbie nodded.

'Fine, so hold that picture of where everyone was. Then at 5:50 p.m. the Sinclairs leave, home to pack as they're on the dawn flight to Barbados.'

'Bit of a feeble excuse,' said Bertie.

'And there's no dawn flight to Barbados,' said Bobbie. 'The dawn flight is to St. Vincent.'

'Maybe it was a private flight,' said Stilton. 'But then they fly when you want them to fly. And it may not be the whole truth, maybe they had somewhere else to go first, another party perhaps. Anyway, one way or another they're off the crime scene.'

'And I them to the Mule and wave goodbye.'

'Typically polite,' said Bobbie. 'I'd expect nothing less.'

'But then,' said Bertie, 'Quentin arrives to see them off too. He was hurrying as if to make sure to catch them. He was surprised to see me, I must say. And I him, for that matter. Then the Sinclairs drove off in their old John Deere Mule.'

'Then what?' asked Stilton.

'Then I started off back to the terrace. I felt a chill on the way and nipped into our room to fetch a light jacket. Then I went back upstairs and on the way thought I better fetch Bobbie a stole. I had to rummage around in her bags to find something.'

'So how long were you away from the others?' asked Stilton.

'Five minutes, maybe less.'

'During which time Alexis de Méné left the group,' said Stilton.

'To fetch something from his Mule,' Bobbie remembered.

'His camera,' Stilton reminded her. 'Now we know he was murdered on his way to the Mule. The camera was still in it. Next fact we know is Simon Stacey slipped out after Alexis, to have a pee.'

'I think he's the prime suspect,' said Bertie. 'So does Michel. Sunny doesn't rate him either. Back then we'd have said he was a rotter.'

'He's got all the makings,' said Bobbie. 'We know it wasn't Bertie. We know it wasn't you. Quentin's too wet. Michel's too aesthetic. David Sinclair was long gone. It's got to be him.'

Stilton paced up and down for a while. 'MMO. Means, motive, opportunity. He scores on all three and no one else does. And yet; and yet. Why do I keep coming back to the camera? Why did Alexis leave like that? And who gains? Who dares and wins? Always remember, follow the money.'

Just then the phone rang. Stilton said: '101 guest cottage. Yes Officer Denbow. You do? Well thank you. That is most interesting. Most interesting indeed. Yes, he's still with me, still under arrest, in my care. Wait a second please, Mr. Denbow. Wait just a second.' Stilton put the phone on the table and paced up and down some more, mumbling to himself: 'Candice came back of course, Stacey of course, why didn't I see it? Staring at me! The camera hoax, it was blackmail. The money. Quentin's alibi. Candice and the Mule, the heliport, red herrings, right in front of me.' Then he picked up the phone again. 'Mr. Denbow, are you still there? Good. Get up to Gentle Breezes please. I want everyone there in half an hour. Ring round, tell the others. Quick as you can please.'

From the terrace came the sound of servants scurrying and through the open shutter doors in walked Princess Margaret.

'Got it all sorted out, have you, Cheesy?'

'Very nearly, ma'am, I think we are making good progress.'

Then to the Woosters she said: 'Top copper, Cheesy. My copper-bottomed copper is what he is. Who are you?'

'Lady Wooster at your service, ma'am,' said Bobbie.

'That's right, we're on some ghastly committee or other. Guilty is he, your husband here?'

'Abso....'

'Don't worry, Cheesy here will get him off, won't you Cheesy? What's next?'

'We are all assembling at Gentle Breezes for the dénouement, ma'am,' said her minder.

'Then I'm coming too. I love a good whodunit – and I can usually get there before Monsieur Poirot. I want to meet the *dramatis personae*,' said HRH.

'I don't think that's a very good idea, ma'am,' said Cheesewright. 'We haven't had a chance to clear the guests or sweep the house.'

'Thank you for your cautious advise, Inspector Plod, but I'm absolutely not going to miss this one.'

'As you please, ma'am,' said Cheesewright.

As she left, so did they; next stop Gentle Breezes.

⁓⁓⁓

Almost exactly twenty-four hours after the guests had first assembled at Gentle Breezes, they reassembled again. The Sinclairs were gone, but now Denbow was added.

In the collective air of apprehension ex-Chief Superintendent set out his stall: 'This has been a hard case to solve as we've had no autopsy and no forensics. We've had to rely on the old chestnut: means, motive and opportunity. And one old golden rule: follow the money, only in this case the lack of money.

'You see, two things haven't made much sense, one of these has been puzzling me and the other puzzling Sir Bertie.

'To me it was why did Alexis say he was going to fetch his camera from his Mule? Everyone knows you cannot take guest photos in Mustique. If he wasn't going to fetch his camera, then what? It had to be that he was meeting someone there secretly. Yet whom? The

Sinclairs had already left, couldn't have been them. Simon followed him out of the room. But why meet there then? We know they disliked each other, rather intensely. It didn't make sense.

'Then there is Sir Bertie's unsolved mystery. The Sinclairs left together in an old two-seater John Deere Mule. But Bertie noticed another Mule there, a new Willys one. We checked it out with Mr. Denbow. It is registered to the Sinclairs. So the Sinclairs arrived in two cars and left in one. Why was that?

'Put these two mysteries together and what do we have? Alexis was going to meet one of the Sinclairs, the one who would have stayed behind. The one with the alibi provided by Quentin. Only they had not reckoned on Bertie's perfect British manners. Instead of one of them leaving in the John Deere and the other waiting for Alexis to come to his Mule, they both had to drive away together.

'But I saw them drive away together,' said Quentin.

'You did and most conveniently too,' said Cheesewright. 'In fact you hurried across the garden to make sure you saw them off. After all, you were their alibi. The alibi being you saw them drive off together, when you had planned only one of them would do so. Do you want to take up the story from there?'

'I don't know what you mean,' said Quentin.

'Oh, I think you do,' said Cheesewright. 'There are only two people in this room who don't have as much money as they'd like to have. One of them is you. The other is, was, Alexis de Méné. I think you were in cahoots with the Sinclairs to murder Alexis de Méné. Something Sunny said tipped me off. Alexis was blackmailing them about something in Candice's past. Only it all went slightly wrong. Do you want to fill in the dots, Bertie?'

Bertie walked around from behind the bar. 'Knowing that neither of the Sinclairs could now kill Alexis, probably by shooting him in his Mule, you decided to do it yourself. The deal with the Sinclairs for La Dama de Noche would remain as long as Alexis was dead. I'm guessing that was the motive?

Unless you have another.'

'You're completely mad,' said Quentin.

The detective took up the story, 'With Alexis gone, you thought Sunny would sell La Dama de Noche. Now she probably will. You wanted to buy it and develop it yourself. But you didn't have the money. And the Sinclairs did. You hatched a plot with them. You'd be their alibi and they'd be your backer. You'd have some finance and they'd have got rid of a blackmailer.

'You were outside. You knew Alexis would soon be on his way to his Mule. You knew where the spear gun was kept. All you had to do was wait a few moments in the pool house, and as he walked past harpoon him in the back and tip him into the pool. You then went to the back of the house and up to the terrace with the others. It was just a matter of time before someone found him, by which time you'd be safely up with the others. Unluckily for you, Simon really did need the loo and found Alexis.'

'You can't prove any of this,' said Quentin in a mild form of outrage.

Cheesewright said, 'I will now inform the FBI to issue a warrant for the Sinclairs' arrest. We don't know which one planned to commit the murder, but they are both guilty of conspiracy. No doubt the truth will come out in court. But for now, Mr. Denbow, I suggest you arrest Quentin Rowbotham for the murder of Alexis de Méné.'

At first in shock, and then in relief, the other guests mingled and then melted away into the night. Only one stayed behind, Princess Sunny von Tripps. She ushered Bobbie away to a corner and said, 'You know for me the Mustique mystique has been broken. I will sell La Dama de Noche but I want to sell it to you. If you want it, and on my one condition.'

'And I'd like to buy from you,' said Bobbie, 'whatever the condition.'

'The condition is, you keep it like it is.'

'The condition it's in,' said Bobbie, 'the condition is the condition it's in. I promise.'

'Then it is done. Quentin gave me a valuation and I will take it. Tomorrow come for lunch and we will arrange everything. For now, I want to be alone in my beautiful home.'

A few minutes after Sunny had left and after Bobbie told Bertie about their new Mustique hideaway, Bertie popped a bottle of Champagne and poured Bobbie and Stilton a glass each. They toasted their old friendship and the Woosters' new home, away from cameras and taxes. From the drive three sets of headlights appeared, heading their way.

'Oh, just when we thought our troubles were over,' said Stilton.

'What's up?' asked Bertie.

'HRH has rounded up some friends and it looks like the party's up here tonight. How are stocks?'

'Low,' said Bobbie, 'we've only just arrived. What do we need?'

'Booze, fags and a piano, basically. I can see you are all right for the piano. I'll make a call. Could be a long one. Cheer-ho!'

Three glasses clinked and three old friends said 'Cheerho!' and Bertie said, 'Well, she'd better get used to us,' and settled in for their next adventure.

– THE END –